African Dilemma Tales

World Anthropology

General Editor

SOL TAX

Patrons

CLAUDE LÉVI-STRAUSS
MARGARET MEAD
LAILA SHUKRY EL HAMAMSY
M. N. SRINIVAS

MOUTON PUBLISHERS · THE HAGUE · PARIS
DISTRIBUTED IN THE USA AND CANADA BY ALDINE, CHICAGO

African Dilemma Tales

WILLIAM R. BASCOM

MOUTON PUBLISHERS · THE HAGUE · PARIS
DISTRIBUTED IN THE USA AND CANADA BY ALDINE, CHICAGO

To Berta and my other students

General Editor's Preface

It is timely that William Bascom's examination of African dilemma tales — tales which are an integral part of moral and ethical training in many African societies — should appear just as scholars are making serious attempts at understanding and defining traditional African values and the relevance that those values will have in the post-colonial political arena. Dilemma tales are clever and popular, and exercise the "puzzle" talents of people. They are not only intellectual puzzles which sharpen the wits and promote discussion; they also point out that in human affairs there are often no answers, but only difficult choices — which call into play conflicting moral values. That this was known to folk peoples from time immemorial — and forgotten by each new generation in cultures which lack such story-telling devices — is a lesson for modern educators. The fact that the lesson is being taught by African folk (under the auspices of Professor Bascom) well illustrates the idea of the Congress to which this book was presented.

Like most contemporary sciences, anthropology is a product of the European tradition. Some argue that it is a product of colonialism, with one small and self-interested part of the species dominating the study of the whole. If we are to understand the species, our science needs substantial input from scholars who represent a variety of the world's cultures. It was a deliberate purpose of the IXth International Congress of Anthropological and Ethnological Sciences to provide impetus in this direction. The *World Anthropology* volumes, therefore, offer a first glimpse of a human science in which members from all societies have played an active role. Each of the books is designed to be self-contained; each is an attempt to update its particular sector of scientific knowledge and is written by specialists from all parts of the world. Each volume should be read and reviewed individually as a separate volume on its own given subject. The set as a whole will indicate what changes are in store for anthropology as scholars from the developing countries join in studying the species of which we are all a part.

The IXth Congress was planned from the beginning not only to include as many of the scholars from every part of the world as possible, but also with a view toward the eventual publication of the papers in high-quality volumes. At previous Congresses scholars were invited to bring papers which were then read out loud. They were necessarily limited in length; many were only summarized; there was little time for discussion; and the sparse discussion could only be in one language. The IXth Congress was an experiment aimed at changing this. Papers were written with the intention of exchanging them before the Congress, particularly in extensive pre-Congress sessions; they were not intended to be read aloud at the Congress, that time being devoted to discussions — discussions which were simultaneously and professionally translated into five languages. The method for eliciting the papers was structured to make as representative a sample as was allowable when scholarly creativity — hence self-selection — was critically important. Scholars were asked both to propose papers of their own and to suggest topics for sessions of the Congress which they might edit into volumes. All were then informed of the suggestions and encouraged to re-think their own papers and the topics. The process, therefore, was a continuous one of feedback and exchange and it has continued to be so even after the Congress. The some two thousand papers comprising *World Anthropology* certainly then offer a substantial sample of world anthropology. It has been said that anthropology is at a turning point; if this is so, these volumes will be the historical direction-markers.

As might have been foreseen in the first post-colonial generation, the large majority of the Congress papers (82 percent) are the work of scholars identified with the industrialized world which fathered our traditional discipline and the institution of the Congress itself: Eastern Europe (15 percent); Western Europe (16 percent); North America (47 percent); Japan, South Africa, Australia, and New Zealand (4 percent). Only 18 percent of the papers are from developing areas: Africa (4 percent); Asia-Oceania (9 percent); Latin American (5 percent). Aside from the substantial representation from the U.S.S.R. and the nations of Eastern Europe, a significant difference between this corpus of written material and that of other Congresses is the addition of the large proportion of contributions from Africa, Asia, and Latin America. "Only 18 percent" is two to four times as great a proportion as that of other Congresses; moreover, 18 percent of 2,000 papers is 360 papers, 10 times the number of "Third World" papers presented at previous Congresses. In fact, these 360 papers are more than the total of ALL papers published after the last International Congress of Anthropological and Ethnological Sciences which was held in the United States (Philadelphia, 1956). Even in the beautifully organized Tokyo Congress in 1968 less than a third as many members from developing nations, including those of Asia, participated.

The significance of the increase is not simply quantitative. The input of scholars from areas which have until recently been no more than subject matter for anthropology represents both feedback and also long-awaited theoretical contributions from the perspectives of very different cultural, social, and historical traditions. Many who attended the IXth Congress were convinced that anthropology would not be the same in the future. The fact that the next Congress (India, 1978) will be our first in the "Third World" may be symbolic of the change. Meanwhile, sober consideration of the present set of books will show how much, and just where and how, our discipline is being revolution-ized.

This presentation of African Dilemma Tales was the longest of over 3,000 papers presented to the Congress, where it was discussed parti-cularly on September 3, 1973. It is the only Congress publication which in one sense consists of a single paper, but in another sense is really an "edited" volume of material collected from the Africans who originated the dilemma tales.

Chicago, Illinois   SOL TAX
December 20, 1974

Table of Contents

African Dilemma Tales

Dilemma tales constitute a large, diverse, and widespread class of folk-tales in Africa. They are prose narratives that leave the listeners with a choice among alternatives, such as which of several characters has done the best, deserves a reward, or should win an argument or a case in court. The choices are difficult ones and usually involve discrimination on ethical, moral, or legal grounds. Other dilemma tales, which border on tall tales, ask the listeners to judge the relative skills of characters who have performed incredible feats. The narrator ends his story with the dilemma, often explicitly stated in the form of a question, to be debated by his listeners. Sometimes the dilemma is resolved by the narrator after his listeners have argued their conflicting points of view, but often it is not.

Even when they have such standard "answers," dilemma tales can evoke spirited discussions. Like many other African folktales, their con-tent is often didactic, but their special quality is that they train those who engage in these discussions in the skills of argumentation and debate and thus prepare them for participating effectively in the adjudication of dis-putes, both within the family or lineage and in formal courts of law.

Several observers have commented on the intellectual function of dilemma tales or have described the lengthy discussions that ensue (e.g. 2:6, 36:15, 38:1, 79:1, 106:1, 122:1, 125:2). N'Djok concludes his interesting remarks on a tale from Cameroun (143:1) with the following:

I am indebted to Ivan R. Dihoff for the translation of 87:4 from Hausa and again to Neil Skinner for his translations of Edgar's many Hausa tales. I am also deeply grateful to Brunhilde Biebuyck for translating Hulstaert and de Rop's important collection of *Rechtspraakfabels van de Nkundó* from Flemish. Without their help this study would have been manifestly deficient.

But what excellent exercise to prepare for the arguments of the village and those of the court! Woe to the inexperienced official! And what preparation again for the political game of the future!   (1958: 86).

In Kpelle tales, Mengrelis says:

Several times, when a character finds himself faced by a dilemma, the narrator questions the people present and asks them the question, "If you had been in his place, what would you have done?" And each responds in his fashion. At the end the narrator concludes, "It is Pepe who is right. The person in question acted in the same way." The subject of a tale often consists of accomplishing a difficult task. The heroes are people or animals who, after extraordinary adventures, succeed in accomplishing together a superhuman task. The question is posed at the end: "To whom should the reward be given, seeing that each of the persons or animals involved have contributed to the success of an important undertaking?" A good lesson in cooperative work!   (1950: 186).

The end is not quite . . . an end. The adventure is finished but it is the audience that gives the conclusion. The end is an enigma to resolve. Here are some examples of the end of tales. The narrator poses the question to the audience: "To whom should he give the cow's tail?" "Which of the three youths was the most cunning?" "Which of the two brothers was right?" "To which young girl, among the claimants, should she give preference?"   (1950: 92).

Unfortunately for our purposes, Mengrelis gives only fragments of some of the Kpelle tales that he discusses, and the dilemmas are sometimes omitted (1:3, 3:3, 36:37, 123:3).

L.-V. Thomas, who calls dilemma tales "riddles-cases of conscience" though he recognizes that they differ from usual riddles, says:

A fairly large number of these riddles-cases of conscience circulate in Dyola country which are, in the evenings and during siestas in the dry season, the points of departure for interminable palavers between young and old, each expounding the arguments which in their opinion ought to triumph. Certainly, these discussions are often formal and relatively "exterior" to the fundamental principles of a profound speculation, but they permit the confrontation of the multiplicity of points of view and the sharpening of a critical sense which is too often lacking   (1958–1959: II, 579).

The cases of conscience are an entirely different type of riddle, since they are not only a serious game, but also they do not call for fixed answers. On the contrary, they raise strangely difficult problems of morality and give rise to interminable palavers. One can say that they summarize Dyola casuistry, but a noble and sincere casuistry which does not aim at pronouncing rules, but at resolving problems. With this new genre of riddle we are halfway between a literary game and the solution of conflicts of duty   (1958–1959: II, 430).

This new aspect of Dyola literature reveals the cultural psychology, since it states precisely a very frequent type of social game and a highly prized kind of intellectual activity; one frequently sees groups discussing thus in the evening, not without passion and sometimes until a late hour in the night (1958–1959: II, 431).

Describing an Adangme tale that ends with a question (36:15), Berry says:

No solution is suggested. Each of the audience must give his views and an *ad hoc* solution is accepted at each telling depending on the consensus of opinion of those present and the weight of the arguments advanced (1961: 10).

One wishes that there were more such comments on the social contexts of African dilemma tales. Too often we are given only the texts and are left to infer that discussions ensue. Unfortunately, for reasons that will become clear later, there was no opportunity to observe the telling of dilemma tales during my field work among the Yoruba of Nigeria.

It is their intellectual function and their relevance to ethical standards, rather than any literary merit, that make dilemma tales interesting. No elaborate plot or surprising denouement is necessary to present a dilemma, and some examples barely qualify as prose narratives (e.g. 129:1). Adam (1940–1941: 137) says of dilemma tales, "These are for us the least interesting. Perhaps the Blacks like them more."

It is perhaps in part because many dilemma tales have little literary merit — a shortcoming greatly exaggerated in my summaries which follow — that they have been relatively neglected by American folklorists; this neglect also reflects the general indifference of American scholars to African folklore, of which dilemma tales seem to be particularly characteristic.

This is not to say that American folklorists have completely ignored dilemma tales. As we shall see, some are included in Aarne and Thompson's *The types of the folktale* (1964), though surprisingly few in terms of the numbers of African dilemma tales that have been published. Farnham (1920) has discussed a number of dilemma tales centering around contending lovers, starting with the Sanskrit "Twenty-Five Tales of a Demon" (*"Vetālapanchavinsati"*) and its interesting "frame." In order for a king to be enthroned, he must cut down a corpse from a tree and bring it back without speaking. A demon in the corpse tells him dilemma tales that compel him to give an answer, and he must start all over again, until he cannot find an answer for the twenty-fifth tale. Several of Farnham's tales, not cited in Aarne and Thompson, are analogous to African dilemma tales (e.g. 36:36, 39:1, 39:2, 124:2).

Jablow's African anthology (1961) includes twenty-five "dilemma tales," several of which have been reprinted by Feldmann (1963). I have not succeeded in locating all of Jablow's sources, but from the original tales that I have identified, it is apparent that a few, omitted here, have been converted into dilemma tales in retelling them (e.g. Jablow 1961: 64–67, 72–74).

African dilemma tales have been reported in the literature under a variety of names, in Spanish as *adivinanzas* (Ramón Alvrez 1951: 147) and in Flemish as *Rechtspraakfabels* (Hulstaert and de Rop 1954: title). In German they have been termed *Rätsel-Erzählung* (Müller 1902: 155), *Rätselfragen* (Westermann 1922: 21), *Fragen* (Frobenius 1921–1928: IX, 150), *Rätsel in Form einer Parabel* (Schönhärl 1909: 105), *Parabeln* (Spieth 1906: 595), *Rechtsfragen oder Parabeln* (Prietze 1897: 30), and *Erzählunger für Gerichtsverhandlungen* (Becker-Donner 1965: 102).

In French they are known as *énigmes* (Bérenger-Féraud 1885: 239), *contes énigmes* (Trilles 1932: 268), *contes devinettes* (Holas 1952: 81), *devinettes-discussions* (Fouda, de Julliot, and Lagrave 1961: 15), *devinettes-cas de conscience* (L.–V. Thomas 1958–1959: II, 579), *cas de conscience* (Trautmann 1927: 99), *choix difficile* (Trautmann 1927: 99), *questions embarrasantes* (Nicolas 1954: 1030), *récits à point d'interrogation* (Adam 1940–1941: 137), *fables juridiques* (Anonymous 1956: title), and *fables de jurisprudence* (Hulstaert 1965: 475).

In English they have been called *riddles* (Rattray 1930: 263), *riddle stories* (Matola 1907: 214), *unanswerable riddle stories* (Courlander 1963: 116), *insoluble riddle tales* (Courlander 1963: 113), *conundrums* (Smith and Dale 1920: II, 331), *conundrums in the form of little stories* (Macdonald 1882: I, 47), *conundrum and problem stories* (Schwab 1947: 447), *problem stories* (Fletcher 1912: 90), *problem tales* (Cardinall 1931: 204), and *folk problems* (Gay and Cole 1967: 25).

In order to give an idea of the wide distribution of dilemma tales in Africa and to avoid tedious repetitions of geographical locations, the groups whose tales are cited are listed below in alphabetical order; those distinguished by asterisks have analogous tales, but without explicit dilemmas.

Adangme, Ghana

Ahlo, Togo

Akan (a linguistic grouping, including the Ashanti), Ghana and Ivory Coast

Ana (a Yoruba offshoot), Togo

Anyi (Agni), Ivory Coast and Ghana
Ashanti, Ghana
Avatime, Ghana and Togo
Bambara, Mali
Bandi (Gbande), Liberia
Baule, Ivory Coast
Benga, Rio Muni
Bete, Ivory Coast
Betsimisaraka, Malagasy
Bulu, Cameroun
Bura, Nigeria
Cape Verde Islanders
Dagomba,'Ghana and Togo
Dangmeli, Ghana
Dyola, Senegal
Edo, Nigeria*
Ewe, Togo and Ghana
Fang (Pangwe), Gabon
Fon, Dahomey*
Fulani, Senegal to Cameroun
Gio, Liberia
Grushi (Grunshi), Togo
Gurma, Upper Volta and Togo
Guro, Ivory Coast
Hanya, Angola
Hausa, Nigeria
Haya (Ziba), Tanzania
Ibibio, Nigeria
Igala, Nigeria*
Ila, Zambia
Jukun, Nigeria
Kabyle, Algeria
Karekare, Nigeria
Khasonke, Mali
Kimbundu (Ambundu), Angola
Kongo (Bakongo), Zaïre and Congo
Kono, Guinea and Ivory Coast
Kpe (Kwele), Cameroun
Kpelle (Guerze), Liberia and Guinea
Krachi, Togo
Lamba, Zambia

Limba, Sierra Leone
Loma (Toma), Liberia and Guinea
Luba, Zaïre
Lyele (Éla), Upper Volta
Malinke, Guinea*
Mano, Liberia
Mbete, Gabon and Congo
Mende, Sierra Leone and Liberia
Mongo (including Nkundo), Zaïre
Mosi (Moshi), Upper Volta
Mpongwe, Gabon
Ngbaka (Bwaka, Ngbaya), Central African Republic and Zaïre
Ngonde (Konde), Tanzania
Nkundo (Mongo), Zaïre
Nupe, Nigeria
Otwa (unidentified)
Ovimbundu (Umbundu), Angola
Popo (Egun), Dahomey
Pygmy, Gabon, Congo and Zaïre
Saho, Eritrea
Samo, Upper Volta*
Sefwi, Ghana
Sikon, Liberia*
Songye, Zaïre
Soninke (Sarakole), Mali
Swahili, Tanzania
Tanga, Cameroun
Temne, Sierra Leone
Tera, Nigeria
Tsimihety, Malagasy
Tsonga (Ronga), Mozambique
Unidentified: Africa, Cameroun, Ethiopia, Gabon, Ghana*, Liberia,
    Mali, Malawi*, Senegal*, Senegambia, Sierra Leone, Tanzania
Vai, Liberia
Vili (Fjort, Bafiote), Congo
Wala, Ghana
Wobe (Ouobe), Ivory Coast
Wolof (Ouolof), Senegal
Yao, Zambia
Yoruba, Nigeria and Dahomey*
Zigula, Tanzania

Compared with the number of African dilemma tales, remarkably few are to be found in Aarne and Thompson's *The types of the folktale* (1964). One that they include is AT 653, "The Four Skillful Brothers," a widely distributed dilemma tale, which is analyzed as follows:

1. *The Four Brothers Tested* (a) Four brothers sent to learn trades return home and are tested. (b) The star-gazer sees how many eggs are in a bird's nest on a tree; the thief steals the eggs; the huntsman shoots them although they are scattered about on a table; the tailor sews them up so that they can be returned. Only a red line is around the neck of the birds when hatched.

2. *Rescue of Princess* (a) A stolen princess is offered in marriage to her rescuer. (b) The astronomer finds her on a rock in a distant sea; the thief steals her; the huntsman shoots the dragon guardian; the tailor sews together the shattered planks on the boat on which they are returning.

3. *The Reward* (a) Each claims to be rescuer of the princess and they dispute as to who shall have her. (b) The dispute is still unsettled; or (c) it is proposed that she be divided and thus the true lover is discovered; or (d) they are given half the kingdom instead.

Over 270 examples are reported from Europe and Asia, 22 for the Americas, 1 for the Cape Verde Islands, and 6 for Africa (Aarne and Thompson 1964: 228–229).

Although they occur together in a Kongo tale (37:3–38:1), as they do also in the version recorded by the Grimm Brothers, the African evidence demonstrates that Part I (37: 1–3) and Parts II–III (38: 1–7) of AT 653 are two separate tale types, as "each is a traditional tale that has an independent existence" (Thompson 1951: 415).

A third dilemma tale is AT 653A, "The Rarest Thing in the World," which is summarized (omitting motif numbers) as follows:

A princess is offered to the one bringing the rarest thing in the world. Three brothers set out and acquire magic objects: a telescope which shows all that is happening in the world, a carpet (or the like) which transports one at will, and an apple (or other object) which heals or resuscitates. With the telescope it is learned that the princess is dying or dead. With the carpet they go to her immediately and with the apple they cure or restore her to life. Dispute as to who is to marry her.

This tale type is reported in small numbers from Europe and the Americas, with one instance from the Cape Verde Islands, and none for Africa (Aarne and Thompson 1964: 229–230).

Actually, AT 653A is the most common dilemma tale in Africa, with thirty-seven examples noted (36: 1–37). Five of the seven African and Canary Island tales cited under AT 653 belong under AT 653A, which was not distinguished in the first edition of *The types of the folktale*, when Klipple made her survey of African folktales with foreign analogues in 1938. Only Klipple's Betsimisaraka tale (37: 1) is an example of AT 653, her Haya tale being distinct enough to be listed separately (7:1).

AT 653B, "The Suitors Restore the Maiden to Life," resembles AT 653 and 653A and ends with the question, "Which shall have her?" It does not fit the general pattern of dilemma tales, however, because the answer is a clever solution rather than a thoughtful choice. Only Indian versions of this tale are reported in Aarne and Thompson (1964: 230), but there is a Sanskrit literary version (Farnham 1920: 252).

AT 976, "Which Was the Noblest Act?" and AT 985, "Brother Chosen Rather than Husband or Son," also seem to be dilemma tales. However, counting AT 653 as two tale types, this gives only five dilemma tales that I have been able to find in the Aarne and Thompson index. This is a very small number indeed compared with the large repertoire of dilemma tales known in Africa.

In his type-index of East African tales, Arewa (1966) concluded that dilemma tales should be classified as a special subgroup of formula tales. Because they are so numerous and so diverse, it would be futile to attempt to squeeze African dilemma tales into types 653, 976 and 985, and many of them do seem to belong with formula tales rather than with ordinary folktales. However, some appear to have been converted from ordinary folktales by the addition of dilemmas.

The following African dilemma tales also have analogues in the Aarne and Thompson index:

30:1.	AT 291	"Deceptive Tug of War"
31:1–2.	AT 1525H₁	"One Thief Steals Egg from Bird's Nest"
48:1–8.	AT 560	"The Magic Ring"
50:1–17.	AT 160	"Grateful Animals; Ungrateful Man"
80:1–2.	AT 1250	"Bringing Water from the Well"
98:1–2.	AT 303	"The Twins or Blood Brothers"
124:1–2.	AT 945	"Luck and Intelligence"
152:1.	AT 1415	"Lucky Hans"

In addition, AT 1418*, "The Father Overhears," constitutes part of one of three versions of the tale of the lover who sleeps with a corpse (165:2). Part I of AT 1525N, "The Two Thieves Trick Each Other," begins and AT 1532, "The Voice from the Grave," ends the dilemma tale about two thieves who hide their spoils in a pit (33–35:1–3). Other African dilemma tales resemble AT 654, "The Three Brothers," (3: 6); AT 1585, "The Lawyer's Mad Client," (88: 1–3); and AT 2042, "Chain of Accidents," (56: 1–3). As summarized in Aarne and Thompson, all these tale types are straightforward narratives and not dilemma tales.

This raises a basic question about the nature of dilemma tales. Do they constitute a separate class of folktales? Or are they simply ordinary folktales that have been converted into dilemma tales by the addition of arguments or questions? We know that the category of explanatory tales is almost meaningless in some societies because explanatory elements can be added or omitted by the narrator at will. Is the same true for dilemma tales? It is to investigate this question that versions of tales that lack explicit dilemmas have been included here.

As is often the case, the answer to this question is not a clear yes or no. The European analogues just cited suggest that standard folktales can easily be converted into dilemma tales, and the evidence can be considerably strengthened if we restrict our attention to African tales, where the probability of historical relationship is greater. Of seventeen African versions of the hunter and the grateful animals (AT 160), only two (Kpelle and Vai) involve an explicit dilemma (50: 1–2). It is of course possible that the dilemma has been omitted in the telling or recording of the other fifteen African versions, but lacking any supporting evidence — either external or internal — we must accept these versions as they are and conclude that the Kpelle and Vai have converted this ordinary folktale into a dilemma tale. Similarly, of twenty versions of "alternate housebuilding," only the Swahili one presents a dilemma (55:1); dilemmas are posed only in the Ashanti version of the youth and his lion friend (51: 1–11) and in the two Nkundo versions of "Dog Finds Ring" (48: 1–8).

Conversely, the evidence suggests that the dilemma may be omitted, though this cannot be as convincingly substantiated. Analogues of versions of the tales considered here have been recorded among the Malinke, but all without dilemmas (1:13, 3:6, 5:2, 8:4–5). By apparently omitting the dilemmas, the Malinke have converted them into tall tales, or improbable tales (*Unwahrscheinlichkeiten*) as Frobenius calls them. It also seems that the Luba have omitted the dilemma from one of their versions (41:10) of the tale of a man who is found and restored to life (41: 1–11). The Mosi version (101:7) of the tale of the wife who lies under the dead lion (or leopard) would seem to be another example.

However, the fact that dilemma tales have so often been distinguished by special terms suggests that they constitute a separate class of folktales. There are two valid reasons for maintaining that this is the case. In the first place, there are African tales which apparently have been recorded only in the form of dilemma tales (e.g. 36: 1–37, 82: 1–6, 96: 1–7, 104: 1–6, 105: 1–15). In the second place, some dilemma tales would hardly be worth repeating if the dilemma were omitted (e.g. 57–73), and if they were not repeated, they could not persist in the verbal tradition. Similarly, I would argue that some explanatory folktales and legends might not persist if their etiological elements were omitted.

The answer to this rhetorical question seems to be that, as in the case of explanatory elements, dilemmas can be added to or omitted from some folktales but that there is a group of tales from which the dilemma cannot be, or at least apparently never is, omitted. As Finnegan (1967: 30) says, "In some plots certainly a concluding dilemma seems an essential feature [she cites 23:3 and 122:1 as examples]; but in many others whether or not a dilemma is stated seems to be a matter of choice for the teller rather than an inherent characteristic of the story itself." When some versions of a tale have an explicit dilemma (e.g. 24: 1–2) and an equal number do not (e.g. 24: 3–4), there is no way of deciding whether the dilemma has been added or omitted. When the only known version of a tale presents a dilemma, it must be assumed that it is a dilemma tale, though a single version is not sufficient to establish that it is a traditional tale. Any final decisions in such cases must wait until further evidence is available.

In an earlier discussion of dilemma tales I concurred with Arewa's suggestion that they should be grouped together as a subgroup of formula tales (Bascom 1972). I am now forced to retract this statement, because the evidence indicates that dilemmas can be added to or omitted from some folktales. (This new conclusion was reached only because a special effort was made to include analogous tales, regardless of whether or not they had explicit dilemmas.) As in the case of explanatory tales, there seem to be some narratives that can exist only as dilemma tales, and these might be so classified. However, this does not justify putting all tales that have dilemmas (or explanatory elements) into a special category as that would mean separating them from tales with similar plots. Any valid attempt at tale typing must be based on the plot, which is the integral feature of narratives, rather than on discrete items such as dilemmas, explanatory elements, or characters, which can be added, omitted, or substituted for one another.

There are other folktales that end with questions, arguments, or debates but which do not qualify as dilemma tales because they do not call for moral or ethical judgements or for choices between relative skills. It is the nature of the issues involved that distinguishes dilemma tales from those with similar questions, including the following tales about clever men, stupid men, and numbskulls:

AT 1577. "Blind Men Duped into Fighting; Money to be Divided." Trickster says that he is giving one of them money to be divided with the others. Gives it to none. They quarrel and fight.

AT 1698A. "Search for the Lost Animal." A inquires for his lost animal. B talks about his work and makes a gesture. A follows the directions of the gesture and happens to find the animals. He returns and offers an injured animal to B in thanks. B thinks he is blamed for injuring the animals. Dispute. Taken to deaf judge.

AT 1225. "The Man Without a Head in the Bear's Den." A man's head is snatched off by accident and his companions did not see what has happened. Debate: Did he ever have a head?

AT 1225A. "How Did the Cow Get on the Pole?" A fool hides his purse on a pole on a cliff. A rascal substitutes cow-dung for the money. The fool is interested only in how the cow could have reached the purse.

AT 1347. "Living Crucifix Chosen." Peasants take their old crucifix to an artist for a new one. The artist asks them whether they want a living or dead crucifix. Argument: Living God takes less for upkeep and he can be killed later.

At least where Africa is concerned, dilemma tales cannot be defined as tales ending with a question (Motif Z16), as has been suggested (Klipple 1938; Berry 1961:6). Some tales that end with a question do not qualify as dilemma tales; some dilemma tales end with an argument rather than a question. When a question is asked in a dilemma tale, it may be followed by an answer provided by the narrator. In the words of Mengrelis, "The end is not quite . . . an end. The adventure is finished but it is the audience that gives the conclusion." Even tales from the same society, which are almost certainly historically related, may or may not have questions (e.g. 87:3, 87:4) and may or may not have answers (e.g. 96:3, 96:5).

An essential feature of the dilemma tale is that it presents an unresolved issue that is to be debated by the audience. The "Judgement of Solomon" (AT 926), which may epitomize a dilemma in the minds of many people, has been omitted because none of the African versions encountered (e.g. Pinney n.d.: 171–172) suggest that the dispute over the child is referred to the audience for discussion. With considerable misgivings I have included a tale that Jablow has classed as a dilemma tale (53: 1). When Frog is called to dine with his two wives at the same time, it is clear that he is faced with a dilemma, but is the audience?

I have also excluded tales that end with a problem, such as how can a man cross a river in a small canoe with a leopard, a goat, and a yam? (Cardinall 1931: 205). These intriguing items of folklore, which are fairly common in Africa, have been classed with riddles as "arithmetical puzzles" by A. Taylor (1951: 1). Arewa (1966: 251, 255; 1971: 229) classes them with prose narratives as "mathematical (logical) dilemma tales," as opposed to "philosophical (moral) dilemma tales." For the sake of simplicity and to avoid confusion, I prefer to restrict the term dilemma tale to the latter, while deferring any judgement on whether "arithmetical puzzles" are folktales or riddles.

Both riddles and arithmetical puzzles resemble dilemma tales in that they also pose questions for the audience to answer, but riddles at least need not be stated in the form of prose narratives. Dilemma tales differ further in that they often have no "answers," and when they do, they are of quite a different nature from the answers to these two other genres. Moreover, even if an "answer" is provided, dilemma tales lead to argumentation and debate, whereas, to my knowledge, riddles and arithmetical problems do not. Put concisely, riddles are to be answered; arithmetical puzzles are to be solved; dilemma tales are to be resolved.

Though L.–V. Thomas considers dilemma tales to be a kind of riddle, he recognizes that they do not call for fixed answers, but "raise strangely difficult problems of morality and give rise to interminable palavers." He also notes that they are taken seriously as a "highly prized kind of intellectual activity," whereas riddles are widely regarded by Africans as meant for children (Bascom 1965: 484).

African dilemma tales are folktales. They are prose narratives, and there is nothing to suggest that, like myths and legends, they are accepted as factual accounts. Rather they seem clearly to be hypothetical cases, and presumably they are regarded as fiction. Most frequently their principal characters are humans, but in some cases they are animals (45–56); in some tales of the Nkundo and other Mongo peoples they are inanimate or are parts of animate beings (57–75). Typically, these dilemma tales do not end with an escape, a departure, or a death, as do many African folktales. Several end with explanatory elements (17:1, 39:3, 42:3, 52:1, 53:1–2, 63:1, 68:2–6, 74:2, 84:3, 105:12), and the same plot may be employed for either a dilemma tale or an explanatory tale (3:7, 42:4, 47:4, 48:6, 50:5, 50:7, 51:5, 51:11, 56:2). Again, some dilemma tales have moral tales as analogues (24:4, 42:5, 48:7, 50:9–10,

92:2, 93:6, 168:2), but very few African tales have both explicit morals and dilemmas (18:3, 122:2).

Despite their wide distribution, dilemma tales do not seem to be appreciated equally by all African peoples. I do not refer only to the hundreds of African groups who are not represented in the tales presented here, as this negative evidence may simply reflect the nature of the available collections of their folktales. However, all five of the Malinke analogues to these tales lack dilemmas, and I have not encountered any tales with dilemmas among the Malinke, who seem to prefer tall tales to argumentation.

Similarly, though I have examined more than 300 different folktales from the Yoruba of Nigeria and Dahomey, I have not found one with a dilemma. The only dilemma tale comes from the Ana, a Yoruba offshoot at Atakpame in Togo. Two versions of the hunter and the grateful animals have been recorded as a moral tale among the Yoruba in Dahomey (50: 9–10) but this is told as a dilemma tale in only two out of seventeen African versions. There is also a Yoruba version from Nigeria of the tale of the snake that took refuge in a person's stomach, but it also ends with a moral instead of a dilemma (93:6). Again, only one of the six versions of this tale has been reported with a dilemma, in this case Jablow's Hausa tale from an unidentified source. The Yoruba also tell the fairly common tale of "The Lawyer's Mad Client" (AT 1585) in a straightforward manner (88:3); its only known dilemma versions are from the Nkundo (88:1–2). However, two dilemma tales (96:7, 97:1) are found in Tutuola's *The palm-wine drinkard* (1953).

On the other hand, dilemma tales are very popular in the area of Liberia and Sierra Leone (among the Bandi, Gio, Kpelle, Limba, Loma, Mano, Mende, Temne, and Vai) and also among the Nkundo of Zaïre. Forty-five Nkundo dilemma tales have been published in Hulstaert and de Rop's *Rechtspraakfabels van de Nkundó* (1954), the most important collection of original African dilemma tales. An anonymous article, "Fables juridiques Nkundo" (1956) in *Annales N.D. Sacré Coeur* is reported to contain two Nkundo dilemma tales with their resolutions, but unfortunately this article has not been accessible. Eighteen additional dilemma tales come from the Mongo, the large cultural group that embraces the Nkundo. More than fifty of the tales considered here are from the Hausa of Nigeria, but this reflects the fact that more folktales have been published for the Hausa than for any other African society; more than a third of these tales lack explicit dilemmas.

I have no explanation for this difference in taste. I suspect that it may somehow be related to different patterns of settling disputes, and perhaps to the importance of the informal "house palaver" or moot among the Kpelle and their neighbors. (However, even if adequate information on legal institutions and practices were available to pursue this suggestion, I suspect that it might not support a rigid hypothesis such as, for example, that dilemma tales are less popular where more formal courts of law are more important.) In addition, whereas the dilemma tales from Liberia and Sierra Leone often end with a question or with the statement that the argument has never been settled, all those in Hulstaert and de Rop's collection are resolved. Moreover, the "answers" to Nkundo dilemma tales are longer and more involved than usual.

Two broad categories of dilemma tales may be distinguished. The first often involves a contest or competition and asks the audience to decide which character is the most skillful, most powerful, greediest, or the like. If they did not present this choice, many of the tales in this category would be tall tales, and it is characteristic of them that the question is seldom answered. Of the ninety-one versions of tales of contest (1–35), two are resolved by magic (1:10, 1:11), but answers are given in only eight cases (2:6, 11:1, 15:2, 17:1, 18:3, 23:5, 26:1, 30:1). One of these (15:2) comes from the Nkundo, all of whose dilemma tales are provided with resolutions, but this is the only tale of contest among the forty-five dilemma tales in *Rechtspraakfabels van de Nkundó*. It would seem that this simpler type has little appeal for the Nkundo, despite their apparent predilection for dilemma tales.

Dilemma tales of the second type (36–168), which are more often resolved by the narrator, involve moral or ethical judgements and are considerably more interesting because of the light that they throw on cultural norms and values. Thus, we see how attitudes toward the mother-in-law, often expressed in no uncertain terms (80–84), vary from one society to another and even reveal a generation gap (81). We also find the question of whether sons or daughters are the more desirable (103) and of whether the eldest or the most loyal son should inherit (111–112). The audience is called upon to judge which of several sons should inherit from his father, when the mother of each has saved the father's life (105). The hero may be forced to choose among several wives, each of whom has expressed her grief at his death in her own way (96) or to decide whether to kill his adoptive father who has been kind to him or his real father who has mistreated him (87). The lengthy resolutions of the Nkundo dilemma tales in particular involve nuances that cannot be presented adequately in these summaries, but their subtlety is at least suggested by the different resolutions of similar dilemmas (111:1, 112:1; 116:1, 116:2).

As might be expected, there is no sharp dividing line between these two categories. For example, most of the versions of 36:1–37 (AT 653A) belong in the second category, but one version asks "Which man performed the greatest miracle?" (36:7), and another asks "Which of the three is the greatest magician?" (36:15). Perhaps it would be better to think of dilemma tales as falling on a continuum between these two extremes. Rather than trying to order them in this fashion, however, an attempt has been made to separate them into two categories, beginning with tales of contest.

Analogous tales have been grouped together under the same initial number, with the individual variants distinguished by secondary numbers. Tales grouped together in this fashion are usually similar enough and often geographically close enough to suggest the possibility of a common historical origin, but no claim is made that they are actually homologues. They are presented only as analogues. Further evidence may show that some of these should be given separate initial numbers or, conversely, that similar tales, which I have tried to place near to each other, should be grouped under the same initial number. Beyond this, it has proved difficult to present the tales in any systematic order despite several reorganizations. In the hope that it may be helpful in locating tales where an index is impractical, a list of "catch phrases" describing the content of each group of tales precedes the tales.

For each of the initial numbers there is at least one version that involves a dilemma. As indicated earlier, it was essential to include analogous tales that lack explicit dilemmas in order to determine whether or not dilemma tales constitute a separate category of prose narratives. A second reason for so doing is the hope that this will be helpful when a tale-type index for Africa is prepared or when the Aarne-Thompson index is again revised.

The most frustrating aspect of assembling the relevant texts was to find a dilemma version of a familiar African tale (e.g. 54:1, 88:1–2, 98: 1–2, 149:1–2) but not to recall where the non-dilemma versions had been encountered and not to have the time to search again through the extensive literature to find them. I have not attempted to summarize again all the African versions of the tale of "alternate house-building" (Bascom 1969: 133) which has been converted into a Swahili dilemma tale (55:1). Nor have I felt it necessary to try to include the many African non-dilemma versions of the well known tale of the tug of war that Tortoise arranged between Elephant and Hippopotamus (AT 291), which the Mpongwe end with the question: "Were they equal?" (30:1).

Rather than restrict this survey to Africa south of the Sahara, or even to the African continent as is often done, I have attempted to include North Africa, Ethiopia, Malagasy, and the African islands. My coverage of these areas may leave much to be desired, but I do not pretend to present an exhaustive survey, if only because of the diverse and often inaccessible sources in which African folktales have been published. Additional dilemma tales and variants continue to turn up, but I have taken the date of my article (Bascom 1972) as an arbitrary cutoff point. I expect that that article and the present study will bring to light many others that I have missed.

1:1–14.   Cross river on smoke, etc.
2:1–6.   Shoot arrow through rock
3:1–7.   Catch arrow in flight (cf. AT 654)
4:1.   Giants and leper
5:1.   Horse in sky
6:1.   Father in sky
7:1.   Cure father's feet
8:1–5.   Counting seeds
9:1.   Needle in pond
10:1.   Dig a well
11:1.   Dipper in air
12:1.   Arrow in air
13:1.   Race up hill
14:1–3.   Horsemanship
15:1–2.   Tree as belt
16:1–2.   Thresh millet with penis
17:1.   Harvesting palm nuts
18:1–3.   Cure blindness and lameness
19:1–3.   The smallest
20:1.   Crafty man and woman
21:1.   Three fools
22:1.   Two fools
23:1–5.   Greedies butcher cow
24:1–4.   Greedies divide bean
25:1–4.   Greedy is buried
26:1.   Overeating and oversleeping
27:1–3.   Sleeping contest
28:1.   Greatest memory: it is sweet
29:1.   Eating own head
30:1.   Tug of war (AT 291)
31:1–4.   Thieves steal from each other (AT 1525H₁)

32:1.　　Thieves disclaim stealing
33–5:1–7. Thieves in pit (AT 1525N, 1532)
36:1–37.　Mirror, etc. (AT 653A)
37:1–3.　Repairing an egg (AT 653)
38:1–7.　Repairing boat (AT 653)
39:1–4.　Rescue from eagle (lion, snake)
40:1–2.　Rescue from crocodile (hippopotamus)
41:1–11.　Where is father?
42:1–6.　Drinking river dry
43:1–2.　Escape with sweetheart
44:1.　　Rescue by liar, etc.
45:1.　　Hunter saved by animals
46:1–6.　Recovering cattle
47:1–4.　Poisoned food in sky
48:1–8.　Dog finds ring (AT 560)
49:1.　　Animal language
50:1–17.　Grateful animals (AT 160)
51:1–13.　Boy and lion cub
52:1.　　Leopard eats child
53:1–2.　Frog's two wives
54:1.　　War of birds and beasts
55:1–20.　Alternate house-building
56:1–3.　Chain of accidents (AT 2042)
57:1.　　Fire and water
58:1.　　Two seasons
59:1.　　Canoe and paddle
60:1.　　Canoe and drum
61:1.　　Mortar and canoe
62:1.　　Mortar and climbing belt
63:1.　　Garden knife and axe
64:1.　　Pitfall and spikes
65:1.　　Net and legs
66:1.　　Manioc and banana
67:1.　　Manioc and plantain
68:1–8.　Oil palm and raffia palm
69:1.　　Bofumbo tree and parasol tree
70:1.　　Tree parts
71:1.　　Two hands
72:1.　　Hand and mouth
73:1.　　Foot and stomach
74:1–2.　Body parts

157:1.   Charm for wealth
158:1–4.   Cure for blindness
159:1.   Cure for impotence
160:1.   Knocked with baobab
161:1.   Husband's rough buttocks
162:1.   Father takes son's bride
163:1.   Deer escapes
164:1.   Fouls his trousers
165:1–3.   Sleep with corpse (cf. AT 1418*)
166:1.   Blind man's proposition
167:1.   Four lovers
168:1–2.   Revenge on chief

Cross River Smoke, etc.

1:1.   (Krachi)   Three travelers came to a large river. One said he could walk across it on his magic sandals. Another said he could cut the waters with his magic cutlass and walk across. The third said that this was too much trouble; he had a magic thread on which all three could cross over. Which of the three men had the most power has never been decided (Cardinall 1931: 201).

1:2.   (Vai)   Male triplets came to a river. One lit his pipe and walked across the river on its smoke. Another walked across on a thread. The third shot arrows to make a bridge on which he crossed over. Who knows which one excelled? (Ellis 1914: 191–192).

1:3.   (Kpelle)   Three cunning young men crossed a river without getting wet. The first fired his gun and walked across on the smoke; the second stuck his arrows in the water and crossed over on them; the third, who was the cleverest, dived into the water and came out on the other side, brushing his clothes and saying, "This dust is uncomfortable" (Mengrelis 1950: 189). No dilemma is presented here, but Mengrelis does not always present complete tales in this article and, as noted in the introduction, he comments on the frequency of Kpelle tales that end in dilemmas.

1:4.   (Wolof)   Three youths came to a huge river. The first split the water with his sword and reached the other bank with dry feet. The second unrolled a band of cloth and made a bridge on which he crossed

over. The third shot arrow after arrow, each striking the other so that
they formed a wooden bridge over the river. Which is the most cunning?
(Guillot 1933: 54).

1:5. (Mosi) Three brothers came to a lake. The eldest threw a piece
of cloth on the water, making a path for himself. The next joined his
arrows together and crossed over on them. The youngest put on his
magic shoes and walked across the water. Which had the best charm?
(Froger 1910: 234–235).

1:6. (Unidentified, Cameroun) Three men returning home with their
brides came to a river in flood. One was a well-known *marabout*
[priest], another was a famous hunter, and the third was a man like you
or me. The *marabout* said that each should cross over with his wife and
they would see who was the strongest. The *marabout* wrote a verse from
the Koran on a leaf, put it on the water, sat on it, and crossed over with
his wife without getting wet. The hunter took an arrow from
his quiver, put it on the water, sat on it, and crossed over with his wife.
The third man uprooted a huge baobab tree and struck the water with
all his force. The water receded, and he also crossed the river. I ask you,
which of the three was the strongest? (Fouda, de Julliot, and Lagrave
1961: 15).

1:7. (Karekare) A *malam* [priest] set out on a journey accompanied
by a fighter and a hunter. On their return they came to a river in flood.
The *malam* put two pieces of paper on the water and walked across,
stepping from one to another and putting the piece behind in front of
him. The hunter shot two arrows into the water and walked across on
them in the same fashion. The fighter struck the water with his club,
parting it so that he could walk across. They came to an old woman and
asked her for food. She said she had put cold water into boiling water
and had poured both onto a mat in order to separate them. They came
to a man digging a well and asked him for food. He said it was so hot
that he was going to move his well into the shade of a tree and then
move it back again when the sun set. Now, which of the five was the
cleverest? (Frobenius 1921–1928: IX, 406–407).

1:8. (Hausa) The King of Wrestlers, the King of Bowmen, and the
King of Prayer were returning home with their brides when they came
to a river in flood. The King of Prayer prostrated himself, spat on his
staff, and struck the water with it; the water parted, and he and his bride

crossed over. The King of Bowmen set his arrows in a line on the water, picked up his bride, and carried her across; then he returned and picked up his arrows. The King of Wrestlers seized his bride and, with a wrestling trick, twisted his leg about hers and jumped over the water. Among them who was better than another? (Rattray 1913: I, 204–208; retold by Jablow 1961: 101–102).

1:9.   (Hausa)   An untranslated version of this tale has been partially summarized by Merrick in a book review: "The learned man, priest or mallam, the archer, the wrestler and the courtesan are represented as traveling together and stopped by a swollen river. Each relies on the instruments of his trade to cross the water." This version ends with the question, "Which was the best?" (Harris 1908: 11–13; summarized in 1909 by Merrick [*Folk-Lore* 20:374]).

1:10.   (Bambara)   A woman promised the hand of her beautiful daughter to the suitor who would bring her home. The three suitors set out together and found her on the other side of a river in flood. The first suitor threw her his *sabara-diala* [garment?] which she put on the water and walked across. The second told her to go back to the other side of the river; he took his arrows and threw them rapidly one after another so that they formed a bridge on which she crossed over. The third took his sword in both hands and parted the waters so that she could return. Embarrassed, the mother slapped her daughter, transforming her into three identical girls, one for each suitor. But of these four persons, which was the greatest sorcerer? (Traoré 1944–1945: 26).

1:11.   (Dyola)   A girl of incredible beauty had four suitors who lived on the other side of the river. They had no canoe and could not swim across because of the strong current and many crocodiles. The first suitor took off his sandals, knocked them together, and flew over in the cloud of dust that came out. The second shot four bullets from his gun, perched on them, and quickly reached the other bank. The third put a strip of cloth on the water and easily crossed over. The fourth parted the water with his machete and passed through dry-footed. Arriving at the girl's village at the same time, they fell before her. Each of the suitors was equally handsome, equally strong, and equally intelligent. What to do? "Don't be afraid," said the girl's mother and, touching her with a wand, she transformed her into four girls of equal beauty. Several days later four weddings were celebrated (L.–V. Thomas 1970: 296–297).

1:12. (Hausa) A *malam* and a grass cutter came to a river in flood. The *malam* spat on his staff and struck the water with it; the water parted and he crossed over. The grass cutter took his sickle, cut the water, tied it into bundles, and stacked it; then he crossed over (Edgar 1911–1913: I, (4); translated by Skinner n.d.: I, (4)).

1:13. (Malinke) Three young men returning home with their brides came to a river in flood. The first took a small piece of wood, put his bride on it, and swam across. The second took out his purse, put all the water in it, and crossed over with his bride. The third took his knife, parted the waters, and walked across with his bride (Frobenius 1921–1928: VIII, 44).

1:14. (Guro) A man went to visit his girl friend, accompanied by six friends. When they came to a river that they could not swim, he shot arrows from his bow, making a bridge. The second parted the water with a blow of his knife. The third drained the river with a calabash. The fourth took burning embers and passed beneath the water without the fire being extinguished. The fifth put on a large gown and walked across. The sixth simply walked over on the water. The seventh threw his loin-cloth on the water and crossed on it as though on a boat. (This tale continues with a second tale type.)

Shoot Arrow through Rock

2:1. (Guro) On the other side they came to a large rock behind which was an elephant. The first man shot an arrow through the rock and killed the elephant. The second went through the arrow's hole and returned the same way with the dead animal. The third skinned it with his thumbnail. The fourth called enough wood to cook it. The fifth formed a circle with his arms and all the meat was put on them. The sixth cut enough peanut leaves to wrap up all the meat. Finally, the seventh carried it to the girl friend's village on his forefinger (Tauxier 1924: 298).

2:2. (Loma) One man shot through a rock and killed an elephant. Another followed the shot, butchered the elephant, and carried it back through the hole. The third picked a louse from his head, skinned it, and sewed up the elephant in the louse's skin. The tale is entitled, "Who did the biggest stunt?" (Schwab 1947: 448).

2:3–4.   (Limba)   Three men went hunting. One shot an elephant; one butchered it with his thumbnail; the third killed a small fly, skinned it, and carried the meat home in the fly's skin. Who was the cleverest? (Finnegan 1967: 221–222). Finnegan notes that she heard a Limba story incorporating this plot but lacking a specific dilemma.

2:5.   (Vai)   One man shot through a rock and killed an elephant. Another went through the hole in the rock and brought the elephant back through the hole. When they reached home, they were served the cooked liver of the elephant they had just killed. They called the people and asked them to judge which of them excelled the other (Ellis 1914: 193–194).

2:6.   (Temne)   A boy shot through a hill and killed a hog on the other side. His twin brother went through the hole and brought the hog home. When they arrived, they found that their sister had already cooked the heart, liver, and lung of the hog that he was carrying. Which of the three surpassed the others? "A lively argument followed this story, and it was evident that there was a difference of opinion. However, the majority seemed to think 'de girl do de big t'in pass all' " (Cronise and Ward 1903: 199–200).

Catch Arrow in Flight

3:1.   (Mosi)   A man climbed to the granary and threw down millet for his wife to make a cake. As he descended, his wife took the millet, pounded it, ground it, cooked it, and said, "Pay attention to this cake that comes out of the oven." The next day the man went hunting and shot at a gazelle. He caught the animal by its horns, stabbed it, and, hearing a whistling sound, caught his arrow in his hand. Which is the speedier? (Guillot 1933: 54; retold in Guillot 1946: 37–38).

3:2.   (Dyola)   A couple noted for their speed in hunting and cooking received an unexpected visitor. Telling his wife to prepare *couscous*, the husband found a magnificent antelope in a few minutes, shot it, and began slaughtering it as the bullet reached its mark. When he returned home, his wife told him to throw down some sheaves of millet. Before he could climb back down his wife cried, "Watch where you put your feet or you'll upset this delicious *couscous*." Frightened at this the visitor fled, saying, "I am among sorcerers," and before he finished speaking, he was at the other end of the Casamance. In your opinion, which of these three was the quickest? (L.–V. Thomas 1970: 235).

3:3. (Kpelle) A hunter shot at an elephant, rushed forward, and killed it with his knife. Returning, he caught the bullet in his hand and said, "It is not necessary for the bullet to spoil the elephant's meat" (Mengrelis 1950: 189–190). As in the case of 1:3, this tale may have had a specific dilemma which was omitted in Mengrelis' summary.

3:4. (Bambara) Two brothers went to the fields after a heavy rain. The younger brother, who carried a basket of seeds on his head, slipped. But before he fell, he put the basket down, took off his white gown and trousers, and put on his old gown and trousers; then he fell. A deer ran past and the elder brother took his gun and shot at it. Impatient, he went himself and seized the deer, butchered it, skinned it, put the meat in the hide, and hung it at his side. Then he caught the bullet, saying, "Don't spoil my meat." When they reached home, the elder brother's wife told the younger brother to get some millet. He climbed into the granary and handed her a small basket full, and then a second. The third time she said, "Don't put seeds in my [cooked] dough." Which of these three is the fastest? (Travélé 1923: 57–58).

3:5. (Hausa) A storm caught Speed King and Dodging King in the bush. Speed cut some grass, collected it, made a booth, entered it, and escaped the rain. Dodging began jigging here and there between the drops until the rain stopped. When Speed came out of his booth he slipped, but before he hit the ground he whipped out a sickle, cut some palm fronds, plaited a mat, and fell on it (Edgar 1911–1913: I, (2); translated by Skinner n.d.: I, (2); cf. AT 654).

3:6. (Malinke) Three men went to harvest millet and were caught in the rain. The youngest, who carried a basket of millet on his head, slipped as far as from Bamako to Kati. As he fell, he reached into a house and picked up a knife, cut grass along the path, wove a mat from it, and laid the mat on the ground so that the millet spilled on it. As he put the millet back into his basket, he said, "If I hadn't been quick enough to make this mat, I'd have had the devil's own job picking up that grain." The eldest took his forty chickens out of their baskets to feed them. As an eagle swooped down at the chickens, he picked up all forty of them, put them in their own baskets, shut the baskets, and seized the eagle, saying, "What do you mean getting fresh with my chickens!" When the

youngest shot at an antelope, the third man jumped up, ran to the antelope, killed it, skinned and quartered it, laid the hide in the sun to dry,
and put the meat in his knapsack. Just then the arrow whistled by. He
caught it with one hand and shouted at the youngest, "Hey! What do you
mean by trying to shoot holes in my knapsack!" (Frobenius 1921–1928:
VIII, 36; translated in Frobenius and Fox 1937: 153–154; partially
abstracted in Waterman and Bascom 1949: 19; retold as a Mende tale
from the Ivory Coast by Courlander 1963: 17–18).

3:7. (Ashanti)   Fly, Moth, and Mosquito went hunting and caught
Anansi but could not subdue him. Anansi said that they could eat him
if they could tell him a story he did not believe; if they did not believe
his story, he would eat them. Moth said that before he was born his
father was injured, so he cleared the forest, cultivated the ground,
planted, weeded, and harvested it; when he was born his father was already wealthy. Mosquito said that when he was four years old and
eating an elephant he had killed, a leopard tried to swallow him, but
he put his hand down the leopard's throat, pulled on its tail, turned the
leopard inside out, and released a sheep, which thanked him and grazed
off into the grass. Fly said that he shot his gun at an antelope, ran forward and caught it, skinned it, quartered it, caught the bullet and put it
back into the gun. Then he climbed a tree, made a fire and cooked and
ate the entire antelope, but he became so heavy and swollen that he
could not climb down. He went to the village, got a rope, and let himself down to the ground with it. Anansi said that he planted a coconut
tree which matured in a month and bore three coconuts containing a fly,
a moth, and a mosquito, but when he tried to eat them, they ran away.
At last he had found them again. No one would admit that he did not
believe the other's tale, but the fly, the moth, and the mosquito fled.
That is why Anansi, the spider, eats them (Courlander and Prempeh
1957: 25–29).

It seems that several distinct tale types — concerning the granary,
catching an arrow or bullet in flight, slipping in the rain, saving
chickens from an eagle, farming before birth, pulling a leopard inside
out, and climbing down from a tree — may be involved here (3:1–7).
For any of these elements to be accepted as a tale type, however, it
would have to be found by itself. In the Kpelle tale (3:3) catching a
bullet in flight seems to fulfill this requirement, but we have no assur-
ance that this tale is complete.

Giants and Leper

4:1. (Wolof)   A giant and his friend went hunting, leaving a second friend near a baobab tree to prepare food. When they returned they were told that the devil of the baobab tree had eaten all the food. The next day the giant took the second friend hunting, but the same thing happened. The third day the giant himself stayed behind to cook the food. When his two friends returned, they found the giant and the devil fighting. The giant seized the devil and crushed him against the baobab with such force that the tree was uprooted and hurled through the air. A giant woman was passing with her giant baby on her back. The baobab fell into the baby's eye and completely disappeared. In anger, the mother began pulling up trees and huge stones to crush the giant and his two friends. They fled, with the mother in pursuit, and came to a leper who hid them in his clothing. The woman hurled pieces of a mountain at the leper, but he had the advantage and she abandoned the fight. The leper loosened his clothing to release the three men, but there was no trace of them. They had been swallowed by the leper's sores. Which is the strongest, the giant, the mother, her baby, or the leper? (Guillot 1933: 87–88).

Horse in Sky

5:1.   (Bambara)   Three men drove their sons from home because one saw too well, another was too skillful, and the third was too strong. While traveling together, the first saw a large horse in the clouds. The second shot it with an arrow. The third stopped its fall, but its force was so great that it bounced out of his hands into a nearby village. They went to look for it and met an old woman carrying its bones. She had caught the horse, killed it, cooked it, eaten it, and gathered its bones to throw them away. Which of the four was the most powerful? (Travélé 1923: 90–91).

5:2.   (Malinke)   Three boys were traveling together. One who saw very well looked up and saw a horse tied above the clouds by a very fine cord. One who shot very well cut the cord with an arrow. One who was very strong spread his arms and caught the horse so that it would not break its legs. They climbed on the horse and rode away (Frobenius 1921–1928: VIII, 45).

Father in Sky

6:1. (Mosi)   One day God picked up a man and tied him to a star by a cord. The man's first son had sharp eyes and saw his father. The second threw his baton, breaking the cord. The third caught his father when he fell. Which of his sons should the father thank? (Guillot 1933: 53).

Cure Father's Feet

7:1. (Haya)   Four brothers named Shooter, Looker, Listener, and Diver found millet to cure their father's feet but lost it on the way home. Listener told where it was in the sky. Looker saw it. Shooter shot it down, but it fell in the water. Diver pulled it out, and their father's feet were healed. Which did the most? (Rehse 1910: 366–367; cited as AT 653 by Klipple 1938).

Counting Seeds

8:1. (Bambara)   Three men set out in a canoe with a basket of eleusine. One had good ears, another was a great counter, and the third had good eyes. The first man said that one of the seeds had fallen into the water. The second counted the seeds and said that one was missing. The third dove into the river and found the seed in the sand. Which was the strongest? (Travélé 1923: 91–92).

8:2. (Unidentified, Sierra Leone)   Three brothers set out on a journey taking a sack of millet for food. The first could hear the slightest rustle of the smallest insect in the grass. The second could see a grain of sand on the path a mile away. The third could count anything from the leaves on a tree to the stars in the sky. They came to a river and started across in a canoe. The first said he heard a grain of millet fall into the river. The second dove into the water to look for it. The third looked through the sack and said, "Yes, you are right. One seed is missing." The second returned with the seed, and they continued their journey. Which of these three, do you think, was the cleverest? (Arnott 1967: 155–157; original source undetermined).

8:3. (Unidentified, Sierra Leone)   Three brothers named Large Ears,

Large Eyes, and Long Hands set out in search of a new crop. Returning home with one millet seed, they crossed a river by canoe. In midstream Large Ears said he heard something fall into the water. Large Eyes saw it in the sand on the river bottom, and Long Hands picked it up. They planted the seed and had a plentiful harvest. The king held a feast and announced he would give his beautiful daughter to the man who had made his kingdom a land of plenty. The three brothers began to quarrel over her. Who do you think deserved to marry the princess? (Baharav 1963–1966: I, 18–20).

8:4. (Malinke)   Three men turned out their sons because one heard so well, one saw so well, and the third counted so well. They loaded a sack of millet on a boat and started across a river. In midstream the first said that he heard a grain of millet fall into the water. The second said he would look for it. The third counted the remaining grains in the sack and said, "He is right. One grain is missing." In the same instant the second man came to the surface and said, "Here it is" (Frobenius 1921–1928: VIII, 45; translated in Frobenius and Fox 1937: 154–155).

8:5. (Malinke)   Three men set out with seven camels laden with millet, and in crossing a stream a grain of millet fell into the water. One man heard the grain fall; the second dove into the water and brought it back; the third counted all the rest of the millet before the second returned and declared that, in fact, one grain was missing. With their loads complete again they went on (Frobenius 1921–1928: VIII, 45).

Needle in Pond

9:1. (Krachi)   A man dropped a needle into a deep pond, threw in a thread, and drew the needle up, properly threaded. Another threw in an empty calabash, then some palm oil, and brought up the calabash filled with palm oil. To this day we do not know which man had more sense (Cardinall 1931: 201).

Dig a Well

10:1. (Dyola)   Two hunters in the forest suddenly became thirsty. One said, "I'll dig a well. You find a bucket." In the same instant he broke open the ground with a mighty kick, and pure fresh water gushed forth. Immediately the second hunter produced a bucket, and they quenched their thirst. Which man was the most worthy? (L.–V. Thomas 1958–1959: II, 430).

Dipper in Air

11:1.   (Ana Yoruba)   One man planted roasted yams, and they grew. Another hung a dipper full of water in the empty air. A third set out fire brands to kill an antelope. The first said that when they returned the yams would be big. The third said they would roast the yams. The second said they would drink the water. Which of the magicians was the greatest? Answer: The one who suspended the dipper of water in the air (Müller 1902: 155–156).

Arrow in Air

12:1.   (Bambara)   A pagan swore to kill the king's son with an arrow. A Muslim swore that a bullet, much less an arrow, would not kill the king's son; he wrote a talisman and fastened it to the neck of the child. The pagan shot his arrow at the child, but it remained suspended between heaven and earth near the child; it did not fall, but it did not strike him. When the child stood, sat, or lay down, the arrow followed without being able to touch him; this lasted three days. When the child entered a room, the arrow hit the door; its head fell to the ground, but its shaft struck the boy who fell down and died. Who is the stronger of these two men? Some say the pagan, but the Muslim had mentioned the arrow and had not mentioned its shaft (Travélé 1923: 84–85).

Race up Hill

13:1.   (Betsimisaraka)   Three brothers raced to a rock at the top of a mountain. The eldest arrived first and struck the rock, half of which turned to water. He cooked rice and ate, and said to the second to arrive, "Get out of the way. I've already held this rock a long time." The second told him to let it go, and when it rolled down the hill, he stopped it with his forefinger. Then he also cooked rice and ate, and said to the youngest when he arrived, "Get out of the way and be careful. I am going to let go of this rock." When it rolled down the hill, the youngest gave it a flick, and it turned into sand. Which was the strongest? (Renel 1910: II, 115–116).

Horsemanship

14:1.   (Hausa)   A chief told his three sons to mount their horses and prove their skill. One thrust his spear through a baobab tree and jumped through the hole with his horse. One lifted his horse by the bit and jumped over the tree. The third pulled the baobab up by its roots and rode up to his father, waving it aloft. Who among them excelled? (Rattray 1913: I, 256–258; abstracted in Waterman and Bascom 1949: 19; retold by Arnott 1962: 40–42 and by Courlander 1963: 50).

14:2.   (Nupe)   A lengthy tale concludes with a father giving each of his three sons a horse. The first son spurred his horse and jumped over a huge tree. The second split the tree open with his spear and jumped through it on his horse. The third son seized the spear, pulled up the tree and its roots, and rode to his father's farm carrying the tree on the end of the spear like a flag (Frobenius 1921–1928: IX, 167–170).

14:3.   (Bambara)   A braggart, who claimed to be without equal in the world as a horseman, was challenged by another man. The braggart galloped to a house with two doors, jumped over it, and landed in his saddle on the other side of the house. The challenger galloped up a baobab tree, broke off a branch, and galloped down again. The braggart admitted that one might say he is without equal in his family but not in the world (Travélé 1923: 86–87).

Tree as Belt

15:1.   (Mende)   A man tied a palm tree around his waist like a belt. His friend hit a large rock and turned it to sand. Which one was stronger? (Kilson 1960–1961: 45–47).

15:2.   (Nkundo)   One man cut down a large tree with a single blow of his knife. A second put it up straight with one hand. A third man twisted the tree like a vine and tied a knot in it. Which of the three do you think is the strongest? Answer: The third (Hulstaert and de Rop 1954: 2–3).

Thresh Millet with Penis

16:1.   (Gurma)   A girl said she would marry the strongest of three suitors, whom she loved equally. Her father told them to thresh his heaps of millet. The first beat the millet so hard with his penis that with one blow all the grains flew from their stalks. The second squatted over the millet and broke wind so powerfully that it blew the chaff away. The third took the skin of his testicles and stretched it until it enclosed all of the millet that his rivals had beaten and winnowed. Which of the three would you choose for a husband? (Equilbecq 1913–1916: II, 96–97).

16:2.   (Hausa)   Four champions visited a town and were given grain, but their hosts had nowhere to thresh it. Horny Head champion said that it could be threshed on his head. Penis champion threshed it with his penis. Wind-Breaking champion blew the chaff away. Testicles champion opened his scrotum, put the grain inside, and carried it home. Which was the greatest? (Edgar 1911–1913; III, (127); translated by Skinner 1969: I, 398–399).

Harvesting Palm Nuts

17:1.   (Baule)   Three young men who wanted to marry came to the village of three beautiful maidens. The first man boasted that he could bring down a cluster of palm nuts by looking at it, the second that he could swallow it in one gulp, and the third that he could excrete it without eating it. Each of the girls promised to marry one of the men if they could do as they boasted. They did so, and each could have had a wife and all would have been fine, but they began to fight over the palm nuts. They took their quarrel to the Sky God, who said that the palm nuts belonged to the first man, but that they would have to divide the women themselves. The first man, who was the strongest, took two wives; the second took one; the third man, who had performed the greatest miracle, had none. He was angry and decreed that thenceforth no men should perform similar feats. So today men do not perform miracles (Himmelheber 1951: 28–30).

Cure Blindness and Lameness

18:1.   (Loma)   A blind man carried a lame man to a palm tree. The lame man directed the blind man to climb up and cut the nuts. The blind man fell on top of the lame man, curing them both. Which had the stronger medicine? (Schwab 1947: 447–448).

18:2. (Gio) A blind man carried a lame man, who shot a monkey. When they returned home, the lame man cooked it and ate it all. When the blind man found only bones, he hit the lame man's knees with them and his lameness was cured. Then the lame man threw the soup in the blind man's eyes, restoring his sight. Which one had the stronger medicine? (Schwab 1947: 448).

18:3. (Vai) A blind man carried a lame man, who shot a monkey. When they returned home, the lame man ate all the meat and cooked only the skin for the blind man. The skin hit the blind man in the eyes, and he could see again. When he saw all the meat, he cut a switch and began to whip the lame man. The lame man was cured and could walk again. They began to argue, each claiming to have cured the other. So they carried the matter to the king, who said that they should let the matter drop, because each had saved the other. You cannot hide dishonesty (Ellis 1914: 236–237).

The Smallest

19:1. (Lyele) One man could put water in the shell of a Bambara groundnut and then dive in and jump about. Another had to fasten a hook to a pole to pick the leaves of a creeping bean plant. Which one was smaller? (Nicolas 1954: 1030).

19:2. (Lyele) One man was so small that he mounted a horse of his own size and entered the house through the cat's hole in the door. The other, suffering from heat, took shelter under a man's big toe. Which one was smaller? (Nicolas 1954: 1030).

19:3. (Hausa) The King of Thinness of Sokoto and the King of Thinness of Wurno met, and each claimed to be the thinner. The one from Wurno jumped on a blade of grass and sat there cross-legged. The one from Sokoto began to dig out the roots of the grass, but by sunset he had not pulled up a single root. Well, now, we want to know, which was the thinner and weaker of the two? (Edgar 1911–1913: I, (66); translated by Skinner n.d.: I, (66).

Crafty Man and Woman

20:1.   (Baule)   A very beautiful woman refused all her suitors because she wanted to marry a very crafty man. A suitor came to the village, and she sent him a plate of food on which there were a spider's thread, a bone, a slice of papaya, and two drum sticks. With these objects he found where she lived. He saw a papaya tree in front of the house, threw the bone to a dog, found two drums at the door, and saw a large cloth at the window suspended by a spider's thread. Knowing that this was her home, he entered. When they were married, the young men of the village were jealous of the stranger and decided to kill him. They attacked him in the bush and were about to strangle him, when he asked to tell something to his wife before he died. He asked them to tell her, "I owe money to the vulture, and you will find it by a red feather under my bed." When she heard this she sent help to him. By the red feather she knew he was red with fear. By the vulture, she understood that he was afraid of death in the forest, where only vultures are interested in the dead. Which was the craftier, the man or the woman? (Guillot 1933: 89).

Three Fools

21:1.   (Bambara)   Three men drove their sons from home because one knew nothing, another was a fool, and the third was stupid. They met in another village where their landlord sent one to find string, another to catch fish, and the third to gather baobab fruit; but they returned empty-handed. The first said that he could not find any string to tie his bundle of string. The second said that thirst had prevented him from bringing his basket of fish, because he could not find any water. The third said that he had climbed the baobab tree and had put his hand on the fruit to touch it to his stick, but when he descended and threw the stick, it had failed to detach the fruit. Which of the three was the most foolish? (Travélé 1923: 56–57).

Two Fools

22:1.   (Mosi)   Two brothers were given a sheep by the king. One pulled it from the front, and the other pushed it from behind, but the sheep escaped. While the first held on to the rope, the other went to look for the sheep. The second asked how the sheep escaped; the first asked why it was lost. Which was the greater fool? (Froger 1910: 236–237).

Greedies Butcher Cow

23:1. (Kono) Two greedy brothers went hunting and killed two large buffaloes. When they were roasted, the elder brother sent the younger for water. The younger brother could not refuse, but fearing that the elder would eat all the meat in his absence, he walked backward, fell into an abyss, and was killed. The elder brother said he would eat all the meat, but his stomach burst before he could eat his own half. Which of the two brothers was more greedy? (Holas 1952: 84–85).

23:2. (Temne) Three men were given a cow, and they decided to kill it. One hung his mouth underneath the cow to catch its blood, and his head was chopped off by mistake. Another went for water, but, fearing that the third would eat all the meat in his absence, he walked backwards, fell into a well, and was drowned. The third then went for water and returned to find a gazelle stealing the meat. The gazelle's feet became stuck in the pot, but it escaped. The man chased the gazelle, caught it, and tried to lick its foot, but the gazelle kicked him and burst his throat. Which of these three men was the greediest? (Cronise and Ward 1903: 205–209).

23:3. (Limba) Boy triplets were given a cow. One lay beneath the cow when it was slaughtered and was killed when the cow fell on him. Another was so excited about the meat that he fell into water and was drowned. The third saw a deer step on the carcass. He chased it and sucked at the meat on the deer's leg, but the deer kicked him and he was killed. A pregnant woman came and ate all the meat, not noticing that she was giving birth to a child. The child took all the bones and ate them before the mother and child reached home. Of the child and the mother, which was the more amazing? (Finnegan 1967: 229–230).

23:4. (Vai) Three greedy men were given a cow and sought a place without flies to butcher it. One lay down under the cow to catch its blood, and his throat was cut by mistake. Another went for water to make soup, but, fearing that the third would eat some of the meat in his absence, he walked backward, fell into a river, and was eaten by crocodiles. The third man went for water and returned to find that a red deer had stepped in the pot of soup. He caught the deer, licked its feet, and set it free. During his absence a pregnant woman ate some of the soup, delivered her baby, and put the baby in a bowl with some of the meat. When she reached home, the meat was gone, and the baby said, "I ate it all." The question to be decided is, of the three men and one woman, which is the greediest of all? (Johnson and Moore 1972: 391–394).

23:5.   (Mano)   Two men killed a wild animal and butchered it. While it was cooking, the first man sent the other for water, but he refused. The first man went himself, walking backward in order to watch the other. He fell into a hole, broke his foot, and sat there watching. An antelope came and stepped in the pot, and the second man grabbed its foot and licked it. The antelope crushed his eye and escaped. People came and asked what had happened. They said, "These two people are very greedy, but the one whose eye was knocked out by the antelope surpasses the other in greediness." (Becker-Donner 1965: 75–77).

Greedies Divide Bean

24:1.   (Bambara)   Three men drove their sons from home because they were greedy. Each son was given a basket of beans, and they met and ate together. Fearing that one would take more than the others, they ate the beans one by one. When only one bean was left, they began to fight over it. A passing hunter divided it, cutting it into three parts with his sword. Then he licked the sword for the little that stuck to it. Which of these four was the greediest? (Travélé 1923: 100–102).

24:2.   (Kpelle)   Four brothers were driven away by their father because they ate so many beans. The chief had a hut built in the forest and had it filled with beans. The boys ate all but one bean, disputing over who should have the last one. A passing hunter divided it into four equal pieces, and each boy took a piece. The hunter licked his knife for the traces that were left and cut off his tongue, which fell to the ground. Which of these five people loved beans the most? (Mengrelis 1950: 192).

24:3.   (Dyola)   Two men, who left home because they ate so much, met and stole all the beans from a field. They cooked and ate until only one bean remained. Each hesitated to let the other divide the last bean, fearing that he would take the larger part. A passing traveler cut the bean in two equal parts for them and then licked the knife until he cut his tongue deeply. Seeing someone even greedier than they were, the first two men lost their appetites (L.–V. Thomas 1970: 280–281).

24:4. (Ngbaka) Two men, driven from home because of their greed, met under a tree laden with fruit. They divided it piece by piece, until only one was left. One man cut the piece in two with his knife and then licked one side of the knife. The other licked the other side, but the knife cut his tongue. My fathers, my mothers, my brothers, you must know how to overcome hunger. Do not gorge yourself with food or fill your belly with wine. Master your appetites (J. Thomas 1970: 432–441).

Greedy Is Buried

25:1. (Loma) A sponger visited a greedy couple and would not leave. When the wife finished cooking, she slipped upstairs and ate her part of the meal. Her husband put his dish aside, saying he was not hungry. Then he pretended to die. The sponger guarded the food while the wife called the neighbors, who came to mourn, filling the house with people. The grave was dug and the corpse was wrapped in a mat and lowered into the grave. Suddenly the dead man sat up. He was asked about his miraculous recovery, and finally had to admit that the sponger had prevented him from eating. The crowd was indignant, fearing that two such evil persons would spoil the name of their village. They informed the King, who ordered that the guiltier one should be put to death. The people argued about which one was more guilty. And you, whom would you condemn? (Guilhem n.d.: II, 227–231).

25:2. (Temne) Greedy vowed never to give food to Watch-pot (a sponger). Watch-pot put clothes and carpenter tools in a box and took it to Greedy's house, waiting all day for him to eat. Greedy feigned death and his wife told Watch-pot to go to town and announce the death, but Watch-pot said that this was the task of women. She told him to go and buy white clothes for the corpse, but he took them out of his box. She told him to buy planks for a coffin, but he cut planks from a log and made a coffin. She told him to dig a grave in the bush, but he said he would bury the corpse in the house. She hid their hoe, but he took a shovel from his box. He dug the grave, lowered the coffin into it, and began to cover it with dirt. Greedy got up. He said Watch-pot could have

food, but he must bring a calabash. When Watch-pot went for the calabash, Greedy and his wife ran away with the food, but they forgot their
calabash and spoon. Watch-pot brought them and was allowed to eat.
Which of these two was the more cunning? (Cronise and Ward 1903:
300–310).

25:3.   (Temne)   A sponger waited while a greedy man cleared his
field, hoed it, and planted rice. Then he built a house near the rice and
waited for it to ripen. Meanwhile the greedy man sent his own children
away so that he would not have to feed them, and even refused food to
his own brothers and his father's brothers. When the rice was ripe, the
greedy man pretended to die. The sponger said that there was no need
for him to go to town because he had a hoe to dig the grave and clothing
in which to bury the greedy man. The greedy man's wife refused these
clothes and they waited until her husband's namesake brought a cloth.
They dug the grave, put the body in it, and started to fill the grave. The
greedy man got up, and he and his wife ran away with the rice, forgetting
a spoon. The sponger brought the spoon, and they all ate and laughed
together. They went back to town, where the greedy man's father gave
the sponger twenty pounds and thanked him (N. Thomas 1916: III, 2–
7).

25:4.   (Limba)   A miser made a farm, and when his rice was being
harvested, a scrounger came to visit him. He sat down and waited while
the rice was harvested, thrashed, and dried. Miser said that Scrounger
was not going to eat his rice, but when it was cooked, Scrounger was
still there. Miser became ill and died. Scrounger refused to go to the
village to tell the people, sending his child, while he remained with the
corpse. Scrounger refused to go with the people who carried the corpse
to the village but followed behind with the rice. Miser's wife said to the
corpse, "They are going to dig your grave and bury you." Miser asked,
"Is Scrounger still there?" His wife answered, "Yes. Did you really die
for the sake of the rice?" Miser said, "Yes. If Scrounger is still there, I
am dead." As they put him in the grave, Miser said, "Don't throw in the
dirt. Let us go and eat the rice." Scrounger arose, and as they ate, Miser
said, "You really are a scrounger, begging from me when you thought I
was dead!" Scrounger said, "You truly are a miser, dying for rice!"
(Finnegan 1967: 203–204). Finnegan (1967:30) remarks that "a dilemma could perfectly well have been added as an explicit question for the
audience."

Overeating and Oversleeping

26:1. (Tanga) Overeating went to visit Oversleeping and greedily swallowed all the food in his house. When Oversleeping returned the visit, Overeating went hunting to provide food for his guest. When he returned, Oversleeping was fast asleep, and Overeating thought that his guest had been killed. He killed other people to revenge his friend's death and returned to find that Oversleeping had awakened. People called a council and accused Overeating, but he said that Oversleeping should be accused. The elders in council decided that Overeating was the guilty one (Nassau 1915: 34–35).

Sleeping Contest

27:1. (Vai) Two men engaged in a sleeping contest. One man slept by a fire and his leg burned to the knee, but when he was awakened and told that he was on fire, he said that he should have been left to continue his slumber. The second man slept in the street and was washed to sea by a heavy rain. He was swallowed by a fish, which was caught by a fisherman. When the fish was cut open, he said that he was just taking a nap and asked why he had been awakened. The judges were unable to settle the matter, so they submitted it to the people, who are still undecided as to which of them won the bet (Ellis 1914: 186–187; retold by Jablow 1961: 88–89).

27:2. (Temne) Sleepy Villager met Sleepy Stranger and they fell asleep by the road. Sleepy Villager was swallowed by a snake, which was swallowed by a crocodile, which was swallowed by a water monster, which was killed by a hunter. When he was found inside, Sleepy Villager said, "I believe I nearly fell asleep." He went back and found Sleepy Stranger fast asleep, though the villagers were making a great noise preparing their fields for planting, cutting down trees near him, burning the branches close to him, and hoeing all around him. Tired of seeing him sleeping while they worked, one of the villagers hit him with a hoe. He got up and said, "I believe I nearly went to sleep." Weren't they a pair of sleepyheads! (Musson 1957: 20–22).

27:3. (Temme) Two sleepy men met and went to sleep. One was swallowed by a python, which was swallowed by a crocodile, which was swallowed by a water animal, which was killed by a hunter. When the man was found inside, he said, "I nearly slept." He went back to the place where he had gone to sleep and found that the bush had been cut and burned. People scratching with a hoe found the second man, who said, "I nearly slept" (N. Thomas 1916: III, 1–2).

Greatest Memory: It Is Sweet

28:1. (Bambara)   Two brothers went to plant millet. The younger brother stopped suddenly and said, "It is sweet." They went on, planted the millet, cultivated and harvested it, and waited for the next rainy season. Then they went again to plant millet, and when they came to the same spot, the elder brother asked, "What?" The younger replied instantly, "Honey!" Which one had the better memory? (Travélé 1923: 59).

Eating Own Head

29:1. (Vai)   One man said he had seen two birds fighting: the first bird swallowed the second, and then the second swallowed the first. Another said he had seen a man who had cut off his own head and who had it in his mouth, eating it. A third man said he had seen a woman carrying a house, a farm, and all her possessions on her head. When he asked her where she was going, she said she had heard that a man had cut off his own head and had it in his mouth, eating it, so she had left town in fear. Which told the biggest story? (Ellis 1914: 239–240). Here the choice is among three tall tales.

Tug of War

30:1. (Mpongwe)   Tortoise enticed Elephant and Hippopotamus into a tug of war, which neither could win. Were they equal? Answer: Yes, they were equal (Nassau 1914: 37–41; retold by Jablow 1961: 95–98). For obvious reasons I do not attempt to summarize here the African non-dilemma versions of this well-known tale type, AT 291.

Thieves Steal from Each Other

31:1. (Fang)   Three thieves argued over which was the greatest, and a contest between them was arranged. One stole the eggs from the nest of a dove without disturbing it. The second stole them from the first thief, and the third stole them from the second. Which was the greatest thief? (Ramón Alvarez 1951: 147; AT 1525H₁).

31:2. (Kpelle) A king made a law that no one could steal in his town, but two boys made a bet about which was the greater thief. This was overheard and reported to the king. He summoned the two boys and their mothers, and the boys admitted making the wager but said that they had not stolen anything. The king ruled that they could continue their bet for four days, but that they must not steal in his town. He also demanded that each give a woman as a bond, and each gave his own sister. The boys left town but for three days could find nothing to steal. On the fourth day they found a dove hatching its eggs. One boy stole the eggs without the dove's knowledge and presented them to the king. The second boy asked the first, "But where is your loin cloth? I have stolen it." Everyone laughed, but the king had to decide which surpassed the other in stealing. That is the question (Westermann 1921: 424–426).

31:3. (Ewe) Two men saw an antelope eating, and one said he could steal the grass from its mouth without being noticed. The other said he could steal the jacket of the first man without being noticed. Which of the two performed the harder task? (Schönhärl 1909: 106).

31:4. (Otwa) Two thieves stole yams from a rich man's storage hut. On their way home the man behind took yams from the basket of the one in front and put them in his own basket. Which was the more proper thief? (Jablow 1961: 62–63; source and identity of Otwa undetermined).

Thieves Disclaim Stealing

32:1. (Fulani) A Fulani swindler from Macina met a Moorish swindler from Timbuktu. While the Fulani milked a deer, the Moor stole his trousers. Together they stole a chief's horse. The Fulani said, "They must not say we have stolen this horse." The Moor said, "I did not. You are the thief." The Fulani said, "Then it is understood. I alone am the thief." They traded the horse for goods, which they divided, and then parted. That night each came to steal the goods of the other, and they met on the road. Which was the greater thief? (Equilbecq 1913–1916: II, 235–238).

Thieves in Pit

Three separate tale types are variously combined in the seven following tales, making it difficult to present them separately. The first is "The Exchange of Spurious Articles," which is Part I of AT 1525N, but which "has an independent existence" in 33–35:5. The second is the episode of hiding stolen goods in a pit or well and pulling them out again; this occurs by itself in 33–35:6–7. The third is a variant of AT 1532, "The Voice from the Grave." 33–35:4 consists of the second and third parts, and all three occur together in 33–35:1–3.

33–35:1.   (Hausa)   A Kano trader colored wood with indigo, wrapped it in a cloth, and went toward Katsina. A Katsina trader took a bag, filled it with grass, put cowries on top, and went toward Kano. They met and exchanged their loads, learned that they had been cheated, returned, and joined forces. They went to another city and, pretending to be blind, were allowed to sleep in a rest house for traders. During the night they stole the traders' loads and threw them into an empty well. Later the Katsina man climbed into the well, and the Kano man drew out the loads. Warning that it would be a heavy load, the Katsina man wrapped himself in a skin and was pulled out of the well and put with the other loads. The Kano man threw wood into the well, hoping to kill him, but the Katsina man carried the loads to another place. When the Kano man could not find them, he tied his sandals to his head like long ears and brayed like a donkey. The Katsina man came to get it to carry the loads and was caught. They went to Katsina, sold the loads, and divided the money, but one gown was left over. The Kano man told the Katsina man to sell it, saying that he would return for his share in fifteen days. When he returned, the wife of the Katsina man said that her husband had died, and the Kano man asked to see his grave. In the night he came back to it, howled like a hyena, and scratched at the ground. Frightened, the Katsina man rose out of the grave and divided the price of the gown. Which excelled in cunning? (Mischlich 1929: 138–142).

33–35:2.   (Hausa)   A Kano rascal dyed baobab bark with indigo, and a Katsina rascal put 200 cowries on top of a bag of gravel. They met and exchanged their loads, learned that they had been cheated, met again, and demanded that their goods be returned. Deciding that they were equal in cunning, they joined forces. They found gourds and calabashes and, pretending to be blind, camped near some traders, stole their wares, and hid them in a well. In the morning they complained of the loss of their gourds, and the traders went on their way. The two rascals returned to the well and, after arguing, the Katsina man went into the well and began tying the loads on a rope. The Kano man pulled up each load, carried it away, and returned with a stone that he placed by the well. The Katsina man got inside the last load, after warning that it would be a heavy one. The Kano man pulled it up, carried it to the other loads, and filled the well with stones. Meanwhile the Kano man moved all the loads to another hiding place. When the Kano man found the loads gone, he brayed like a donkey; the Katsina man came and was caught. They carried the loads to the Kano man's house and the Katsina man went home, saying he would return in three months. After two months the Kano man had himself buried in a false grave and had his wife tell the Katsina man that he had died. The Katsina man went to the grave at night, made noises like a hyena and began to dig up the grave. The Kano man came out, and they divided the goods (Edgar 1911–1913: II, (35); translated by Skinner 1969: I, 185–188 and by Johnston 1966: 212–215; retold by Carey 1970: 66–74). Johnston comments, "It is difficult to believe, *pace* some anthropologists, that such tales ever had any purpose but to entertain."

33–35:3. (Hausa) In a lengthy tale whose narrative charm is lost in this summary, a thief from Katsina filled his sack with stones and put 200 cowries on top; a thief from Kano filled his sack with dyed leaves and put a cloth on top. They met and exchanged their loads, learned that they had been cheated, returned, and demanded their goods back again. They joined forces and went to Kano together, pretending to be a blind man and a cripple. After begging for a few cowries, they found lodging in the warehouse of a wealthy trader and stole many of his bales of silk, hiding them in a deep hole in the forest. Later the Katsina thief climbed into the hole, and the Kano thief pulled up bale after bale, carrying each one into the forest to hide it and returning each time with a large rock. The Katsina thief tied himself in the last bale and, after warning that it would be the heaviest, was pulled up and carried to the place where the other bales were hidden. While the Kano thief threw the rocks into the hole to kill his confederate, the Katsina thief hid the bales in another place in the forest. The Kano thief slept for a while, then got up and brayed like a donkey; the Katsina thief came and was caught. When they could not agree on dividing their spoils, the Kano thief took them all to his house and the Katsina man said he would return in three months for his share. Before he arrived, the Kano thief had himself buried in a grave, but the Katsina thief saw his wife bringing him food and drink. That night the Katsina thief cried like a hyena and scratched at the grave. The Kano thief came out, and they divided their spoils and separated (Frobenius 1921–1928: IX, 290–299).

33–35:4. (Hausa)   A Kano man and a Katsina man exchanged loads, thinking that they were trading cloth for cotton. Learning that each had been cheated, they returned, met, and joined forces. As agreed, the Kano man sold the Katsina man for two loads of salt and a load of dates. The Katsina man escaped that night and rejoined the Kano man, and they hid their loads in a dry well. Later the Kano man climbed into the well and the Katsina man drew the loads out and hid them in a forest. The Kano man rolled himself in a cow hide and, after warning that this load would be very heavy, was pulled up and placed with the other loads. The Katsina man went back and filled the well with stones. Meanwhile the Kano man hid the loads in the house of an old woman. When it was dark, the Katsina man brayed like a donkey, and the Kano man was caught. They went to divide the loads, but while the Kano man went for beasts of burden, the Katsina man rehid the loads. He dug and hid in a grave, telling the old woman to say that he had died and that the chief had taken away the loads. She showed the Kano man the grave, and that night he scratched at the ground like a hyena. In his fright, the Katsina man hit his head against the grave's wooden cover. He came out, and they divided the loads (Mischlich 1929: 142–146).

33–35:5. (Gurma)   A swindler put a quarter of a bar of salt on a rag and set off to sell it as a full load of salt. Another swindler took a strip of cotton to sell as a full load of cloth. When they met, the first said that in his country women had to go naked because there was no cloth. The second said that in his country it was salt that was lacking. They exchanged loads and parted, each thinking he had cheated the other, but when they reached home, both cried, "He robbed me!" Which one was the greater thief? (Equilbecq 1913–1916: III, 227–229).

33–35:6. (Bambara)   Dark Moussa and Light Moussa were driven from home because they were rogues. They met, found a donkey, and stole it. Dark Moussa sent Light Moussa for herbs for the donkey and left with the donkey while he was gone. After dark, Light Moussa went to the place where they had found the donkey and brayed. Thinking that there was a second donkey, Dark Moussa went back to steal it and was caught. They sold the donkey and divided the money. They came to a deserted village whose inhabitants had left after hiding their wealth in a pit. After a long discussion Dark Moussa agreed to climb into the pit. He put the goods in a basket, and Light Moussa pulled them up and hid them in a thicket, returning each time with a large stone. Dark Moussa said that the last load would be heavy, and climbed into the basket. Light Moussa pulled him up, carried him to the goods in the thicket, and went back and filled the pit with stones. Dark Moussa took the goods back to the pit, and they divided them. Which of these two men is the greater rogue? (Travélé 1923: 165–168).

33–35:7. (Unidentified, Cameroun) Two thieves stole silver, bought three packages of blue cloth with it, and hid the cloth in a hole. When they came to take it, the first asked the second to go into the hole and tie the packages to a rope so that they could be hauled up. The second thief was suspicious that he might be left in the hole but went down into it. After the first and second packages had been brought up, the second thief shouted up, "Pull hard. This package is heavier than the others!" The first thief pulled it up and put it with the others. Then he threw a large stone into the hole to kill his confederate, saying that now the cloths were his. "No," said the second thief, and he took the cloths home. I ask, which was the greater thief? (Fouda, de Julliot, and Lagrave 1961: 17).

Mirror, etc.

36:1. (Kongo) Three brothers told their father that they wanted to marry his niece. To each of them he gave money, saying that the one who brought him the most useful gift would become her husband. One bought a magic carpet, another magic glasses, and the third a magic whip. When they looked through the glasses, they saw that their loved one was dead and flew to her on the magic carpet. When the third brother struck her twice with his magic whip, she opened her eyes, sat up, and asked, "What are you doing in my room?" Each of the brothers claimed her as his wife. To which one did their father give his niece? What would you have done in his place? (M'Bow 1971: 96–101; AT 653A).

36:2. (Bulu) A girl fell in love with three young men who came to court her. Each made a charm for himself and they started home. One man saw in his magic mirror that she had died; the second carried them back to her with his powerful wings; the third restored her to life with his charm. Her father gave her to them without bridewealth, but when they came to the parting of their ways, they quarreled over her. They were not able to settle the matter, even to this very day. Therefore will you, gentle reader, have the kindness to settle this dispute? Which of these three men really has the best claim to take this woman in marriage? (Krug and Herskovits 1949: 355–356).

36:3.   (Vai)   Three brothers were in love with the same girl. One had a magic glass in which he saw that she was dead; one had a magic hammock that carried them home to her; the third had a medicine that restored her to life. Each claimed her and they began to fight. The people came to part them and the whole matter was referred to the judge, who, unable to decide the case, turned it over to the people. To which of the brothers did the daughter belong? (Ellis 1914: 200–201; repeated by Woodson 1964: 165–167; cited as AT 653 by Klipple 1938).

36:4.   (Sefwi)   A Sefwi analogue of this Vai tale (36:3) is mentioned, though no text is given (Berry 1961: 6).

36:5.   (Krachi)   Three brothers set out to seek their fortunes and met again after a year. The youngest had a mirror in which they saw that their father was dead. The next had a pair of sandals that carried them immediately to his grave. The eldest had a small calabash of medicine that revived him. Now which of these three has done best? (Cardinall 1931: 201–202).

36:6.   (Swahili)   There were three brothers. One had a mirror in which they saw that the king's daughter was dead. Another had magical shoes that carried them to her. The third had medicine that restored her to life. In gratitude the king offered them his daughter in marriage. Which brother deserved to marry her? (Matola 1907: 214–216).

36:7.   (Kono)   Three young men were in love with the same girl. One had a mirror in which they saw that she was dying. Another had a flying cloth that took them to her side. The third had a cow-tail switch that cured her. Which of the three performed the greatest miracle? (Holas 1952: 85–86).

36:8.   (Wolof)   Three youths, each with his charm, went to see a girl. One had a magic telescope in which he saw that she was dead. Another had an animal hide that took them to her. The third had a powder that revived her. To whom did the girl belong? (Guillot 1933: 51).

36:9.   (Kpelle)   Three young men fell in love with the same girl, but her father refused them because they were poor. They went away to work for a chief who rewarded them with a magic mirror, a magic canoe that flew through the air, and a magic spear. Meanwhile an evil forest spirit had changed itself into a handsome man, had brought many gifts to the girl's father, and had been granted permission to marry her. In his mirror, the first youth saw that the marriage was about to take place; the second carried them home in his canoe; the third killed the spirit, which turned back into an ugly serpent. In gratitude the father agreed that she should marry one of the young men. But which of them deserved her most? (Pinney n.d.: 87–88).

36:10.   (Ashanti)   Three brothers were in love with the daughter of the chief, who said that she could marry whichever brought him one of the Little People of the forest. While searching for them, the first brother looked in his magic mirror and saw that the girl was dead. The second had a magic hammock that carried them home instantly. The third used his magic to restore her to life. The chief said his daughter should marry the one who did the most. Which one deserved the reward? (Courlander 1963: 28–31).

36:11.   (Ashanti)   Three young men in love with the same girl went to the coast to buy things. One had a mirror in which he saw that the girl was dead. Another put medicine on their knees and they returned immediately to her side. The third sprinkled her with medicine that restored her to life. Of these three people, which did best? (Rattray 1930: 262–263).

36:12.   (Limba)   Three brothers in love with the same girl bought a magic glass, a magic tail, and a magic skin. In the glass they saw that the girl was dead; they were carried home on the skin; she was revived with the magic tail. All three claimed the girl. Which one owned her? (Finnegan 1967: 218–219).

36:13.   (Kpe)   A girl was engaged to three men, named Intelligence, Feet, and Hands, who went to work for a European to earn bridewealth. Intelligence dreamed that the girl was dead; Feet had a machine that took them home the same day; Hands had a medicine that restored her to life. But the girl no longer wanted to marry, and the youths were given thirty goats to dissolve the betrothal. Each claimed twelve. How should the goats be divided? (Bender 1922: 110).

36:14. (Betsimisaraka) Three brothers went walking. One saw a corpse; one provided a charm; one outstripped the others and restored the corpse to life. The parents gave them two cows and they argued about how their reward should be divided. And you, what do you think? (Renel 1910: II, 111–112).

36:15–18. (Adangme, Akan, Dangmeli, and Vai) "Three brothers are on a trading expedition. One acquires a magic mirror in which he sees that the chief's daughter, with whom all three are in love, has died. The second has a magic hammock (or basket or mat), which takes them back before the girl can be buried. The third resurrects the princess by means of a magic medicine. Each claims her as a wife, and the judge, to whom the case is referred in the Vai version, is unable to decide who has done the most towards saving her. In the Adangme variant, the tale ends quite simply with the question 'which of the three is the greater magician?' No solution is suggested. Each of the audience must give his views and an *ad hoc* solution is accepted at each telling depending on the consensus of opinion of those present and the weight of the arguments advanced" (Berry 1961: 10).

36:19. (Tanga) A wise man announced that a great queen was ill and that her doctors could not cure her, but he said nothing more. A doctor who heard this said that if he were there he could cure her, but he said nothing more. A strong worker said that he would take the doctor there in a large canoe that he had made. The doctor cured the queen and was handsomely rewarded. The strong worker complained that the queen could not have been cured if he had not taken the doctor to her. The wise man said that the queen would have died if he had not brought the news of her illness. The other two replied that his news was of no use by itself. The three continued to argue. They never were able to decide which was the greater: Knowledge, Skill, or Strength (Nassau 1915: 30–32; cited as AT 653 by Klipple 1938).

36:20. (Yao) Three brothers bought a glass to see everywhere, a mat to fly anywhere, and a medicine to revive the dead. They returned home to restore their friend to life. When they quarreled over who owned him, their father reproached them for disturbing the peace by trying to excel all other men (Werner 1906: 247–249).

36:21. (Unidentified, Tanzania) Three brothers used a magic telescope and saw that the bride-to-be of the eldest was ill. They rode home

on a magic wagon, and the youngest cured her with a magic spoon. When
they disputed about who should marry the girl, her father said that, to
avoid endless arguments, the eldest should do so (Faessler 1962: 224–
227).

36:22. (Wala)   Three men were traveling. One had a mirror in which
he saw that their lovers were dead; the second had a medicine that took
them home; and the third had a magic wisp with which he wakened their
lovers. Which of the three was the most powerful? Which was the
greatest one? Answer: The one who saw their lovers was the most powerful. Had he not seen them, would they have known that their lovers
had died? (Fikry-Atallah 1972: 437–438).

36:23. (Saho)   A devil, a demon, a man, and a werewolf traveled
together. They sought the favor of a maiden, but she became ill. The
devil brought medicine from a year's distance in a day. The man opened
a book and learned the remedy. The demon changed into wind and
brought the medicine in an instant and the maiden recovered. They
began to fight and went to court. The demon won the maiden and
married her (Reinisch 1889–1890: I, 126–127). The werewolf, who said
he could breathe on the girl and make her well, is not mentioned again.

36:24. (Cape Verde Islands)   A man gave each of his sons money
and a horse so that they could go out and see the world. Before leaving,
the youngest went to ask his godmother for her blessing, and she gave
him as a remembrance three handkerchiefs, the color of the moon, of
the sun, and of the stars. He gave the handkerchiefs to a princess who
had refused his brothers admission to her palace, and she let him and
his brothers in. Each asked to marry her, and she said that she would
marry the one who obtained the most knowledge and skill. They acquired a magic spread, a magic mirror, and a magic candle. They saw
in the mirror that the princess was dead, flew home on the magic spread,
and revived her with the candle. They argued about who should marry
her, but she chose the owner of the candle. The two other brothers went
to work for a demon who tried to kill them. The demon gave one some
pigs to take to a friend. The youth cut off their tails and stuck them in
the mud so that the demon fell into the mud when he tried to pull them
out. The two brothers lived on in his house (Parsons 1923: I, 110–113).

36:25. (Nkundo)   A man had a looking glass in which he saw that a
woman had died in a distant village. He told a medicine man, who told

a driver. They left in the driver's car, and the medicine man revived the woman. Her father-in-law wanted to reward all three men, but each claimed the entire reward for himself. To which of the three should he give the reward? Answer: To the medicine man (Hulstaert and de Rop 1954: 26–29).

36:26.   (Nkundo)   Three brothers heard of a beautiful woman who refused all her suitors. The eldest brother asked his father for money for bridewealth so that he could try to marry her. The second also asked for money so that he could try if his elder brother failed. And the third asked for money so that he could try if both his brothers failed. Their father gave each 1,000 rings, and they set out together and parted at a crossroads. Each found a magic object – a charm to live, a charm to disappear, and a charm to see from a distance — and they met again. One used his charm and saw that the woman was near death; another made them disappear and reach her immediately; the third cured the woman of her illness. Her father gave her to the three young men, but when they returned home, they began to fight over her. Their father asked the woman which brother she wished for a husband, but she did not know. The father asked other people to settle the dispute. Which of these three young men is the owner of the woman? Answer: The eldest, who conceived the idea, but he should compensate his brothers for their cooperation (Hulstaert and de Rop 1954: 18–23).

36:27.   (Nkundo)   A father gave a bicycle to each of his three sons, and they left home. They parted at a crossroads and later met there again. The first had found a mirror in which he could see everything; the second had found an airplane; the third had found an ivory trumpet that could revive the dead. The first saw that their sister was dead; they flew home in the airplane, and the third brother restored their sister to life. Their father wanted to reward them with an expensive ring, but there was only one ring. To whom will he give the ring? Which son did best? Answer: The three sons had done equally well, but it is good that the ring be given to the eldest son because he is his father's heir (Hulstaert and de Rop 1954: 22–25).

36:28.   (Nkundo)   A father gave a bicycle to each of his three sons, and they left home. They parted at a crossroads and later met there again. The eldest had a mirror in which he could see everything; the second had a valise that could fly like an airplane; the youngest had an ivory trumpet that could revive the dead. The eldest saw that their sister was dead; the second carried them home; the youngest blew three times on the trumpet, and their sister, who was already in her grave, revived. Their father wanted to reward them with a ring, but there was only one ring. To whom should he give it? Answer: There is no winner or loser, and it is best that the father give the ring to the eldest son because he inherits from his father (de Rop 1956: 162–165).

36:29. (Temne)   Four men in love with the same woman went on a trip. Far Seer dreamed that she was ill, and they returned to find her dead. Waker awoke her, and Life Restorer revived her. When they argued about who should marry her, Fast Walker suggested that they go to the chiefs and let them decide. They found all the chiefs dead and revived them. The chiefs decided that the woman should be given to Fast Walker because he was the eldest (N. Thomas 1916: III, 12–14).

36:30. (Ngonde)   There were three brothers: a doctor, an airplane pilot, and a telephonist. The telephonist heard that a beautiful woman had died in a distant town; the pilot flew them there; the doctor restored her to life. Which brother deserved her as wife? I myself think that their claims are equal and that they should let their father marry her. What do you think? (Berger and Gemuseus 1932–1933: 151–152; cited as AT 653 by Klipple 1938).

36:31. (Zigula)   A father gave each of his three sons ten goats so that they could find wives and get married. They traded their goats for dream magic, travel magic, and magic to revive the dead. When they met again, the first dreamed of the death of a distant Sultan's daughter; the second took them to her; the third restored her to life. They fought about who should marry her but finally decided that their father should do so because he had provided the goats for bridewealth (Reuss 1931: 122–123).

36:32. (Swahili)   Three brothers were in love with the same woman. One had a looking glass in which they saw that she was dead; one had a prayer rug that carried them home; one had medicine that restored her to life. Who married the woman? Answer: Their father, and his sons called her "mother" (W. E. Taylor 1932–1933: 9–11; cited as AT 653 by Klipple 1938).

36:33. (Tsonga)   Three brothers, named Mirror, Wind, and Powder, were in love with the same girl. Their father gave each a boat and they left together on a trading voyage. Mirror saw her lying dead; Wind carried them home in his magic basket; Powder restored her to life. Each claimed her as his wife. An elder said that she should go to the first one who said "Mama" (Junod 1897: 304–309).

36:34. (Ovimbundu)   A girl sent her three lovers to bring back something never before seen in her village. One bought a casket of dreams, another a bow and arrow, and the third a snuffbox. The first dreamed that the girl had died. The second carried her home on one of his magic arrows. The third put snuff to her nose; she sneezed and revived. Each claimed the right to marry her, and their dispute was taken to the king. The king said that their claims were equal, and he married the girl himself (Ennis 1962: 89–91).

36:35. (Hanya)   A girl sent her three suitors to the coast to buy something to give her pleasure. One bought a beautiful box, another a bow and arrow, and the third a snuffbox. The first dreamed that the girl was dead; the second carried them home on his magic arrow; the third put some snuff in her nose, and she sneezed and awoke. Each claimed the right to marry her. The king said that their claims were equal, but because there was no solution, he would marry her himself (Hauenstein 1967: 196–197).

36:36. (Ibibio)   Three brothers with a medicinal fruit and a magic horn returned home on a magic mat to cure the girl they all loved. When each of them claimed her as his bride, her father set them the task of shooting an arrow twelve miles. The first two failed, but the third succeeded and took the girl as his wife (Jeffreys 1967: 134–135; cf. Farnham 1920: 272–273).

36:37. (Kpelle)   Three young men were in love with the same girl. The first could see very far; the second could run very fast; the third could prepare a charm against all illness (Mengrelis 1950: 189). This summary is obviously incomplete because it does not even include the girl's recovery; the dilemma may also have been omitted (cf. 1:3).

Repairing an Egg

37:1. (Betsimisaraka)   A hunter, a thief, and a woodworker found some eggs. The hunter shot, hitting only one egg. The thief stole the other eggs without being noticed. The woodworker repaired the broken egg. Having shown what they knew how to do, they went home. Which of the three was the most skillful? (Renel 1910: II, 118–119; AT 653A; cited as AT 653 by Klipple 1938).

37:2. (Ewe) A king set an egg on a post at a distance. A hunter said he would shoot and hit it. Another man said he would gather it up and put it together again. A third said that he would give it to a hen and that the hen would hatch it. Which of them did the most? (Westermann 1907: 149).

37:3. (Kongo) A wizard, a hunter, a carpenter, and a thief set out to find a boy's lost parrot. Before leaving, they demonstrated their skills. The thief stole an egg on which a fowl was sitting, without its knowledge. The hunter shot and hit the egg from a great distance. The carpenter put the egg together again. (As in the Grimm Brothers' version, this narrative continues with a second tale type).

Repairing Boat

38:1. (Kongo) Then the wizard announced that the parrot was on a ship, and all four set out in pursuit in a glass boat. They caught up with the ship and the thief stole the parrot. The ship's captain sent rain and then lightning, twice breaking the glass boat, but the hunter shot and killed them, and both times the carpenter repaired their boat. When they returned the parrot, the boy rewarded them with a fowl that laid beads or whatever else they wanted. The four men argued over the fowl and, when they could not agree, they killed it and divided it in four pieces. Now, which of these four foolish ones should have had the fowl? (Weeks n.d.: 43–45; AT 653).

Weeks comment:

This story excited a great amount of discussion. Some argued that this one should have had the fowl, and others argued with much gesticulation that another should have taken the fowl. Each character had his supporters; but all agreed that they were four fools not to let the fowl lay plenty of beads and share them.

38:2–3. (Ewe) A thief, a hunter, and a mender went by boat to rescue the king's daughter, who had been carried away by an eagle. The thief stole her from the eagle's claws, and the hunter shot the eagle when it pursued them. The eagle fell into their boat and broke it, but the mender repaired it. Which of the three did the greatest work? (Spieth 1906: 595–596). A very similar version of this tale is recorded by Westermann (1907: 149).

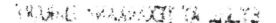

38:4. (Ewe) A thief said that he could rescue the king's only son, who had been carried off across a river by a seven-headed bird. The king promised a large reward, and sent a hunter, a rower, and a boat maker with him. The thief stole the boy from the bird, and they started back in their boat. The bird came and carried the boy off, but the hunter shot it, and one of the bird's heads fell into the boat, making a hole. The boat maker repaired the hole and the rower brought them safely to land. The king gave each of the four men a cask of gold. Then he brought a very large cask of gold and said that the one that had done the most in saving his son could have this besides. Which of them received it? (Schönhärl 1909: 111).

38:5. (Ewe) A couple sent each of their three sons into the world to learn a trade before the next child was born. Their fourth child was a girl. The rainbow turned itself into a young man and asked for her hand in marriage. The parents agreed against their will, and the young man took her to his home across the sea. He put her in a room that no one could enter and kept the key under his pillow when he slept. The three brothers returned home, learned about their sister, and set out by boat to find her. The first had become a thief, the second a hunter, and the third a mender. The thief stole the key and brought his sister to the boat, taking with him beads and gold from the rainbow's store of wealth. The hunter shot the pursuing rainbow, which fell into the boat and broke it to pieces. The mender repaired the boat and they reached home safely. Which of these three brothers did the most? (Schönhärl 1909: 122–125).

38:6. (Popo) A thief, a hunter, and a carpenter set out by boat to rescue the king's daughter, who had been carried away by the Rainbow God. The thief stole her; the hunter shot the pursuing deity, who broke the boat in two by his fall; the carpenter repaired it. Which was the most worthy? (Trautmann 1927: 100).

38:7. (Dyola) Three friends were in love with the same girl. While bathing in a stream, she was carried away by a monster. The first friend said that he would save her if he had a canoe, which the second procured. The third knew how to repair canoes. They found the monster and beat it with sticks. The first friend extracted the girl from its mouth, but it charged their canoe and broke it in two with its tail. The third friend repaired the canoe, and the girl was returned to her parents. Her father decided to give her in marriage to the most deserving youth. Which one deserved to marry the girl? (L.–V. Thomas 1958–1959: 678–679).

Rescue from Eagle (Lion, Snake)

39:1. (Mbete) Three brothers, named Dreamer, Blacksmith, and Hunter, saw their sister carried off by an eagle. Dreamer dreamed where she could be found; Blacksmith forged-the bullets; Hunter shot the eagle. Each claimed that without his efforts their sister could not have been saved. To whom should she give her reward? (Adam 1940–1941: 137; cf. Farnham 1920: 253).

39:2 (Ila) A woman sent her four sons in search of their missing sister. The eldest saw her in the clutches of a lion, fifty miles away. Another made himself invisible and stole her from the lion's claws. The third killed the lion, but the girl was dead when they reached home. The fourth brother interrupted the funeral preparations and, with his magic, restored her to life. The mother wanted to reward all of them with meat, but they asked that it be given to only one of them — the one who had done the most to bring their sister back alive. To whom should the reward be given? (Smith and Dale 1920: II, 332; cf. Farnham 1920: 271).

39:3. (Avatime) A man and wife had six sons: a farmer, a hunter, a trader, a palm-wine tapper, a snuff grinder, and one who stayed with his father. Their seventh child was a girl, who was carried away one day by a python to a termite hill in the bush. They searched for seven days without finding her, and the father asked his sons what they should do. The farmer said she was in the farm; the hunter said he knew where she was; the trader said that if it were he who knew, he would tell them; the palm-wine tapper said she was in the palm grove. The hunter said she was in a termite hill in the bush, and they found her there sur-rounded by three pythons. The trader flew through the air like a bird, dived into the termite hill, and carried his sister home. It was time for the daughter to marry. Whom should she marry? Her father said that she should marry a hunter. Hence the custom that the cloth with which a father's corpse is washed is moistened five times in the mouth of the most intelligent son (Funke 1911–1912: 46–49).

39:4. (Cape Verde Islands) The daughter of a king married the Devil, who courted her in the form of a man with gold teeth, but turned into a snake when they reached his home. Her father offered half of his fortune to anyone who would rescue her, and a diviner sent Eater, Shooter, and Seer to do so. When the snake was asleep, they carried the girl away. The snake pursued their boat, but Seer saw it and pointed it out. Shooter shot the snake twice, and where it fell to the ground there was a fire. The king divided his wealth with the diviner and the others (Parsons 1923: I, 106–107). In this tale Eater did nothing.

Rescue from Crocodile (Hippopotamus)

40:1. (Unidentified, Ethiopia)   A beautiful girl had many suitors, the most ardent of whom were a musician, a hunter, and a swimmer. While washing her clothes in the river, she was about to be eaten by a crocodile. The musician played his harp, causing the crocodile to listen with its mouth open in amazement. The hunter shot it, and the swimmer brought the girl to shore. Who should marry the girl? What is your judgment? (Baharav 1963–1966: III, 22–23).

40:2. (Saho)   Four men courted a girl. She fell in a river and was swallowed by a hippopotamus. One man blew his trumpet and the hippopotamus came to the surface; the second man shot and killed it. The third man swam to the hippopotamus and cut open its belly; the fourth brought the girl to shore in a boat. The girl was still alive, and each of the men asked to marry her. They went to court and stated their cases. The court decided that the girl should marry the trumpeter, who brought the hippopotamus to the surface (Reinisch 1889–1890: I, 50–52).

Where is Father?

41:1. (Temne)   Four sons asked about their father, who had not returned from the hunt. The youngest found his father's gun and skull. Another dived into the water, collected his bones, and put them together. The third molded mud to form his body. The fourth put a magic horn to his father's nose and blew in it; his father sneezed, got up, and went home. Now, which of the four sons made their father? They are still arguing this question today (Cronise and Ward 1903: 200–205).

41:2. (Limba)   After a hunter had been eaten by crocodiles and hippopotamuses his wife gave birth to triplets, and when they grew up, they went in search of their father. One led the way to the pool where he had died; the second cut the animals open and recovered the bits that were left of their father; the third put them on a mat and brought them to land. Then the first fitted the pieces back together; the second gave their father breath; the third used medicine to restore his sense. But when they reached home, their mother cooked all the foods known to man together in a tiny pot, and yet served them all separately. Now, which was the most amazing? (Finnegan 1967: 214–217).

41:3. (Bulu)   A man fell from a tree and was restored to life by his five wives, named Remembering, Finding-Path, Sounding-Fords (who helped them cross a river), Picking-Things-Up, and Bring-to-Life. They argued over who should have their husband and took their case to a judge. He said that the husband belonged to all of them (Schwab 1922: 212–213).

41:4. (Bulu)   A man who died in the forest was restored to life by his three wives, named The-Finder-of-the-Path, The-Gatherer, and The-One-Who-Brings-People-Back-to-Life. They quarreled about the possession of their husband and called people to settle their dispute. Answer: All three of these women should have this man as their husband (Krug and Herskovits 1949: 355).

41:5. (Vili)   A man who was killed while hunting was restored to life by his three wives, named Dreamer (who dreamed he was dead), Guide, and Raiser-of-the-Dead. To settle their argument about who had done the most to save him, each wife cooked food, and they waited to see from whose pot he would eat his first meal. He ate from the pot of Raiser-of-the-Dead, explaining that even after the other two had performed their feats, he had not yet been able to eat. Most people agreed, but many women said he should have eaten from all three pots (Dennett 1898: 33–34; retold by Feldmann 1963: 217–218).

41:6. (Nkundo)   A man who was killed while hunting was restored to life by his three wives, named Dreamer, Tracker, and Life-Giver. On the way home he killed a pig, and each wife claimed it. Which one really owned it? Answer: The largest share should go to the wife who revived him with her medicine (Hulstaert and de Rop 1954: 56–59).

41:7. (Nkundo)   A hunter was lost in the forest. His younger brother waited for him in vain, then went home and told his mother. She sent a man who saw where he was, a man who followed his spoor and found that he was dead, and a man who put a charm in his nose and revived him. They brought him back home, and the mother wanted to reward them. Who should receive the largest portion? Answer: They deserved equal shares, but the one who revived the hunter should receive somewhat more than the others (Hulstaert and de Rop 1954: 24–27).

41:8. (Nkundo) A man and his three wives went into the forest to gather copal. While they were away, he fell from a tree and was killed, and his wives searched for him. One led the way, and the second discovered the body. They carried it home and were about to bury it, when the third wife stopped them and revived their husband with her medicine. The elders were astonished at this deed and promised the third wife a slave as a reward. The other two wives claimed the slave for leading the way and for finding the body, but the third wife insisted that without her their husband would still be dead and that without her act no slave would have been offered. The judge forbade them to quarrel and tried to settle their dispute. Who will win it? Answer: The first wife, because without her they would not have known where to look for their husband, and the others could have done nothing (Hulstaert and de Rop 1954: 92–99).

41:9. (Unidentified, Liberia) A hunter went into the forest but did not return. His family wondered what had happened, but after some months they forgot about him. Then a son was born to his wife and, when he began to talk, the first thing he said was, "Where is my father?" His elder brothers repeated his question and decided to do something about it. They searched through the forest, and each time they lost their way, one of the brothers found it again. Finally they found their father's scattered bones and rusted weapons and knew that he had been killed in the hunt. Another brother put the bones together. One covered the skeleton with sinews and flesh. A fifth put blood into the hunter's veins. A sixth put breath into his body. A seventh gave him the power of movement. And the last gave him the power of speech. After the hunter had been purified, a feast was held. He announced that he would give his cow-tail switch, which all had admired, to the one who had done the most to bring him home. His sons began arguing over it, and the whole village joined in the argument. Finally, calling for quiet, the hunter gave the cow-tail to his youngest son, who had asked, "Where is my father?" (Courlander and Herzog 1947: 5–12; adapted as a film cartoon entitled *The Cow-Tail Switch* by the Learning Corporation of America).

41:10–11. (Luba) A twist to this tale is provided in the following version: A honey gatherer was killed in a fall from a tree, but he was revived by his three sons, named Hear-it-however-faint-the-sound, Follow-it-however-great-the-distance, and Put-it-together-however-small-the-pieces. While arguing about who was the most important, their father fell again and again they restored him to life. When he fell and was killed a third time, however, the first son did not tell his brothers, and their father really died (Burton 1961: 40–42). There is no dilemma here, but another Luba version of this treatment of the tale ends with the question, "If each of us really needs the other, who is to judge who is best?" (de Bouveignes 1938: 39–43).

Drinking River Dry

42:1. (Grushi) A chief's daughter fell in love with a python that appeared in the form of a handsome man. During the night it resumed the form of a python, swallowed the girl, and carried her off to its home in a large lake. In the morning the chief ordered his people to follow, but they found no tracks. A man who could smell everywhere followed their trail to the lake. A man famous for his thirst drank the lake dry. A famous worker dug out all the mud, revealing a hole so deep that its bottom could not be reached. A man whose arm could reach all over the country pulled out the python. It was killed, but when they cut open its stomach the girl was dead. A man who had medicine to raise the dead restored her to life. Now, which of these five men did best? Answer: They were equally good, and the girl never married again (Cardinall 1931: 203–204).

42:2. (Ewe) The mother of three children died, and they grew up with their grandmother, thinking that she was their mother. When their playmates said that their mother was dead, their grandmother told them the whole story. One child said he knew the way to the place where their mother had been buried in a stream; another drank the water; the third gathered her bones. Which of these children did the most? Answer: The one who drank the stream dry (Spieth 1906: 595).

42:3. (Ashanti) Anansi failed to return from a journey, and his six sons set out to rescue him. Able-to-See-Trouble said Anansi had fallen into a river in the forest; Road-Builder made a path; Able-to-Dry-Up-Rivers dried up the river; and The-Skinner-of-Game cut open the fish that had swallowed their father and released him. A large hawk seized

Anansi and flew away with him, but Stone-Thrower hit the hawk, and Lie-on-the-Ground-Like-a-Cushion softened his father's fall. Then one day Anansi found the Moon and asked the Sky God to award it to the son who had done the most to rescue him. The six sons argued over it, and the Sky God could not decide which one deserved it. Finally he became impatient and went back to the sky, taking the Moon with him (Courlander and Prempeh 1957: 59–62; adapted as an animated cartoon entitled *Anansi* by Landmark Educational Films).

42:4.   (Baule)   A hunter was eaten by a lion, which then was drowned in a swamp. Seven years later his seven sons were taunted for being orphans and learned what had happened. The eldest named himself Searcher-for-the-Father-Missing-Seven-Years and led them to the swamp. The second named himself Water-Drinker and drank the swamp dry. The third called himself Bone-Searcher and found the bones. The fourth named himself Medicine-Searcher, and the fifth Bone-Gluer. When the bones had been put together, the sixth washed them with herbs, and their father stood up alive and healthy. Since that time the loss of the father is not concealed from his children (Himmelheber 1951: 105–107).

42:5.   (Kono)   A woman went to the forest for firewood and did not return. The eldest and wisest of her seven sons called his brothers together to discuss her fate. The second, who had a subtle sense of smell, led them to her decomposing corpse, which was scattered in a pool of water. The third, who was a great drinker, knelt by the pool and drank it dry. The fourth gathered all her bones. The fifth put them together and gave her flesh. Just as the sixth was about to give her the breath of life, a sorcerer appeared in the form of a bird to prevent him. The seventh, a great hunter, shot the bird, and their mother's life was saved. Since that day children love their mothers, and mothers love their children (Holas 1952: 26–27).

42:6.   (Nupe)   A man who had seven sons was swallowed by a fish. His sixth son saw it happen and called his brother, who was a great drinker. He drank the river dry and then called another brother, who knew every fish in the water. He identified the one that had swallowed their father and called another brother, who was a surgeon. He cut open the fish, carried their father home, and called another brother, who was skilled in using a strike-a-light. He made a fire to dry their father, but a great bird came and flew off with their father, so the son called another brother, who was a good stone thrower. He hit the bird and called the sixth brother, who caught things on his back. He caught their father when he fell and called the seventh brother, who was a water carrier. He brought water and washed their father (Frobenius 1921–1928: IX, 258-259).

Escape with Sweetheart

43:1. (Hausa) A chief's son set out to win the beautiful young wife of a neighboring chief and was joined by a thief, a warrior, a carpenter, a paddler, a hearer, a seer, a thrower, and a catcher. Through an old woman he sent presents to the girl, who sent back symbolic presents, which, when interpreted, told him how to pass the guards and visit her in the palace. The chief heard them talking and called out his guards, but the hearer and seer announced that their master was in trouble. The thief helped them escape, and they all fled. When they reached a river, the warrior held off their pursuers, the carpenter fashioned a canoe, and the paddler took them across. Then one of the pursuers turned himself into a hawk, snatched the girl, and flew off with her. The thrower hit the hawk with a stone, and the catcher caught the girl in one hand. Now which was the most skilled of all these people? (Edgar 1911–1913: II, (48); translated by Skinner n.d.: II, (48) and by Johnston 1966: 195-201).

43:2. (Karekare) A great lover, a warrior, a canoeman, a hunter, a catcher, and a thief were sent by a king to prove their skills. They met an old woman, who told them that her king had a wife whom no one was allowed to touch. The lover sent her to this wife, who told the old woman how the lover could pass the palace guards, and that night he slept with the king's wife. The king found them in bed and had his people surround the palace. The old woman told the other men, and the thief turned himself into a white cat, like one owned by the king. He found the couple and turned them into a spider and a rat. He took the spider in his mouth and the rat in his teeth and rejoined the others. They resumed their human forms and fled to a river, where the canoeman felled a tree and turned it into a canoe and a paddle. They started across when the king arrived with his horsemen. He turned one of his men into an eagle, which seized the woman from the canoe. The hunter threw his club at the bird and it dropped the woman, who was caught by the catcher. Another eagle seized the woman and was hit by the hunter's club. As they reached the other bank, the king's horsemen plunged into the water, but the warrior killed them all. When they returned to their own king, he asked his people which man had done his work best. No one could answer. Then he asked the woman herself, but she said each was as brave as the others. Then the king himself took her into his palace (Frobenius 1921–1928: IX, 408–413).

Rescue by Liar, etc.

44:1.   (Hausa)   Five young men set out to rescue a girl who had been carried away. By telling lies, one got food for them to eat. One borrowed mats for them to sleep on. To secure lodging, a cunning one had them close their eyes so that people would think that they were blind and then open them and explain that they had been miraculously cured. One stole the girl; another defeated their pursuers. When they reached home, the girl's mother told her to choose one of the men as her husband. She decided that the liar, the thief, the cunning one, and the fighter would not make good husbands and chose the one who had borrowed mats and returned them the next morning (Edgar 1911–1913: II, (58); translated by Skinner 1969: I, 388–390).

Hunter Saved by Animals

45:1.   (Vai)   One feature of African dilemma tales is that human characters predominate, but there are some in which animals are the principal characters. Eagle, Dog, and Otter fell in love with the daughter of a hunter, who had disappeared in the forest. The girl's mother promised her daughter to the one who brought back her husband. Dog followed the hunter's trail to a pool. Otter dove into the water and found the hunter, who was held captive; he convinced the Water People to release the hunter in return for 100 monkeys. Eagle captured the monkeys and threw them into the pool. When the hunter was released, he agreed to his wife's promise. Which of the three animals most deserved the girl? (Pinney n.d.: 134–135).

Recovering Cattle

46:1.   (Kono)   A chief sent Spider, Tsetse Fly, and Anteater to reclaim a cow that he had entrusted to a wealthy subject. Spider stretched out his thread so that they could cross a river. Anteater dug a hole through a high mountain, and they reached their destination. However, their host was not only wealthy, he was also greedy. He prepared poisoned food for the three envoys, but Tsetse Fly smelled the poison and they refused the food. They left with the cow but were pursued and encircled. Anteater dug a subterranean passage, and they reached home safely. Each claimed the cow. To whom should it be given? (Holas 1952: 82–84).

46:2. (Mbete) Mole, Dog, Spider, Fly, and Firefly set out to receive an inheritance. Spider spun a bridge so that they could pass over a river. Firefly lit the night, preventing all from falling over a precipice. Dog found the right way at a crossroads. Mole dug a tunnel under a cliff. Fly discovered poison in the food, put there by the step-parents, who did not want to give up the inheritance. Together they inherited five wives. There was one for each, but each claimed to have earned all five for himself. To whom should they be given? (Adam 1940–1941: 138).

46:3. (Kpelle) A chief sent Fly, Horse Fly, Mole, Spider, Wood-Borer, and Wind to bring his cow from a distant land. Mole dug a tunnel through an impassable mountain and Spider spun his cloth over a large river so that they could pass over. They reached their destination, and Fly warned them that the chief had poisoned their food. The chief announced that they would be killed if they could not fell a large tree in the middle of town without hitting any of the houses. Wood-Borer weakened the tree, and Wind blew it down safely. Horse Fly identified their master's cow. The chief set fire to their house, but again Mole dug a tunnel, and they escaped with the cow. Returning, they crossed the river and mountain as before and finally reached home. The chief wanted to reward them with the cow's tail, but each of them claimed it for what he had done. You, who have heard this folktale, to whom should he give the cow's tail? (Mengrelis 1947: 29).

46:4. (Samo) A rich man's cattle were stolen by a man with powerful magic, and he sent his seven sons to recover them. A large ape helped them over a large escarpment that they could not climb; a spider wove a rope so that they could cross over a large pool; a tsetse fly identified their cattle, whose color had been changed by magic. They returned home with the cattle (Guilhem n.d.: II, 73–77).

46:5. (Tera) A chief stole a blind man's cattle. The blind man set out in search of them and was joined by a tree stump, a cattle egret, a wild pig, and a tsetse fly. When they reached the chief's village, the fly warned them against poisoned food, and the stump got in the way of the servant who brought it, causing him to stumble and break the dish of food. The fly also warned that their hut was to be burned, and the pig dug a hole by which they escaped. Finally the fly brought word that the blind man's cattle were to be mixed with the chief's herd, but the egret identified them. Returning home, the blind man shared his cattle with the fly, the egret, the pig, and the stump (Newman 1968: II, 200–213).

46:6. (Guro) Ram's grandfather loaned fifty packages of *sombés* (iron currency) to a man who lived in the sky. Ram set out to claim the debt but did not know how to climb up. Rabbit told him to make a cord, and Spider attached it to the sky. With the Flying Rat, the three climbed up to the sky and demanded repayment of the debt. The debtor denied owing it and proposed the sasswood ordeal to settle the argument. Flying Rat drank the sasswood without dying, and the debtor gave them a fine ox in payment of the debt. When they returned to earth, each claimed the ox for what he had done. The people gathered and judged that it certainly belonged to Ram, but that it would be best if he killed it and gave some to the other animals and shared what was left with the assembled crowd. That is what was done (Tauxier 1924: 309–310).

Poisoned Food in Sky

47:1. (Vili) The Earth Goddess refused to allow anyone to marry her beautiful daughter unless he brought lightning from heaven. Spider offered to try if others helped him. Spider suspended his thread from the sky, and Woodpecker pecked a hole in the roof. They asked the Sky God for lightning, but he tested them to see if they really came from the Earth Goddess. Tortoise went back to earth and brought back a bundle of bamboo. Rat stayed under the bamboo, which was burned, and came out of the ashes unharmed. Sandfly learned that the lightning was kept in five cases in the fowl house. Then the Sky God gave one case to Spider, and Tortoise carried it down to earth. Spider presented the lightning to the Earth Goddess and was given her beautiful daughter in marriage. Each of the other animals claimed her, but the Earth Goddess said she belonged to Spider, who undertook to bring the lightning. However, because the others would make her daughter's life miserable if she lived with Spider, the Earth Goddess would give her to none. She then gave them all equal rewards, and the girl remained un-married and waited upon her mother (Dennett 1898: 74–76; retold by Feldmann 1963: 212–214).

47:2. (Limba) In a lengthy tale, a chief, whose daughter had been carried away by the Sky God, allowed Spider, Fly, Rat, Anteater, and Chameleon to live with him, despite the protests of his subchiefs. They climbed up to the sky on Spider's thread. Fly warned them against poisoned food. Rat stole other food for them to eat. When their house was burned, Anteater dug a hole by which they escaped. The Sky God said that they should see who had the best clothing. He put on a gold gown, gold trousers, and a gold hat; Chameleon also dressed in gold. Fly identified the girl, and they climbed back down on Spider's thread. Each claimed her as his wife, but instead they were given a cow to eat (Finnegan 1967: 276–280).

47:3. (Limba) The Sky God sent a girl to earth to be raised, and when she was grown he came and took her up above. Cane Rat, Ant-eater, Cockroach, Spider, Woodpecker, Fly, and Cat went to bring her back. Cane Rat cut through grass on the way. Cockroach spread his wings and carried them across a river. Spider hung his thread from the sky and they climbed up it. Woodpecker knocked a hole in the sky and they went in. They explained to the Sky God that they had come to take the girl back, and he said that they could do so if they could identify her. Fly bit her, and she jumped; Cat came and rubbed against her. They recognized her and were allowed to take her. Woodpecker knocked a hole in the sky. Spider stretched out his web, and they descended. Cockroach spread his wings, and they crossed the river. Cane Rat cut a road through the grass, and they reached home. They asked, "Is it she?" Her foster father said, "Yes, it is she. I thank you" (Finnegan 1967: 274–276).

47:4. (Vili) Spider spun a thread to the sky. Woodpecker climbed up it and pecked at the sky, making holes that we call stars. Man climbed up to the sky and fetched down fire. But some say that man found fire where fiery tears fell from the sky (Pechuël-Loesche 1907: 135).

Dog Finds Ring

48:1.   (Nkundo)   When offered many good things at a feast, a poor
man chose a dog with scabies. At other feasts he took only a chicken, a
hawk, and a rat, and everyone laughed at his stupidity. The dog helped
him catch a python, which gave him a ring when he spared its life. The
ring produced a beautiful house, a village, and wealth for him, and he
took a wife. The python had warned him not to give his ring away, but
one night when he was drunk, his wife stole the ring and fled. His
village and wealth disappeared and went to his wife's family. The hawk
carried the rat to the wife's village. The rat swallowed the ring but was
killed. The hawk flew off with the rat's body, but the rat fell into a
river and was eaten by a fish. The chicken found a nail, made a fish-
hook, and caught the fish. The dog ate its intestines and found the ring,
and the man's wealth returned. When the man died, the animals argued
over his inheritance and invited people to settle their dispute. Who do
you think owned it? Answer: The dog, because he found the lost ring
and found the python in the first place, but the others should receive
their portions (Hulstaert and de Rop 1954: 38–47; AT 560).

48:2.   (Nkundo)   A man had four children: a servant, a hawk, a dog,
and a rat; he also had a magic ring that gave him a wife and a village.
The wife made him drunk and stole his ring. Her family became rich,
and he became poor. He asked his children to retrieve his ring, but they
either refused or failed until the hawk carried the rat to the woman's
village. The rat bit the ring off the woman's finger; it was killed, but the
hawk flew off with its body. The rat came to life and quarreled with the
hawk about the ring. The ring fell into the water and was swallowed by
a fish. The servant caught the fish. The dog ate its intestines and found
the ring, and the master's wealth returned. Which one of the four did
the best and deserved to inherit the ring? Answer: The servant, because
when the ring was lost, he brought it out of the water (Hulstaert and de
Rop 1954: 46–51).

48:3.   (Fon)   A hunter, who owned a dog and a cat, spared the life of
a serpent. The serpent gave him a ring that produced two-story houses,
and he became rich. The serpent had warned him that a fat woman
would come to him, but that he should never tell her the secret of the
ring. He told her, and she stole the ring and went home. The hunter's
houses vanished, and he was poor again. The cat and the dog went to
get the ring. The cat stole it but dropped it in a river. They went to the

Sky Goddess, who told them to go back to the river and buy the first fish caught by a fisherman whom they would find there. They found the ring inside the fish, gave it to the hunter, and his wealth returned (Herskovits and Herskovits 1958: 225–227).

48:4. (Hausa) While his elder brother obtained a goat, a bull, two slaves, and two brides, a boy bought a scraggy dog, a skinny cat, and a wizened old woman. The woman was really the daughter of a king and had been captured in a war, and the boy went to ransom her. Following her advice he refused in turn 1,000,000 cowries, 1,000 head of cattle, 1,000 horses, and 100 slaves; instead he chose a ring from the king's finger. He went to live in the forest, and a big city magically appeared. He lived there with his mother and brother and his cat and dog. A bad woman came and begged for his ring; he gave it to her, and she gave it to her lover. The city arose around the lover, and the one around the youth disappeared. Setting out to retrieve the ring, the dog carried the cat across a river. The cat began killing thousands of mice, and the lover ordered that it be brought to kill mice in his palace. The mice asked the cat why it was killing them, and it told them about the ring. A mouse stole the ring from the lover's mouth and gave it to the cat, and the dog carried the cat home. The youth's city reappeared, and that of the bad woman and her lover vanished (Tremearne 1913: 244–251).

48:5. (Nupe) A precocious child, born from his mother's knee with a knife, bow, and arrow in his hands, went immediately to help his father on the farm. He announced that he wanted to be a trader, and his father gave him 20,000 cowries with which he bought a dove, a rat, a frog, a dog, and a cat. The dove said it would wake him every day; the rat said it would steal kola nuts for him; the frog said it would pray all day for him; the dog said it would help him hunt. When asked what it would do, the cat told the boy to come into the house, where it turned into a beautiful maiden. She told him to take her to her father, who would ransom her, but to refuse all offers and demand her father's red cap. The boy refused in turn 400,000 cowries and 200 cloths, but the father refused to part with his cap until the girl's mother insisted. The girl turned into a cat again and went home with the boy. With the cap the boy became rich through trading. Then he took a wife, who refused to sleep with him until he told her about the cap. She stole it. All his houses, horses, clothes, and weapons burned, and he had nothing left. The dove explained why this had happened and offered to show where the cap was. The five animals set out, with the frog stopping at a body of water. The dove lit on the house where the cap was. The cat rubbed against the woman, keeping her attention, while the rat scratched a hole through the wall, found the cap, and gave it to the dog who was waiting outside. Then the animals fled. When they came to the water, a man threw the dog a bone, and it dropped the cap in the water. The frog picked it up, and they returned to the boy, whose wealth was restored (Frobenius 1921–1928: IX, 230–237).

48:6.   (Ashanti)   A boy asked his mother for £4 worth of gold and with it bought a dog, for £5 worth and bought a cat, for £6 worth and bought a pigeon. The pigeon said that it was a chief from another village and that the boy would be rewarded if he took it home. The boy did so and was given much gold dust and a ring that did anything he commanded. With the ring he built houses, assembled people, and became a chief. Anansi, the spider, sent his niece to steal the ring, and with it Anansi built a big town. The boy sent his dog and cat to steal back the ring, warning them that Anansi had placed poisoned meat on the path. When they reached the meat, the dog stayed behind to eat it, but the cat went on. In Anansi's room the cat caught a mouse but released it on condition that it fetch the ring. Carrying the ring, the cat rejoined the dog, and they came to a river in flood. The dog took the ring but tired in midstream and dropped the ring, which was swallowed by a fish. The cat threatened the fish, and it vomited up the ring. The cat returned it to the boy and related what had happened. The cat was promised its reward and the dog its punishment. That is why a cat sleeps only on the best mat and eats only from a plate. And that is why a dog stays in the courtyard and sleeps in ashes to keep warm, and why a dog is flogged (Rattray 1930: 110–119; retold by Carey 1970: 27–39).

48:7.   (Cape Verde Islands)   A boy went fishing and caught a siren, who gave him a charmed ring in return for her freedom. He gave the ring to his mother to take care of it, and it built her a house with everything she needed. The boy brought home a dog, a cat, and then a rat. The mother's sister stole the ring. The dog smelled where the ring was and carried the cat and rat across the water. The rat found the ring, and the cat helped it escape. As they were recrossing the water, the dog dropped the ring, but the crabs retrieved it. The three animals took it back to the boy, and he took charge of it himself, saying, "The man who trusts in a woman ends up in jail or in the hospital" (Parsons 1923: I, 258–261).

48:8. (Bambara) A generous blind man was the only one left alive after his village had been attacked by warriors. He wept day and night, wishing that he too had been killed. A genie gave him a book, saying that he could have whatever he named while tapping the book, but that he must never tell its secret to a woman and that he must take care of a dog and a cat. He tapped the book, and his sight was restored. Tapping again, he got wives, children, and wealth and became a king without equal. A woman whose village had also been destroyed offered herself to him in marriage and became his favorite wife. Every night when they were in bed, she asked him how he became king, but he told her nothing. But one night, after she promised not to reveal the secret, he told her about the book. When he was sound asleep, she stole it and fled to her own country. There she tapped the book, naming everything that the king had and everything else that she wanted, and saying that the king should become blind again. After the blind man had spent three days and nights weeping, the genie came again and told him that it was his own fault. The genie said that he should not forget the dog and cat and sent them to get the book. After everyone was asleep, the cat stole the book and took it to the dog, who had waited outside the woman's village. The dog took the book in its teeth, put the cat on its back, and fled back to the blind man. After thanking the dog and cat, he tapped the book and his sight and his former property were restored, as well as the property of the woman. He had her arrested and, after reproaching her, he killed her (Travélé 1923: 195–200).

Animal Language

49:1. (Anyi) A hunter caught a python in his trap. In return for its freedom it gave him two gourds that gave him a large house and the ability to understand the language of animals. A mangy dog warned him of impending famine, and he hoarded his harvest and sold it at a high price. Later it warned him against a plague, a fire, and a flood. Twenty years later it said that he would die if he did not return the first gourd and become poor again. The hunter hesitated. Which decision would you have made? (Dadié 1955: 96–104).

Grateful Animals

50:1. (Kpelle) A man and his wife went to live in the forest, where she gave birth to a son. When the mother died, the father buried her, but when the father died, the boy, who knew nothing about death, thought he was sleeping. His corpse smelled. The boy went to look at his father's trap and found a mongoose. It said, "Don't kill me. Save me, and I will save you." The boy released it. The next day the mongoose went to the king's house, stole kola nuts, and dropped them on the ground, leaving a trail leading to the boy's trap. The king's people followed the trail and found the boy, who had come to look at his trap. They seized the boy and took him to the king, who sentenced him to death. They locked him in an abandoned house and an old woman brought him rice, which he shared with a cat. The cat caught a rat, which the boy gave to a snake. The snake bit the king's wife and she died, but it gave the boy medicine, and he restored her to life. The king divided his town in two and gave half to the boy. Who made the boy rich: the mongoose, the snake, the old woman, or the cat? (Westermann 1921: 434–436; AT 160).

50:2.   (Vai)   A man caught a deer in his trap but released it when it promised to make him rich. It carried him near a large town and left him there. He gave cassava to a 'possum that promised to make him rich. It stole kola nuts from the king's house and felt a trail of them leading to the man, and he was arrested. The man caught two rats and gave them to a snake that promised to make him rich. It bit the king's son and then gave the man medicine to cure the boy. The king divided his town in two and gave half to the man. The three animals came to the man, each claiming credit for having made him rich. Which of the three — the deer, the 'possum, or the snake — made the man rich? (Ellis 1914: 230–231).

50:3.   (Sikon)   A deer trampled on the crops of a man's new farm. When asked to stop, the deer said that this had long been its land, and it offered to make the farmer rich if he would leave the farm. The deer led the farmer to a spot to spend the night, stole a hamper of the chief's kola nuts, and left a trail of them leading to the sleeping farmer. In the morning the chief's warriors followed the trail. Weeping at his betrayal by the deer, the farmer was put in prison, where he found rats. After he had killed six rats, a snake entered and said that it had been sent by the deer to help and would do so if the farmer gave it the rats. The farmer did so, and the snake gave him three leaves to cure snakebite. Hearing that the chief's first son was dead, having been bitten by a snake, the farmer revived him and was rewarded with wealth and a high position (Pinney n.d.: 230–232).

50:4. (Baule) A hunter found a leopard, a gazelle, a snake, and a man in a pit. The animals promised to help him if he rescued them, so he pulled them out, and he pulled out the man also. The leopard brought him game, and the gazelle brought him a pot of gold that had been owned by Anangama, the Sky God's brother. The man told Anangama, and the hunter was seized. The snake gave the hunter medicine to cure snakebite and then bit Anangama's son. The hunter cured the youth, and was given the heart of the traitor (Himmelheber 1951: 37–39).

50:5. (Ashanti) Hunter rescued Man, Leopard, Snake, and Rat from a pit after asking each to mend its ways. In thanks, Leopard brought Hunter meat. Rat brought him gold dust that it stole from the Sky God. Man brought only a little pot of palm wine, which Hunter refused, telling what the others had brought. Man took his palm wine away, went to Sky God, and said that Rat had taken the gold dust to Hunter. Sky God had Hunter flogged. Snake gave Hunter medicine to cure snakebite and then bit the child of the king's favorite wife. Hunter saved the child's life, using the remedy mixed with the blood of the tale teller. That is how tale telling came to the Ashanti (Rattray 1930: 58–63; cited as AT 160 by Klipple 1938).

50:6. (Ashanti) A hunter rescued a rat, a snake, a leopard, and the chief's messenger from his pitfall. Each promised to reward the hunter, but the man failed to keep his promise. The leopard killed game for the hunter; the rat brought him a bag of gold; the snake taught him a cure for snakebite. When the chief's treasurer discovered that a bag of gold was missing, the chief's messenger accused the hunter, who refused to defend himself at his trial for fear of getting his friends in trouble. The snake bit the chief's daughter and the hunter cured her, using the blood of the man who had betrayed him. The hunter married the chief's daughter, and they lived long and happily (Appiah 1969: 100–105).

50:7. (Akan) A poor hunter found a man, a leopard, a snake, and a rat in a pit in the forest. Each begged the hunter to help him out. He asked the man where his sense of gratitude was; the leopard if it would not eat his sheep, goats, and hens; the snake if it were not the one that had killed his brother; the rat if it would not disturb his palm nuts. Each one promised to reward the hunter, and he helped them all out of the pit. The snake gave the hunter an antidote for snakebite. The man went home with the hunter and stayed with him for three days. The leopard brought game for him to sell, and the rat brought him a large pot filled with gold that it had stolen from the king. The hunter became wealthy, and his compound was full of slaves. When the rescued man heard this, he told the king that the hunter had stolen his gold. The king had the hunter, his wife and children, his slaves, and all his possessions brought to the court. The hunter admitted that his accuser was his friend and then asked if this ingratitude was his reward. While the hunter was speaking, a messenger brought news that the king's son was dying of snakebite. The hunter cured the king's son and chose the traitor's head as his reward; all his property was returned to him. Hence the proverbs, "That is the thanks of man!" and "If your friend takes you to where you find life, don't take him to where he finds death." (Christaller 1894: 65–69; repeated by Seidel 1896: 282–289, who refers to a Malayan parallel; cited as AT 160 by Klipple 1938).

50:8.   (Unidentified, Ghana)   A hunter helped a leopard, a serpent, a rat, and a man out of a pit. The three animals promised to reward him, but the man said he was very poor, and the hunter took him home with him. The serpent gave the hunter medicine to cure snakebite. The leopard killed game and brought him food to eat. The rat gave him cloth, gold dust, and ivory, and the hunter built a fine house. When the theft of the king's treasures was announced, the hunter's envious guest went to the palace and, when promised a reward, accused his host of the theft. The hunter was brought to court, and no one would believe his story. While the preparations for his execution were being made, a serpent bit the king's eldest son. The hunter offered to cure him, asking for the blood of a traitor to mix with his medicine. His ungrateful guest was beheaded, the king's son was cured, and the hunter was sent home loaded with honors (Barker and Sinclair 1917: 163–166; retold by Woodson 1964: 32–35, Green 1967: 15–19, and Arnott 1967: 81–85; cited as AT 160 by Klipple 1938).

50:9.   (Yoruba)   A hunter rescued a leopard, a serpent, a rat, and a woman from a pit. The animals promised to reward him, and he took the woman home with him. The leopard brought him game. The rat dug a tunnel from his house to the palace of the king, stole things, and brought them to his house, and the hunter became wealthy. The woman told the king that the hunter had the king's missing property, and the hunter was thrown into irons. The serpent brought him medicine to blow into the eyes of the king's son to revive him. He did so and received a reward of 200 slaves and 200 cloths. This is the reason why one should not be envious and should not take anything from the king's palace (Bouche 1884–1885: 49–50; cited as AT 160 by Klipple 1938).

50:10. (Yoruba) A hunter rescued animals and a woman from a pit. The leopard and the rat promised to reward him. One of the animals warned him about the woman, but he took her home with him. The leopard brought him game, and the rat dug a passage to the king's palace and stole things for him. The hunter became wealthy, but the woman told the king that his missing treasure was in the hunter's house. The hunter was thrown in irons; he said that the rat had given him the stolen things. A serpent brought him medicine to blow into the eyes of the king's son. He revived the boy and received a reward of 200 slaves and 200 cloths — all that he wished — and he became rich again. Learn from this not to take anything from the king (Bouche 1884–1885: 51–52; cited as AT 160 by Klipple 1938).

50:11. (Fulani) A man found a lion, a hyena, a serpent, and a man in a deep pit. He pulled out the animals after each had promised to reward him, and then he pulled out the man. A famine came, and the lion brought him game each day. The hyena gave him a golden jug that it stole from the king's palace. The man he had pulled from the pit accused him, and he was imprisoned. The serpent came and said that it would bite the king's son, and told him what to do. When the youth was bitten, the man told the king that he must kill the slanderer, remove his brains, and rub them on the snakebite. This was done, the youth was cured, and the man was freed (Gaden 1913–1914: I, 174–177; cited as AT 160 by Klipple 1938).

50:12. (Unidentified, Mali) A farmer found a blacksmith, a lion, a hyena, and a snake in a pit. The lion begged him for help, promising to reward him, and the farmer released them all. The lion helped him clear his fields, and the hyena brought him a pot of gold stolen from the royal treasure. The farmer gave the gold to the smith to work, but the smith betrayed him, and the farmer was condemned to death. The snake bit the king's favorite son, and the farmer said that he would cure the youth, but he needed the brains of a smith. The traitor was decapitated, the king's son was cured, and the farmer was rewarded with animals and part of the gold (Mabendy 1966: 106–107).

50:13. (Swahili) On successive days a hunter found an ape, a snake, and a lion in his traps. He freed them when they said, "Save me from rain, that I may come and save you from sun." Each also warned him not to do good for a man because the man would do him harm. The hunter found a man in his traps and freed him also. Later the hunter was lost in the forest, and the ape stole papaya, bananas, and a calabash of water for him to eat and drink. Lost again in the forest, the lion brought him game to eat. He went to get water from a well and in it saw the snake. The snake gave him gold and silver chains. The hunter came to a town and was invited to eat with the man he had freed, but the man went to the sultan and accused the hunter, who was seized and bound. The snake came to where the man was. The townspeople asked the hunter to send the snake away, but it stayed until the hunter was untied. When the hunter told his story, the sultan had the ungrateful man drowned at sea (Steere 1899: 422–431; retold by Bateman 1901: 81–96 and by von Held 1904: 34–39; cited as AT 160 by Klipple 1938).

50:14. (Unidentified, Malawi) A man ran away with the chief's wife, built a hut in the forest, and became a hunter. One day he found a man, a lion, and a snake in his game pit. Despite the animals' warning not to free the man, he helped them all out. The man told the chief that he had found the one who had run away with his wife; the chief had the hunter seized and bound. On the day of his trial, the lion began to kill people on the way to their gardens, and when the hunter was being questioned, the snake bit the chief. The hunter cured him with medicine the snake had given him, and the chief announced that when he died, the hunter should succeed him (Young 1933: 44–45).

50:15. (Edo) A great wrestler was chided by his chief because he did no work. He began trapping but freed every animal he caught. He slapped a wife of the king because she stole a rabbit from his trap, and later he saw the king's wives bathing in a stream. For these two crimes he was condemned to death. A rat told him that the animals he had freed would save him. On the day that he was to be killed, a snake bit the king's daughter. The wrestler revived her as instructed by the animals. He married the daughter and the king gave him lands and a fine house (Brown 1966: 40–43).

50:16. (Bura) A *waikil* [who ranks next to the chief] fell into a well with two snakes. They were pulled out by a man, who came to the *waikil* for the reward that had been promised. The *waikil* had the man driven away, but one of the snakes brought him a mouthful of gold. When the chief learned the man's story, he gave him the *waikil*'s position (Helser 1930: 89–92; cited as AT 160 by Klipple 1938).

50:17. (Ashanti)   A poor hunter spared the life of a rat and a deer that promised to help him and took them home with him. Each night the rat brought him a nugget of gold it had stolen from the house of a miser, and the hunter became rich. The deer warned him that his house was to be searched and saved him from disgrace by swallowing the gold. When the deer died of old age the hunter buried it. He decided never to kill animals again or to eat meat, and he grew even richer because animals never invaded his farms. Until he grew old he always spoke of the gratitude and faithfulness of animals, which far surpassed that of human beings (Appiah 1967: 25–32).

Boy and Lion Cub

51:1. (Ashanti)   A woman lost in the forest built a shelter near a shea-butter tree; there she gave birth to a son. A lioness that lived nearby gave birth to a male cub. The boy and the cub became friends, playing together when their mothers were out hunting food. One day the lioness killed the woman, but the cub refused to eat. The cub swore to take care of the boy until it could avenge the woman's death. Each morning the young lion measured its paw against the footprint of the lioness, and when they matched, it killed its mother. Later it helped the youth to marry the chief's daughter and warned him never to take a second wife. Every Friday night the youth sent his wife to visit her family, and the lion came to visit him. Then a wealthy woman asked to marry him; he refused but compromised by letting her live with him. Not understanding why she was also sent off every Friday, she hid herself and saw the lion coming to the house. She called a hunter who shot the lion. When the youth saw the dead lion, he stabbed himself, and his real wife hanged herself. Which of the three — lion, man, or wife — did best? (Cardinall 1931: 190–192).

51:2. (Loma or Mende)   A woman gave birth in the forest near a cave in which a lioness gave birth to a female cub. The boy and cub met, played together, and learned to love each other. The lioness killed the boy's mother, but the cub refused to eat her flesh. The boy killed the lioness and lived in the cave with her cub. When they grew up, the boy went to town and fell in love with the chief's daughter; the young lioness helped him to marry her. When the youth sent his bride to spend the night with her mother, she suspected that he had a lover. One night she returned and found him in bed with the lioness. She reported this to her father, and he sent his warriors, who killed the lion. The youth killed himself, and his wife killed herself (Pinney n.d.: 71–73).

51:3.   (Vai)   A woman, driven away by her husband, gave birth in the forest near a lioness and her cub. When their mothers were away, the boy and the cub became friends and played together. The lioness killed the woman, and the cub killed the lioness. When they grew up, the young man went to town and was married. When he occasionally spent the nights in his own room, his wife became jealous. Finally she threw open the door, saw him with the lion, and screamed. Neighbors came and wounded the lion, and when the young man found its dead body, he stabbed himself (Creel 1960: 93–100).

51:4.   (Igala)   A woman gave birth in the forest and left her son there. He was raised by a leopardess with her cubs, and when he grew up, the leopardess stole clothes for him. Later it left him near a town, where he settled a quarrel and was proclaimed king. When the leopardess was about to die, it came to bid him farewell. He begged it to stay, but it ran away and died in the forest. The youth followed, flung himself on its body, and died also (Mockler-Ferryman 1902: 283–284).

51:5.   (Unidentified, Senegal)   A boy, whose mother had a cotton field, found the lair of a lioness and her cub. The two young ones became playmates and friends. One day the lioness brought home a human leg and hand. The cub refused to eat it and, to revenge its friend, dug a pitfall over a fire and baited it with the arm of the boy's mother; the lioness fell in and was burned to death. The boy and the lion lived together and separated when they grew up, the lion returning to the forest and the youth going to town. The lion promised to warn him if he was in danger but said he must never speak of its foul mouth. The boy was circumcised, and when the king announced that he would give his daughter in marriage to the man who brought him a living lion, the lion let itself be taken. The boy married the king's daughter and later became king. One night when he was tired from a journey, he heard the lion and mentioned its foul mouth. Insulted, the lion demanded that the youth kill it with his sword. The lion died, and since then men and lions have been enemies (Socé 1948: 205–213).

51:6.   (Bura)   A woman gave birth to a son in a cave. A lioness came to the cave and gave birth to a cub. The woman hid in the back of the cave and went for food when the lioness did, and the boy and the cub became friends and played together. The lioness killed the woman, but the cub refused to eat her flesh and promised to feed the boy and avenge the woman's death. After months had passed, the young lion killed its mother and then provided food for the boy's circumcision. The young man fell in love with the chief's daughter, and the lion helped him to marry her. The young man, his wife, and the lion lived together happily ever after (Helser 1930: 169–172; repeated in Helser 1934: 63–66).

51:7. (Hausa) One day a hunter captured only a locust. He gave it to his pregnant wife to cook. It escaped, and he ordered her to recapture it. She set out in pursuit, but each time she approached, it fled. Finally it entered a cave; she followed and gave birth to a son there. At the same time a lioness gave birth in the cave, and in time the boy and the cub became friends and played together. The lioness killed the woman, but the cub refused to eat her flesh. It promised the boy it would kill its mother, and when its footprint matched hers, it killed the lioness. When the boy grew up, the young lion captured a barber to circumcise him and paid him with goods it stole from traders. Afterwards it captured the king's daughter and let his young friend rescue her, after he had been promised he could marry her. The young man told his wife that he had a lion as a friend. She accepted this, and it came to visit him each Friday. Against the lion's warning, the young man allowed a prostitute to live with him. He told her about his lion friend, but when she first saw it, she screamed, and people came and shot it. The young man and his wife followed the lion, found it near death and stabbed themselves, but a priest gave them medicine, and they recovered. The lion then killed the prostitute (Mischlich 1929: 84–93).

51:8. (Hausa) One day a hunter caught only one locust, and his pregnant wife let it escape. The hunter ordered her to bring it back, but each time she approached it, it jumped away. That night she took refuge in a hollow tree, where she delivered her son. The boy made friends with the cub of a lioness that lived nearby. The lioness fed them both, and the boy took food home to his mother. One day the lioness killed the boy's mother, but the cub refused to eat her flesh. When the young lion grew up, it killed its mother. The young man went to town and married, and the lion came to visit him. One day the wife saw the lion and fled in fear. Heartbroken, the lion went away and died. When the young man found its body, he stabbed himself (Tremearne 1913: 198–201).

51:9. (Hausa) Tremearne cites another Hausa version in which the youth went to look for the lion and revived it with medicine provided by a guinea-fowl. Then they separated, with the youth returning home and the lion going off into the forest (Tremearne 1913: 201).

51:10. (Hausa) One day a hunter caught a large locust. His pregnant wife prepared to cook it, but it escaped. Her husband ordered her to catch it, but each time she struck at it, it flew away. That night she slept in a hollow tree; there she gave birth to a boy. While she searched for food, the boy went to visit the cub of a lioness that lived nearby. One day the lioness killed the boy's mother, but the young lion was angry and refused to eat her flesh. When the young lion grew up and its footprint was as large as its mother's, it killed the lioness, but the boy refused to eat its flesh. When the boy grew up, he decided to live in town. The lion stole clothing, spears, axes, knives, and arrows from passing traders for the young man, who went to town and married. The lion came to visit him each night, but one night his wife saw the lion and screamed. The lion fled into the forest, where it died. The man sharpened his knife and went into the forest; when he found the lion's dead body, he killed himself (Schön 1885–1886: I, 129–132; II, 85–88).

51:11. (Hausa) An orphan woman went into the bush and gave birth to a son. Nearby a lioness gave birth to a cub. The lioness killed the boy's mother, and the boy lived with the lioness and her cub. When the boy grew up, the lioness had a barber circumcise him and, saying that he was a man, sent him to live in the village where he married a daughter of the chief. The young lion visited the young married couple and became their best friend. Later the man wanted to marry the daughter of the chief bowman, but his first wife warned him that the bowman would kill the lion. He took his second wife anyway. One day two children saw the lion enter his house. They cried out that the lion was going to eat the chief's daughter and all the village came. The lion fled, but the chief bowman killed it with an arrow. The man came, pulled out the arrow, and drove it into his stomach. His first wife came and pulled the arrow out of his stomach and plunged it into hers. A passing lion prayed to Allah to revive them. Allah did so and told them, "You, humans, stay in your village and the lions will stay in the bush. You should not live together" (Guillot 1933: 70–71).

51:12–13. (Hausa) Two untranslated Hausa versions are "The boy and the Lion Cub" (Charlton 1908: 25–30, [12–17] and the "Story of a Boy's Friendship with a Lion" (Harris 1908: 75–77). Neither of these appears to pose a dilemma, but one may be the tale (51:9) cited by Tremearne (1913).

Leopard Eats Child

52:1. (Pygmy) Long ago men and animals lived together in the same village. One day a leopard ate a baby boy, and his mother went crying to the chief. The leopard denied its guilt, saying the boy was lost in the forest. An ape said it had seen the boy running toward the river. But a dog said it had been in the woman's house eating a bone and saw the leopard eat the boy. The chief pronounced the sentence. The leopard was banned from the village, and men, aided by dogs, would try to kill it and its children. It was war to the death. The ape, which had also lied, was banned from the village and could enter only when tied by the neck; it was to live in the trees and be mocked by all the animals, and men would eat its flesh and make clothing from its skin. The dog, because it had not defended the woman, was made the slave of man and ordered to guard women in their homes. Was the chief right to punish the leopard, the ape, and the dog? Which one was happiest with its sentence? (Trilles 1932: 278–280).

Frog's Two Wives

53:1. (Kimbundu) Frog built huts for his two wives at opposite sides of his compound and spent the days in its center. Each wife cooked food and sent her son at the same time to call Frog to eat. He asked, "What shall I do?" He knew that if he went to either wife, the other would be jealous. He began croaking, "I am in trouble! I am in trouble!" That is what Frog is still saying whenever he is croaking (Chatelain 1894: 216–217; retold by Seidel 1896: 156–157 and, as an "Mbamba" tale, by Jablow 1961: 99–100).

53:2. (Kongo) Frog built a house in Ndumbi for his first wife and a house in Ndala for his second wife. Each wife made manioc pudding and sent for him at the same time to come and eat. Not knowing what to do, Frog began croaking, as he does today, "I am in trouble, I am in trouble!" (Courlander 1963: 58–59).

War of Birds and Beasts

54:1.   (Ewe)   Elephant wanted Cock's wife for himself and went to tell
her so. Cock came and asked, "What does this fat one want here?" She
told him. Cock said that his wife should choose between them, and she
said that Elephant was too fat. Elephant declared war and gathered all
the four-footed animals to help him. Cock assembled all the winged
creatures, including the bees and wasps. They met at the battle field and
Fox tried to seize Cock, but Eagle grabbed him by the throat. Then
Elephant came with his other helpers, and Cock sent the bees and
wasps to fight them. Which side won? (Schönhärl 1909: 125–126).

Alternate House-building

55:1.   (Swahili)   Lion and bushbuck, working on alternate days, built
the same house, and when it was finished, both claimed it. Which owned
the house? (Lademann, Kausch, and Reuss 1910: 84).

55:2.   (Mongo)   Working alternately, a house was built by a porter,
who did not know how to kill game, and a hunter, who did not know
how to carry game. When it was finished, they decided to live together.
On the first day, the hunter killed seven wild boars, and on the second
day, six boars and four chimpanzees. Each day the porter carried them
all home at once. Each man feared that the other would kill him, and
they went back to live in the village. Their relatives came to take the
game that they had left behind, but the hunter's relatives kept it all for
themselves. Hulstaert comments that this tale gives the impression of
being a "fable de jurisprudence," like those in *Rechtspraakfabels van
de Nkundó* (Hulstaert 1965: 472–475).

55:3.   (Wolof)   Working on alternate days, the hyena and the lion
built the same house. It had two sections with a hole in the wall between
them. The hyena was in one part, and during a storm an old woman
took refuge in the other. Through the hole she offered some food to the
hyena, in thanks for his hospitality. In fear, the hyena opened the door
to rush out, just as the lion came in. The two animals tumbled into the
sand, got up, and ran away. Stopping at a stream, each asked the other
why he was running. They asked the giraffe to see who was in the house.
It stuck its head through the hole in the wall, and the old woman tied
her red kerchief around its neck. When it returned to the other two

animals, the hyena told the lion that the giraffe was bleeding. They fled again, with the giraffe following. The other animals saw them and fled with them. The elephant ran so hard that it made holes in the ground, and the little frog, following as best he could, cried, "Watch out for the ponds" (Guillot 1933: 4–5).

55:4–20.   Seventeen other African non-dilemma variants of this tale are summarized in Bascom (1969: 133).

Chain of Accidents

56:1.   (Nkundo)   A blacksmith sharpened a woman's knife so that she could clear the undergrowth for a garden. He warned her not to put it in her basket because it would pierce the basket and cut her leg, not to cut a liana because the knife would wound her, not to threaten any-one lest it kill him, and not to threaten any animal because it was very sharp. He said that when she reached her field, one blow with the knife would cut all the undergrowth, and that if she did not believe him, it was not his affair. On her way the woman met a cobra in the path and, in fear, she cut it in two. The piece with the head ran away and entered the hole of a Gambia rat. The rat fled, and a wildcat asked why. When the rat did not answer, the wildcat thought it was a sign of something really dangerous, and it ran also. Seeing a chicken, the wildcat said, "I cannot run past my food," and struck it in the eye. The chicken screamed. A cuckoo heard it, thought it was a warning that war was coming and called. A pheasant heard the cuckoo and, thinking the same thing, also called. A monkey heard the pheasant, reached the same con-clusion and ran. It broke a dead branch which fell on a liana, and the liana awakened an antelope. The antelope broke the eggs of a night swallow, which broke the eggs of a nectarine bird, which crawled into the nose of an elephant. The elephant trampled the garden of a man, who, upon seeing the damage, hanged himself. The elephant was charged and told to pay compensation.

In the manner typical of such cumulative tales, each character accuses the one before him, repeating the subsequent action. Finally, when the woman blamed the blacksmith, he said it was her fault because she did not heed his warning and cut the cobra in two. Then the cobra went to the rat's hole, the rat found the wildcat, the wildcat called but the rat did not answer, the cat scratched the eye of the chicken, the chicken cried alarm, the cuckoo answered, the pheasant answered, the monkey broke the dead branch, the branch fell on the liana, the liana woke the antelope, the antelope broke the eggs of the night swallow, the night swallow broke the eggs of the nectarine bird, the nectarine bird crawled into the nose of the elephant, the elephant trampled the field of the man, and the man hung himself. In this palaver, how many are right and how many are wrong?

Answer: The woman wins because she only asked to have her knife sharpened, and though she cut the cobra in two, a woman does not step over a snake lying in the path. The other winners are the rat, because it left its house to the cobra; the cuckoo and the chicken, which made their calls as always; the pheasant, which only spoke with its mouth; the dead branch, which the monkey broke; and the liana, which the dead branch carried with it and which did not harm the antelope. The losers are the blacksmith, because he bewitched the woman's knife; the cobra, because it blocked the woman's path; the wildcat, because it wounded the chicken; the monkey, because it broke the dead branch; the antelope, because it broke the night swallow's eggs; and the night swallow, the nectarine bird, and the elephant, because they were brutal and wanton in their vengeance (Hulstaert and de Rop 1954: 134–147; cf. AT 2042).

56:2.   (Nkundo) A fly frightened a cobra, which entered the hole of a rat, which frightened a young mother, who called for help. A pheasant beat the war drum, and a monkey ran away dragging some fruit, which dragged dry branches, which dragged a liana. The liana awakened an antelope, which jumped through the fence of the stupid one, who wounded the fighter, who insulted the mother of the dumb person, who set fire to the harem of a mantis. The mantis broke the eggs of a night swallow, which broke its wings in fighting the mantis. The mantis was charged and asked to pay compensation. Again each character blames the one before him and recites the subsequent action, but in this case there is no separate answer. The tale ends with people going to kill the fly when it refuses to pay compensation, and with the explanatory element: Therefore we kill flies without the slightest palaver (Hulstaert and de Rop 1954: 146–157). Hulstaert and de Rop comment:

There is no other solution in this case. The solution is, in fact, part of the narration. The fable was recorded as such and was not presented as a judiciary fable, but as an explanation of why flies are killed. It boils down, however to the same thing. The fly is put entirely in the wrong as the first cause and fault of the entire complicated story. She must pay compensation to the night swallow, but she refuses frankly without even wanting to give an explanation. So she is guilty of the death sentence.

56:3. (Guro) Spider and Stone made a trap together and shared the game they caught. One day Spider said he would take his share to the village and Stone demanded to know why. As they argued, they stepped on a centipede, which jumped on the trunk of an elephant, and the elephant ate the yams of an old lady. She told her dog to gather the rest of the yams and bring them to her, but the dog refused, and she gathered them herself. When she returned, she struck the dog, reproaching it for disobeying her. The dog fled to the refuse heap, making a bird fly up into a tree. Then the dog went to the stream where the antelope was bathing. The antelope fled and disturbed the Koukouo bird, which beat the drum. Its brother, the Dagboué bird, came immediately, fell on a passing man and killed him. Meanwhile Spider and Stone continued their argument (Tauxier 1924: 308).

Fire and Water

57:1. (Unidentified, Gabon) Fire claimed it was greater than Water because without it no food could be cooked. Water replied that it was greater because without it there would be nothing to drink. People tired of their endless, repetitious dispute and went into council to settle the argument. They decided that the two were equal and that they should cease their dispute (Nassau 1915: 38). The appearance of inanimate objects as characters, which is also found in some other African folktales, seems to be particularly characteristic of dilemma tales of the Nkundo and other Mongo groups, in which even parts of the body are personified.

Two Seasons

58:1. (Mongo) The fruit season claimed that it was better than the dry season because it provided caterpillars and many kinds of fruit for people to eat. The dry season replied that it made the sun shine so that people could plant their crops and dried up the streams so that people could catch fish. The rainy season, saying that it was impartial because it gave very little food, heard the argument and gave its verdict: the dry season wins the argument because the fruit season provides little food (Ruskin 1921: 60–61).

Canoe and Paddle

59:1. (Mongo) The canoe claimed it was superior to the paddle because it was larger, and the paddle, claiming to be equal, went away. A man loaded the canoe with his goods, but it could not travel. The man went to call the paddle, but it asked that the case be tried. The paddle won the case, the verdict being that the paddle and the canoe were equals (Ruskin 1921: 68–69).

Canoe and Drum

60:1. (Nkundo) The drum asked the canoe what use it was. The canoe replied, "I carry our master wherever he goes, carry others who pay him for the ride, and because of me our master catches fish. Of what use are you?" The drum replied, "I am the mouth of our master and of the entire clan. I warn people when war comes, and I send messages when our master wants to speak with someone at a distance. During the dances my voice speaks with joy and gives enthusiasm to the dancers. Am I not the most important of our master's servants?" They went to their master to settle the argument. He bent over to think but has not yet spoken. Which has the noblest work? Answer: The canoe, because the drum can not bring or provide food (Hulstaert and de Rop 1954: 82–85).

Mortar and Canoe

61:1. (Mongo) The mortar claimed it was superior to the canoe because it lived with men rather than with fish and because they used it to pound their food. The canoe replied that it took men fishing, hunting, and trading and carried their weapons, food, and other goods. The matter came to trial, and the canoe won the case (Ruskin 1921: 66–69).

Mortar and Climbing Belt

62:1. (Nkundo) A man went to gather palm nuts, using his climbing belt to climb the tree. When he returned home, he hung his belt on the front of his house. His wife took an axe, loosened the nuts, and pounded them in a mortar. The climbing belt asked the pestle and mortar why they always ate palm nuts when they did not go to the palm grove or climb the trees. They said that the belt should ask their master, who gave them the nuts. In anger, the belt threw them a proverb, "The pestle has the palm oil, the mortar has the thick oil, the climbing belt which fetched the nut goes to the front of the house." The pestle and mortar went to the judges and accused the belt of throwing sarcastic proverbs at them. Who will ever win this palaver? Answer: the climbing rope, by means of which its master reaches the nuts (Hulstaert and de Rop 1954: 110–113).

Garden Knife and Axe

63:1. (Mongo) The garden knife claimed it was superior to the axe because it cleared gardens, planted crops, weeded and dug the earth, and when it cut a man, he was wounded. The axe replied that they were equals as far as food was concerned because it felled the trees and bushes to make the gardens; but it also made canoes, mortars, pestles, and paddles and cut firewood and palm nuts. The hawk and the crow heard the case and decided in favor of the axe. They asked the axe for a reward for their verdict, but it refused, saying that it was the senior. The hawk and the crow became angry, and since then they have killed man's chickens (Ruskin 1921: 60–63).

Pitfall and Spikes

64:1. (Mongo) The pitfall claimed that it had killed an animal that had fallen into it. Its spikes did not argue but went away. Then a wild boar fell into the pit, but it climbed out and ran away. The spikes returned and told the pitfall, "You say you kill all the animals, but you did not kill that one, did you?" The pitfall admitted that it was not successful alone, and they agreed to work together again (Ruskin 1921: 72–75).

Net and Legs

65:1. (Mongo) The net decided that it would hunt alone, but it could not catch any animals. The legs also tried alone and failed. So it was decided that the net and the legs should go together so that they could catch game (Ruskin 1921: 68–69).

Manioc and Banana

66:1.   (Nkundo)   The banana, the most important crop above ground, quarreled with manioc, the most important underground crop. It said that it and its "children" that bore fruit above ground, like the oil palm and the avocado, gave mankind tasty food. The manioc said that it, the yam, the sweet potato, and others were the ones that fed people and that without them people could not exist. Their vehement quarrel was taken to intelligent people for settlement. Which one feeds people? Answer: Those underground win the argument, because all crops come from roots below the ground, even if their fruit is above (Hulstaert and de Rop 1954: 126–127).

Manioc and Plantain

67:1.   (Mongo)   The manioc and the plantain each claimed seniority. Afterwards a man made a garden and planted manioc in one part and plantain in another. He harvested the manioc roots and replanted its stems, and they continued to grow. He cut down the plantain and its stump died, but new shoots grew up from its roots. This happened again the next season, but after a while the plantain was dead while the manioc was still growing. The council of elders heard the case and decided that manioc was the senior because it goes on bearing almost without end, whereas plantain can be cut only two or three times from the original planting (Ruskin 1921: 68–71).

Oil Palm and Raffia Palm

68:1.   (Nkundo)   The trees met to eat and drink together. When food cooked in palm oil was brought in by a woman dressed in fine clothes, the oil palm could not restrain its pride. It stood up and said, "I produce good oil, palm sauce, palm wine, salt, palm slats, leaf stems for brooms, and nuts for oil. Who is equal to me?" The raffia palm stood up and said, "I surpass you. I provide clothing and fibers for traps. My leaf stems make better brooms than yours, my nuts give oil, and my salt is good. People make beds with my frond stems." Their quarrel became serious and people went into secret assembly to settle it. Which surpasses the other? Answer: The raffia palm, because it produces clothing. One can walk hungry in front of people, but not naked (Hulstaert and de Rop 1954: 84–87).

68:2. (Nkundo) One day the oil palm and the raffia palm argued about which was the better. The raffia palm said, "I am, because my raffia is woven into clothing, my fibers are made into traps to catch animals, my leaves make very good brooms, and my frond stems are made into beds to sleep on." The oil palm replied, "No, I am the better. Palm sauce is made from the oil from my nuts, and I give salt. My heart is good to eat, and my wine is good to drink. When my nuts are sold, they bring much money. And I have many other good things." The chimpanzee came to settle the argument and said that the oil palm was better. When the raffia palm heard this, it took away the chimpanzee's raffia clothing. The chimpanzee fled in shame into the bush and never again lived with men (de Rop 1956: 162–163).

68:3. (Mongo) The oil palm claimed it was superior to the raffia palm because its nuts gave oil for cooking and for anointing the body, its flowers gave salt, it produced palm cabbage and edible worms and caterpillars, and it yielded palm wine. Also its stems were used for roofing houses, its leaves as remembrances in court cases, and its fibers for patching canoes. The raffia palm replied that it also had edible worms and that its fibers were made into thread, into petticoats for women, and into fish lines and fish nets; they were also used to fasten traps. After considering the case in private, the chimpanzee, the judge, announced that the oil palm won the argument. In anger, the raffia palm snatched away the chimpanzee's cloth, leaving it naked. So the chimpanzee is always seen naked in the forest (Ruskin 1921: 70–73).

68:4–6. (Mongo) The oil palm and the raffia palm each claimed seniority because it kept men alive. The raffia palm said that edible grubs were found in its trunk and that man took its fibers to trap animals, the stems of its leaves to make brooms, its laths to make beds, and its raffia to make clothing. The oil palm said that these were only five things and that its own were more numerous. It yielded edible grubs and palm wine, and men ate its fruit and its palm cabbage. They wove mats and baskets from its fronds and made salt from it, oils from its fruit and its nuts, brooms from the stems of its leaves, and fences and torches from its laths; they also used its fibers in kindling fire. The chimpanzee, who judged their dispute, declared that the raffia palm was the loser. The raffia palm demanded its raffia cloth, and the chimpanzee fled into the forest, shamed by its nudity. It went to live where there were no men, and since then it has been called chimpanzee (Hulstaert 1970: 24–27). Hulstaert cites a Mongo variant in *Buku Ea Mbaanda I* (1935: 26) and another in de Witte (1913–1914: 177).

68:7–8. (Dyola) The *cad* tree and the mango tree argued about which had the better fruit. The mango said that all animals liked its fruit and that humans liked it the most. The *cad* said that its fruit was liked by goats and that goats were above humans. They went to a butcher, who chopped them both down (L.–V. Thomas 1968: 74). A second Dyola version ends with the argument being referred to the lion. Saying that it detested the fruit of both but needed *cad*'s wood for cooking and mango's leaves for its bed, the lion mutilated them both (L.–V. Thomas 1968: 74).

Bofumbo Tree and Parasol Tree

69:1. (Nkundo) A man and his wife went into the forest to make a hunting fence. After three days they had no fire and no water, and the wife gave birth to a child. A *bofumbo* tree (used for fire drills) took pity on them and told the man to rub two pieces of its wood together to kindle a fire. A parasol tree told him to cut beneath its roots to get water to bathe his wife. This he did, and when the fence was finished, they caught much game and returned home. Later the two trees came to the couple, and each asked to marry the girl born in the forest. Until now, the couple has not been able to decide what to do. To which, or both, should they give their daughter as wife? Answer: Water and fire are equally useful, but the *bofumbo* tree wins because it was the first to take pity on the man and woman and thus has seniority (Hulstaert and de Rop 1954: 74–77).

Tree Parts

70:1. (Nkundo) The name "tree" was claimed by its root, trunk, sap, bark, and leaf. Which is the rightful owner? Answer: the root, without which the tree cannot stand (Hulstaert and de Rop 1954: 64–65).

Two Hands

71:1. (Mongo) The right hand said to its wife, the left hand, "I will not give you any more meat. You never kill any animals." The left hand replied that then the right hand would have to butcher meat, cut vegetables, chop firewood, weave baskets, and carry game by itself. The right hand tried and tried but had to leave its meat to rot in the forest. Finally the right hand asked the left hand to help, and they worked together again. The case was heard and the verdict was given that the left hand had won the argument, but that the right hand had come off better because it had admitted its inability to do without the help of the left hand and had asked for its assistance (Ruskin 1921: 62–65).

Hand and Mouth

72:1. (Mongo)   The mouth asked the hand what right it had to all the food. The hand replied that it was the one that procured it, cutting plantains, digging manioc, killing animals, and catching fish. The mouth became angry and bit the hand on the finger. The elders heard the case and rebuked the mouth, reminding it that, but for the hand, it would not taste any food (Ruskin 1921: 64–65).

Foot and Stomach

73:1. (Mongo)   The stomach told the foot that it wanted all the food for itself. The foot did not argue, and the stomach ate up all the food. Afterwards a man wounded an elephant. The foot told the stomach to go and eat it, but the stomach could not. The elders heard the case and gave their verdict in favor of the foot (Ruskin 1921: 66–67).

Body Parts

74:1. (Nkundo)   A man was sleeping one night when he heard with his ears that a man was insulting his mother. Unable to restrain himself, he stood up with his legs and took a spear with his arm, his eyes showed him the way outside so that he could fight the stranger. The stranger hid, but the eye saw him, and the arm threw the spear and killed him. When the stranger's family came to retaliate, the notables stopped them, but they told the man to pay compensation. He refused, saying that his ears should pay because they told him his mother was being insulted. The ears refused to pay, saying that it was the leg that came outside. The leg refused, saying that it was the arm that killed the stranger with the spear. The arm refused, saying that it was the eye that showed him where the stranger was hiding. The notables then said that the eye should pay because when the stranger hid, the leg did not see him, the arm did not see him, and the ears did not see him, but the eye saw him and instructed the arm to kill him. The eye denied this, blaming the leg that brought it outside. The leg blamed the ear that told it. The ear said it had no weapons and that the arm was to blame because it had a spear. They were about to fight, but the elders intervened and went into council. Which do you think wins this palaver? Answer: The winners are the leg, the arm and the eye because they would have slept quietly through the night if the ear had not told them about the insults. The ear is guilty and must pay the compensation (Hulstaert and de Rop 1954: 98–103).

74:2.   (Ewe)   Ear, Mouth, Eye, Foot, and Hand went hunting. Ear heard a man in the forest; Eye saw him; Mouth told the limbs. Foot ran to him, and Hand seized him. Each claimed the man. Mosquito, who was the judge, said that Foot alone was responsible. All the villagers grumbled at this unjust decision, and Mosquito was deposed as judge and driven into the forest. Mosquito himself felt that he had not judged correctly and that Ear, who had first heard the man, especially had been wronged. For this reason Mosquito always comes to the ear at night to say that the man belongs to him, but the ear calls the hand to drive him away (Schönhärl 1909: 79–80).

House Parts

75:1.   (Nkundo)   A man locked his house, went away for three years, and returned to find all his possessions safe. Thieves had tried to break in, but the door latch was strong and had held. A reward was claimed by the latch for keeping the thieves out, by the door because without it the latch could not keep out thieves, by the wall because without it the latch and the door could do nothing, by the house post because it supported the whole house, by the beam because it supported the roof, by the thatch because it covered the house and all its parts and contents, and by the liana that tied the members of the house together. They quarreled and asked for the judges to settle their case. Which has the right to the reward? Answer: All of them, but a larger share should go to the house post because it is the "headman" (which must be erected before the other parts of the house can be added) (Hulstaert and de Rop 1954: 58–63).

Dividing Bread

76:1.   (Ahlo)   A man whose wife was dead had two sons and a daughter. During a famine he had only a bit of bread, and if he divided it among the three children, all would die. If he gave it all to one, the other two would die. To whom must he give the bread? (Westermann 1922: 21).

Worship Two Gods

77:1. (Nkundo)   A blacksmith set off to sacrifice a chicken to the god of the trees and the god of iron, both of which lived in different places far from his smithy. The god of trees said that if he went to the god of iron, he would give him no charcoal; the god of iron told him that if he went to the god of trees, he would receive no iron. The smith halted, not knowing which god to worship first. Which is the more useful for the work of the forge? Answer: He should pray first to the god of the trees who can give him charcoal and fire; then let him look for iron (Hulstaert and de Rop 1954: 124–125).

What's in a Name?

78:1. (Nkundo)   One man asked another why he had named himself Tsotale, and Tsotale replied, "Why shouldn't I?" They began to fight with knives, but people stopped them. The lords said they would settle the case when the war of the whites was finished. Who will win the case? Answer: Tsotale, because the other man deliberately insulted him (Hulstaert and de Rop 1954: 160–163).

Shooting Mosquitoes

79:1. (Kongo)   A boy went down to the river on the same day that he was born. A hunter came and fired his gun, and the boy asked what he was shooting at. The hunter said he was shooting at the mosquitoes that were eating his wife's cassava. The boy said that the hunter was upsetting the proper order of things by shooting a gun at mosquitoes; the hunter said that the boy was doing so by bathing himself on the day he was born. They took their argument to the chief, who heard their case and then announced that his mouth was locked up in a room and that his wives had taken the key away. The boy and the hunter accused the chief of upsetting things. They looked for someone else to settle their argument and stated their case to a palm wine tapper. He heard them and then said that one day he fell from a palm tree, broke into pieces, and then went into town to get someone to carry the pieces home. They accused him of upsetting things, and they are still arguing as to which was the most to blame (Weeks n.d.: 122–123).

Weeks comment:

At the conclusion each actor in this tale of wonders had his staunch adherents among the little crowd of listeners. Some contended that the baby had performed the most wonderful feat, and was therefore to be greatly blamed. Others stood by the hunter, for 'whoever before had heard of shooting mosquitoes?' 'Did you ever hear of a man talking with his mouth locked up in another room?' aggressively asked a backer of that wonder. 'You are all wrong,' shouted a big fellow with a loud voice, 'the man who broke to pieces and yet went for carriers to convey the pieces into his town did something that surpassed all the other marvellous deeds.' Feeling ran high, words were bandied about, innuendoes respecting the sad lack of sense that some folk exhibited were freely exchanged   (Weeks, n.d.: 122–124).

Mother-in-law in Well

80:1.   (Bura)   A man, his mother, his wife, and his mother-in-law grew thirsty. To get water, three of them were lowered into a well. The wife at the top held the feet of the man, who held the feet of his mother, who held the feet of his mother-in-law, who dipped water from the well. The man's mother became tired and dropped the mother-in-law into the water. When told what had happened, the wife said to her husband, "Do you want to let go of your mother and let her fall into the water, or shall I let go of both of you?" This puzzled the young man. What was he to say? Here was his mother still in his hands, but he loved his wife more than he loved his mother, and he let his mother fall. Then he and his wife went home (Helser 1930: 133–134; cf. AT 1250).

80:2.   (Hausa)   A man, his mother, his wife, and his wife's mother grew thirsty. They came to a well but had no bucket. The wife at the top held the feet of the man, who held the feet of his mother, who held the feet of his mother-in-law, who fell into the water. The man's wife said he should let go of his mother or she would let go of him. What would you do? (Edgar 1911–1913: III, (170); translated by Skinner 1969: I, 401–402).

Break the Old Lady's Jaw

81:1.   (Vai)   Several other dilemma tales also involve the mother-in-law. A man's helpless mother was fed by his wife. One day she bit the wife's hand and would not let go. Not knowing what to do, the man asked the judge, and the judge asked the people. The young people said, "Break the old lady's jaw." The old people said, "Cut off the young woman's hand." The judge was unable to decide the case. What would you do under such circumstances? (Ellis 1914: 217–218).

Rescue Mother-in-law?

82:1. (Kono) A man was traveling with his wife, his mother, and his mother-in-law. While they were crossing a river, a large crocodile stopped their canoe and climbed in with them. It said that it would let the man go, but he must give it one of the three women. What would you do? (Holas 1952: 86–87).

82:2. (Bete) In the course of crossing a river, a man's canoe capsized, and he found himself in the water with his sister, his wife, and his mother-in-law. None of the women could swim. Which one should the man save? The narrator added the following commentary: "If you save your sister and leave your wife to drown, you must give bride-wealth again (to acquire a new wife). If you save your wife and abandon your sister, your parents overwhelm you with reproaches. But if you choose to save your mother-in-law, you are an idiot" (Paulme 1961: 38).

82:3. (Lamba) A man, his wife, his mother, and his mother-in-law were attacked by a marauding band. They fled to the river, but his canoe could take only the man and one passenger. Which did he take? Doke comments, "The solving provides much merriment. Of course NOT his mother-in-law. His wife then? No, he can get another wife! But he could not get another mother" (Doke 1947: 119).

82:4. (Ila) A man, his wife, and their two mothers were attacked by wild animals. They escaped to a river full of crocodiles and found a canoe that held only three people. Which was to be left to die? "The man sacrificed his mother-in-law, you say. No! His wife would not allow him. She would not desert her mother, nor he his: the elders would not forsake their children. How did they get out of their difficulty? They all sat down on the river-bank and died together" (Smith and Dale 1920: II, 332–333; repeated by Cole-Beuchat 1957: 149).

82:5. (Dyola) Choices of this type do not always involve the mother-in-law: A man was traveling with his mother and his fiancée. Their canoe was capsized by a sudden storm. The man was an excellent swimmer, but he could save only one woman. Which one should he choose? (L.–V. Thomas 1958–1959: II, 431).

82:6.   (Popo)   A man was crossing a river with his wife and his mother when a giraffe appeared on the bank. When he raised his gun to shoot, the giraffe said that if he shot, his mother would die; if he didn't, his wife would die. What would you do if you were in his place? (Trautmann 1927: 99).

Death or Mother-in-law

83:1.   (Ewe)   Death comes to you and tells you to work his farm or else you must die. Your mother-in-law comes to you and tells you to work her farm or else she will take back your wife. Whom will you follow? (Schönhärl 1909: 106).

The Missing Eye

84:1.   (Bura)   There were four blind people: a man, his mother, his wife, and his mother-in-law. On a journey the man found seven eyes. He gave his wife two eyes and took two for himself. He gave one eye to his mother and one to his wife's mother. "He had one eye left in his hand. 'Kai,' a stalling thing had happened. Here was his mother with one eye looking at him. There was his wife's mother with her one eye looking at him. To whom should he give the one eye he had left? If he gives it to his mother, he will be ashamed before his wife's mother, and before his wife, because both of them are looking at him. If he gives it to his wife's mother, he fears the heart of his mother, because a mother is not something to be played with. This is very difficult indeed; what shall he do? Here is the sweetness of his wife, and the sweetness of his mother. Which would be easier? If this thing would come to you, which would you choose? Your mother or your wife's mother — choose! This is a real problem. Dare any man choose?" (Helser 1930: 39; abstracted in Waterman and Bascom 1949: 19; retold by Jablow 1961: 52–53 and repeated by Feldmann 1963: 201–202).

84:2.   (Mosi)   A man's wife and mother-in-law each dropped one of her eyes in the mud, and he could find only one eye. To whom should he give it? (Guillot 1933: 53; retold in Guillot 1946: 37).

84:3. (Hausa) A man went on a journey with his mother, his younger sister, his wife, and his wife's mother. Growing thirsty, they went in turn to a well inhabited by a spirit, and when they looked in, each dropped an eye into the well. A passing soldier agreed to retrieve the eyes if he could keep one for himself. The husband took one of the other four eyes for himself, leaving three. Well, to whom would you give those three? To whom would you not give them? People argue about this. And that is the origin of the saying that if you want something, don't be in too much of a hurry to make an offer for it (Edgar 1911–1913: III, (169); translated by Skinner 1969: I, 400–401).

Knock Out Father's Eye

85:1. (Hausa) A boy and his father, who were so poor that they shared a single loincloth, married a rich girl and her mother. In a quarrel the boy's father knocked out one of the eyes of the girl's mother. The girl demanded that the boy put out one of his father's eyes or else leave her and all her wealth. What should he do? (Edgar 1911–1913: II, (43); translated by Skinner 1969: I, 384–386).

Knife to Father-in-law

86:1. (Hausa) A man had three sons. Abdu, the eldest, earned money so that he could be married, but his father gave it to his brother. When this happened a second time, Abdu was upset and set out to seek his fortune. He acquired more money and married the daughter of a rich man, and she bore him a son. These four set out and met Abdu's father, who dashed the infant against a tree, killing him. The rich man seized Abdu's father, and they began to fight. Abdu drew a knife. The rich man asked Abdu for it to kill his father, but the father said he should have it. To which of the two people should he give the knife in order to kill the other? (Edgar 1911–1913: III, (72); translated by Skinner 1969: I, 394).

Left Unconscious

87:1. (Hausa) A man whose only work was catching ground squirrels went hunting with his son. The boy let one escape, and his father knocked him unconscious with a hoe handle. An Arab, who had never had any children, found the boy and took him home. He had him bathed and dressed in fine clothes, and he gave him a fine horse, telling him to do whatever the other riders did. The rich merchants, doubting that this was the Arab's son, told their sons to give their horses away, and the boy did likewise. Then they gave their sons extremely valuable horses and told their sons to kill them; the boy did likewise, and the merchants were convinced. Then the boy's father came to take his son home. The Arab had three horses saddled and rode out of town with the father and his son. He gave the boy a sword and told him to kill him or his father. Well, that's the question — the Arab, who had given him so many things? Or his own father, who had struck him unconscious because of the ground squirrel? Which should he kill? (Edgar 1911–1913: I, (29); translated by Skinner 1969: I, 381–382).

87:2.   (Hausa)   A man who was skilled in catching ground squirrels went hunting with his son, who let one escape. In anger his father struck him with a club and left him lying there. A rich man who had no son found the boy, bathed him, and adopted him. Doubting that this was the rich man's son, the king said that he should be given a horse to race with his own son and that after the race each would kill his horse. After each had killed ten horses in this way, the king was convinced and gave the boy his daughter in marriage. The boy's father came and asked for his son. The rich man offered him wealth if he would keep the secret, but the father would not agree. The rich man gave the boy a sword and told him to kill him or his father. The boy cut down his real father and went back to live with the rich man. Now, for the sake of argument, do you think the boy did right or wrong? (Tremearne 1909–1910: 1062; retold in Tremearne 1913: 347–349).

87:3.   (Hausa)   A hunter and his son caught only one rat, which the boy threw away. In anger, the hunter struck his son with an axe and left him there. The boy secretly took his things and went to the chief of another town, whose son had been lost in battle. After the boy promised to keep the secret, the chief announced that this was his own son. Some of the people were doubtful and told their sons to ride with the boy and then to kill their horses. The boy also killed his mount, but the people were still not convinced. They gave their sons beautiful slave maidens to kill; the boy did likewise, convincing the people. One day the hunter came to take his son home. The chief promised him whatever he wished if he would keep the secret, but the hunter refused. The chief gave the boy a sword, and they went out of town with the hunter. Then the chief ordered the boy to kill him and take all his possessions or else kill his own father, the hunter. The boy did not know what to do. Now if it were you, O white man, between them which would you kill? (Rattray 1913: I, 284–294; retold by Jablow 1961: 90–94 and repeated by Feldmann 1963: 205–208).

87:4. (Hausa) The following is given in full because it was published in the Hausa text only:

There was a certain town whose only occupation was catching squirrels (ground squirrels). There was a man in this town who excelled at catching squirrels. One squirrel was so smart that it eluded everyone in town. It was said that only this man had the skill to catch it. So this man said to his son, "Come, let's go catch the squirrel." They took an axe; they found the squirrel near its hole. Then the squirrel ran and entered its hole. They searched out all the holes, then they stopped them up. Then the man said to his son, "Don't let the squirrel get out of its hole." He answered, "Okay." But one hole wasn't stopped up, and the squirrel escaped. When it escaped, the father came to his son and said to him, "Why did you let it escape? If I go home now, I will be ashamed." He grabbed the axe and struck his son. Then he went on his way and left his son unconscious. Ants began to fill his eyeballs and his ears; vultures were circling above him.

In the afternoon, the head-man of a rich caravan arrived at the spot. As he arrived, he set up camp. Then he got up and went for a stroll and saw the boy. He called his slaves to take him and have him washed and shaved. The boy recovered. The head-man had no offspring. When he took the boy, he decided that he would make him his son. He sent a message to the chief of the town, telling him that he had an offspring, that he was happy he had become a complete man, and that he would now receive the gifts due to him.

The chief said, "This is a lie. He is not his son. If he is his son, then let him come that I can see." Then the head-man arrived in town. The chief gave his sons horses worth ten pounds. He said, "Go and join the son of the head-man. Have a race. When you finish give these horses away" (forcing him to do the same). They did it and they returned. The next day, the chief again gave them horses worth ten pounds. They did as the day before. They did it five times. They ran out of horses. Then the chief said, "Indeed, it is his son. I have run out of horses. If it weren't his son, he wouldn't agree to let him give his own horses away to match the presents." Then the chief summoned his daughter. The Galladima brought his to help. The Madaki also gave, and the Makama gave. Altogether, four wives. The chief gave a big house. The head-man came and brought twenty concubines and gave to his son. There was continuous feasting.

Then one day the son saw his father, the one who had knocked him down with the axe because of the squirrel. The father came to the house of his son and said, "Throw away your gown and start catching squirrels."

The slaves of the head-man said, "This is a crazy man, let us all strike him." The boy said to him, "This is my father, the one who sired me." The head-man said, "I have already lied to the chief. Let us keep the secret. I will give your father wealth. Let him go home. Should he want to see you, let him come to visit you. If you want to see him, then you can go and visit him." The real father said he did not agree. Then the head-man said, "Well then, let us go out in the countryside." They went. The head-man unsheathed his sword. He handed it to the son, and said, "Kill one of the two of us." Here ends the story   (Fletcher 1912: 90–92).

87:5.   (Karekare)   A poor man with three sons and three daughters lived in the forest and supported them by catching field rats. In the city there was a rich man who had many wives and 400 slaves but no children. The king asked the rich man who would inherit his wealth; he replied that he had a son in the forest, and the king said the son could marry his own daughter. Though the rich man had 200 horseman, he left them at home and rode off alone into the forest. That same day the poor man and his sons were hunting rats. One of the sons let a rat escape; his father struck him on the head with an axe and left him on the ground, bleeding. The rich man found the youth, washed him, dressed him in fine clothes, and took him home. The youth married the king's daughter and became the most beloved and most powerful man after the king. The youth's poor father came looking for his son. The rich man promised him a farm and cattle if he kept the secret, but he refused, and the rich man accompanied them out of town. Then he gave his sword to the youth and told him to kill him or his father. Should he kill his father, who had almost killed him for a rat? Should he kill the rich man, who had helped him and made him wealthy, and go back to catching rats? He stood between the two men, not knowing what to do. If all three have not died, they are still standing there today (Frobenius 1921–1928: IX, 404–406).

87:6.   (Hausa)   While traveling, a man found a boy lying in the road. His mouth was full of ants and dirt, and they thought he might have been killed. But they bathed him and took him home, and the man said that the boy was his son. The townspeople did not believe him, and as a test, each gave his son five camels to be killed. The man did the same, and some thought the boy must be his son. Then each of the townspeople gave his son ten horses to kill, and the man had the boy kill twenty. As a further test, the boy and five other youths were sent to court a very beautiful maiden. The man put gold in one of the boy's pockets, silver in another, and gold and silver in his mouth. The maiden rejected the five other youths, but she smiled at the boy and silver poured from his mouth. She asked, "Have you no gold?" and he poured gold from his pocket. She promised to marry him, and the townspeople agreed that he was the man's son (Tremearne 1913: 345–347).

Crazy Client

88:1. (Nkundo)   Two men worked as hunters for a wealthy man, who paid them well. But one of them hated his master. Unable to kill him, he killed his master's beautiful daughter and fled to his mother, who denounced him publicly. When his master sent for him, he asked his companion for advice. He was told to take off his clothes, rub his body with mud, and pretend insanity. When his master saw him, he sent for a doctor to treat him. When he was well and had returned home, his companion came to ask payment for his advice. The man refused, saying that if he had not killed anyone his companion would not have had that wisdom. They went to the elders, but up to now they have not settled the palaver. Who will win it? Answer: The companion, because if you are sick you pay the doctor who heals you, and before going to court, you seek advice, and the companion's advice was best (Hulstaert and de Rop 1954: 78–83; cf. AT 1585).

88:2. (Nkundo)   Two young men hunted game for an important man. One of them killed his master's daughter and fled to his mother, who denounced him publicly. His master sent for him, and he asked his friend what to do. His friend told him to take off all his clothing and cover himself with mud. His master thought he had gone crazy and had him bound until he could be cured. He took none of the doctor's medicine but announced that he was well and went on with his work, took a wife, and had many children. One day his friend came and asked to be paid for his advice. The man refused, saying that if he had not killed his master's daughter, he would not have taken the friend's advice. His friend called people to settle the quarrel. Which of the two wins? Answer: The response is identical to the answer in 88:1 (de Rop 1956: 164–167).

88:3. (Yoruba)   For half of the money, a lawyer offered to free a man charged with theft. He advised his client to pretend madness and answer "Ree" to all questions asked of him. When the judge dismissed the case, the lawyer asked for his share of the money. "Ree" was the client's only answer. The lawyer went away, angry with himself that he had not taken his share before the trial (Walker and Walker 1961: 55–56). As noted in the introduction, no attempt has been made to retrieve the other African non-dilemma versions of this tale.

Smoking Husband's Corpse

89:1.   (Nkundo)   I-Was-Not-Mistaken was the wife of I-Did-Not-Know. They went to the forest to inspect their traps. The husband climbed up a tree to repair a trap, fell from the tree, and was killed. His wife carried his body back to their camp, and that night a leopard came to eat it. She did not want to abandon it in the forest, and it was too heavy for her to carry home. She decided to smoke it like meat. She cut it up in pieces and smoked it like an animal. In the morning she packed the parts of her husband's body in a large basket, filling it. She carried the basket home, weeping on the way. People asked about her husband, and she told his relatives what had happened. She unpacked the basket, saying, "Two arms, I was not mistaken. Look! Two legs, I was not mistaken. Look! The head, I was not mistaken. Look! The trunk, I was not mistaken. Look! The buttocks, I was not mistaken." She produced the entire body, but her husband's family blamed her for being so callous as to smoke him like an animal. She complained to the judges about the way they treated her, and the judges retired to deliberate. In this case, who seems to be the winner? Answer: The husband's family, because I-Was-Not-Mistaken could have sent a message for help in carrying the corpse home, or she could have buried it in the forest. But by cutting it up like an animal, she dishonored the corpse of her husband (Hulstaert and de Rop 1954: 162–167).

Cutting Husband's Throat

90:1.   (Bulu)   A wife, who found that her husband had been eating their children, offered to trim his beard; she cut his throat in revenge. Now kind reader, if it were left for you to decide, what would you say? Who is to be blamed in this affair, is it the man or is it the woman? (Krug and Herskovits 1949: 354).

Thieves Reveal Secret

91:1.   (Ewe)   Three men stole a goat and decided that no one should ever learn about it. They roasted it, ate it, and started home. On the way they came to a well. The first said, "I am thirsty. I want some water for what I have just eaten." The second said, "You said that no one would speak of it again, and now you do so yourself." The third said, "Has he named anything? Did he say that he wanted a drink for the goat he had eaten?" Now just explain to me, which of these three revealed the secret? (Prietze 1897: 42–43).

91:2. (Baule) Three friends stole a fine sheep, cooked and ate it, and agreed never to speak of the affair. Coming to a house one of them asked for a drink, saying, "I have eaten well and I need water to quench my thirst." The second said, "Now, now. You know we have promised to say nothing." The third said, "But he did not say anything. He did not say we ate a stolen sheep" (Guillot 1933:48).

Barrel of Money

92:1. (Benga) A man went on a journey, entrusting to his friend a barrel that he said was full of food. While he was gone, his wife became pregnant and craved that particular kind of food. The friend opened the barrel and found it was full of money. After ten years the first man returned, and his friend gave him the barrel, refilled with food. The first man claimed that his friend had stolen his money and took him before the elders. They decided that the friend was in the right because he had returned the food. Later the children of the two men began to quarrel about this, and the first man's child asked, "Have you ever seen food lasting for ten years and not rotting?" When the elders heard them, they reopened the case and decided in favor of the first man (Nassau 1915: 32–33).

92:2. (Hausa) A man went on a journey, entrusting to his friend a pot of money that he had filled with oil. While he was gone, the oil turned rancid. His friend found the money, replaced it with gravel, and refilled the pot with oil. After some ten years the first man returned. When he found that his money was gone, he did not want to bring charges because he would be thought mad, but a second friend offered to help him. He made a wax image of the first friend and had the man tie a monkey to it until the monkey was familiar with it. The man then asked for the son of the first friend, named Muhammadu, to help him, and he hid the boy in his home. He took the monkey to his first friend and told him that Muhammadu had turned into a monkey. The monkey recognized the friend from the figure and clung to him. It would not let go; crowds came to stare. Eventually the friend came to the man and asked if his son had really turned into a monkey. The man replied, "If money can become gravel, why can't Muhammadu become a monkey?" The friend took back the pot of oil, replaced the gravel with money, and returned it to the man. If you are going to give something into safe-keeping, give it publicly and appoint witnesses (Edgar 1911–1913: III, (155); translated by Skinner 1969: I, 261–263 and by Johnston 1966: 208–211).

Snake in Belly

93:1.   (Hausa)   A man permitted a snake to enter his mouth and take refuge in his belly, and it refused to come out. A heron pulled the snake out of his throat, and the man imprisoned the heron. His wife released the heron, and it killed her. Which of the three was the most ungrateful? (Jablow 1961: 78–81; original source unidentified).

93:2–3.   (Hausa)   A farmer permitted a snake to hide in his belly. It entered his anus and refused to come out. A heron told the man to excrete, and pulled out the snake. The man asked the heron for medicine for the snake's poison; he was told to bring six white fowls. "White fowls?" said the man, and he grabbed the heron, tied it up, and took it home. He was reproached for ingratitude by his wife, who released the heron, which pecked out one of her eyes (Edgar 1911–1913: III, (7); translated by Skinner 1969: I, 145–146 and by Johnston 1966: 48–49). Skinner refers to an untranslated version of this in *Lakaru na da da na yanzu* (Zaia: N. Nigerian Publishing Company, 1968. First published 19311931) that "substitutes weaver for farmer and mouth for anus (perhaps because it was meant as a school reader)."

93:4.   (Sikon)   A woman permitted a serpent to take refuge in her belly, and it refused to come out. A crow pulled out the snake, and the woman seized the crow. A man offered the woman his favorite hen if she would release the crow. When she did so, the crow pecked out the man's eye (Pinney n.d.: 228–230).

93:5.   (Wobe)   A woman allowed a boa to enter her mouth to take refuge from a forest fire, and the snake refused to leave her stomach. An eagle pulled out the snake, and the woman struck its wings with her machete. When the eagle asked her why, she replied, "Here we return good with evil" (Girard 1967: 339).

93:6. (Yoruba)   A large snake fled from a farmer whose livestock it had been killing. An old man permitted it to enter his mouth and hide in his stomach, and the snake refused to come out. A vulture and an eagle flattered the snake, and when it came out, they tore it to pieces. If your kindness to another brings troubles, you must endure them, but you should not stop doing kindness to others (Gbadamosi and Beier 1970: 1–4).

Fishbone in Throat

94:1. (Vili)   A fool caught fish, but his clever brother took them and gave them to their mother, who cooked them. When the fish bone stuck in their father's throat, the fool, singing of his plight, refused to go for a doctor, and his father died. People argued about his guilt. Answer: The fool was justified (Dennett 1898: 25–27; retold by Jablow 1961: 111–114).

Pregnant Woman Falls from Tree

95:1. (Fang)   Two pregnant women found a fine palm tree in the forest. One climbed up to gather its fruit but fell down on top of the other. Only one child was delivered. To whom did it belong? (Ramón Alvarez 1951: 148).

Lover Killed

96:1. (Mende or Loma)   An orphan, equally in love with two girls, wanted to attend their initiation feasts, but both were held on the same day in different towns. Not wanting to offend either girl, he killed himself at the crossroads. Finally one of the girls went out to meet him and, finding him dead, killed herself in grief. The second came and found the two dead bodies. She brought a powerful medicine man who restored them both to life. The girls insisted that the boy could not marry both of them but must choose between them. Which girl should he choose? The one who had killed herself for love of him? Or the one who had saved his life and her rival's life also? (Pinney n.d.: 64–65).

96:2. (Dagomba)   A man's three wives returned to their parents' homes to bear children. Their husband accompanied them to the cross-roads where their ways parted, and there he fell dead. The first wife hanged herself. The second protected his corpse from vultures and hyenas. The third ran into the forest and met a spirit, who restored the man and his first wife to life. Which of these women is the best? (Cardinall 1931: 202–203).

96:3. (Mosi) A man fell from a tree and was killed, and his three wives were overcome with grief. The first jumped into the hole caused by his fall and died at his side. The second went into the forest to be killed by the first beast she encountered. The third wife, having good sense, went back home to raise his children. The second wife met Satan, disguised as a lion, and returned with him to the pit. Satan restored the man and his first wife to life and told the man he could live if he gave one of the two wives to be killed. The man gave Satan the wife who deserved less to live. Which wife did he choose? (Guilhem n.d.: II, 207–220).

96:4. (Mosi) A man fell from a tree and was killed. His first wife guarded his corpse. The second took care of the children. The third, mad with grief, fled into the bush where she met a fabulous animal that returned with her and revived the husband. The beast demanded one of the wives as reward. Which did he choose? (Guillot 1933: 53; repeated by Bordeaux 1936: 286–287).

96:5. (Mosi) A man fell from a tree and was killed. His first wife killed herself. The second went home to take care of his children. The third kept vultures away from the two corpses. The fourth went into the forest to be eaten by a beast and met a spirit, who revived the husband and demanded one of his wives in payment. Which wife would you choose? Answer: None. You should demand that the spirit return you to death (Tiendrebeogo 1963: 77–78).

96:6. (Nkundo) A man fell from a tree and was killed. His first wife stayed by the corpse, the second returned to his children, and the third ran to throw herself in the river. On her way the third wife met a bogy, who returned with her and revived the husband. Two weeks later the bogy demanded one of the three wives as his reward. Which wife should the husband surrender? Answer: The second wife, who abandoned her husband's corpse, knowing that his family could take care of the children (Hulstaert and de Rop 1954: 66–69).

96:7.   A version of this tale appears in *The palm-wine drinkard*: A man who was traveling with his three wives stumbled and was killed. His senior wife died with him. The second wife went for a wizard who could revive the dead. The third wife stayed by the dead bodies to protect them from wild animals. When the wizard had restored the man and his senior wife to life, he asked for one of the three wives as payment. The man named each of the wives in turn, but each refused. Then he told the wizard to take all three of them. The wives began to fight, were arrested by a policeman and charged in court. Tutuola's hero was asked to choose the wife to be given to the wizard, but he could not choose any of them because each had shown her love for her husband. So he had the case adjourned for a year and meanwhile left town (Tutuola 1953: 113–115).

Debt Collector

97:1.   A second dilemma tale occurs in *The palm-wine drinkard*: A man lived on borrowed money and had no other work than borrowing. When he refused to return a loan, the lender sent a man whose work was collecting debts to his house. The borrower said that he had never repaid a debt in his life, and the debt collector said that he had never failed to collect a debt. They began to fight, and a passer-by stopped to watch them. After a long fight the borrower stabbed himself and died. Then the debt collector stabbed himself, saying that if he could not collect the debt in this world, he would do so in heaven. The third man also killed himself, so that he could see the end of the fight. The book's hero was then asked in court which one was guilty and, not being able to decide, again had the case adjourned (Tutuola 1953: 111–113).

Look-alike Friends

98:1.   (Dagomba) A rich boy and a poor boy were look-alike friends. They set out to see the world and the rich boy fell in love with a beautiful maiden. She said that before she would marry any man, he would, on pain of death, have to stay in her hut for six days and nights without touching food or water. The poor youth provided his friend with water through a hole in the wall, but the maiden discovered this and saved a calabash of water and a wet cloth as evidence. A rat stole the water and cloth, and white ants destroyed them. When asked for evidence, the maiden could not produce it, and she was married to the rich youth. Later the poor youth set out to see the world, saying that if a tree withered his friend would know that he was in trouble. He saved a town from drought by killing a python that, as a river spirit, withheld the water, and he married the chief's daughter, who had been offered as a sacrifice to the python. When he and the townspeople went hunting, they were swallowed by a great rock. The tree withered and the rich youth set out in search of his friend. He was mistaken for the husband of the chief's daughter, but he had foresworn women until he had rescued his friend. He went on and released his friend and the towns-people with his magic knife. Now tell me which of these two was the greater friend? (Cardinall 1931: 183–189; cf. AT 303).

98:2. (Hausa) Two half-brothers, as alike as two peas in a pod, were close friends. The younger brother left on a journey, saying that if his tree withered, it was a sign that he was in trouble. He slew a goblin that withheld water from a town, saved the chief's daughter, who had been left as a sacrifice to it, and married her. When he went out with the townspeople to drive guinea-fowl away, he was swallowed by a rock. The tree withered and his elder brother set out in search of him. The elder brother was mistaken for the husband of the chief's daughter but did not sleep with her. When the guinea-fowl returned, he followed them, smote the rock, and released his brother. The younger brother went to his wife, and the elder brother was given a title (Edgar 1911–1913: II, (51); translated by Skinner n.d.: II, (51) and by Johnston 1966: 79–84). Again, no attempt has been made to retrieve the other non-dilemma versions of this tale.

Abducted Bride

99:1. (Hausa) A lengthy tale concerns two close friends, the son of the chief and the son of the *malam*. The chief's son fell in love with the daughter of another chief, and the *malam's* son arranged their tryst, saved his friend from being executed, and won the girl for him. When the bride was abducted by a Tuareg on his speedy camel, the *malam's* son told his friend that he must stay in his room for a year with a beautiful slave maiden without touching her, which the chief's son did. Meanwhile the *malam's* son raised a foal sired by the Tuareg's camel, with which he rescued his friend's wife. Well, there you are, and people still argue which of the two showed the greater ability — the chief's son or the *malam's* son. What do you think? (Edgar 1911–1913: II, (25); translated by Skinner n.d.: II, (25).

Foot in Water

100:1. (Bambara) A man was bringing his friend's bride to her husband and they came to a river. The woman walked into the water and was eaten by a beast. The man had one foot in the water and the other on land. A second beast said, "You have cheated me." "No," replied the first beast, "This one was female; I give you the male." If it were you, would you go into the water or not? Some say that they would, for fear of spoiling their reputations; others say that they would not (Travélé 1923: 82–83).

Lie under Leopard

101:1. (Pygmy) A man went to bring his friend's wife back from her mother's village, as his friend had been bitten by a snake. On the way home the woman was attacked by a leopard, which the man killed with his knife. She declared her love for him, saying that her husband despised her because she had no child. The man refused her advances and had her lie beneath the leopard's body while he went to inform her husband. During the night she was terrified by the howls of the leopard's mate, but she did not budge. The man reached home and told his friend that his wife was being eaten by a leopard. He rushed there and, bare-handed, seized the leopard's throat. His wife explained that the leopard had been killed and that she just wanted to see if her husband loved her. Her husband made a charm with the leopard's mustache, and his wife bore many children. Now, who was the bravest? The man who killed the leopard with only a knife? The wife who stayed alone under the leopard in the black of night? Or the husband who threw himself barehanded on the leopard? (Trilles 1932: 268–273).

101:2. (Fang) Two friends used to go to a neighboring village to bring their girls home for dancing and story telling. One time only one of them went for the girls, as the other was ill. As they were returning, a lion attacked his friend's girl, but he killed it with an arrow. It fell on the girl, but she was unharmed. He told his own girl to run and tell his friend that he and his friend's girl were being killed by a lion. Then he lay down with his friend's girl beneath the lion. The friend came and, barehanded, sprang on the lion and tore it from them. Which of the two men is the better friend? (Jablow 1961: 85–87; original source undetermined).

101:3.   (Hausa)   Two friends used to go together to bring their girls to visit, but one time only one of them went. As they were returning, a lion attacked his friend's girl, but he killed it with his sword. He told the girl to lie down beneath the lion and sent his own girl to tell his friend. The friend came and, barehanded, sprang on the lion, thinking it was alive. Between them, who was better than the other? (Rattray 1913: I, 254).

101:4–5.   (Hausa)   Two young men went to visit a girl and brought her home with them, but on the way they were attacked by a lion. The youths hurled all their spears but failed to hit it. While one youth went for more spears, the other killed the lion with his knife. He sat the lion up and hid behind it, and the girl lay down beside it. When the other youth returned, he threw away his spears and attacked the lion barehanded, not knowing that it was dead. Which of the two youths showed the greater pluck? (Edgar 1911–1913: III, (114); translated by Skinner 1969: I, 397–398). An untranslated Hausa version of this tale ends with the question, "Which was the best?" (Harris 1908: 11–13).

101:6.   (Bambara)   A man went to bring his friend's girl back from a nearby village. As they were returning, she saw a supernatural panther; the man killed it with his sword. To test his friend's courage, he had her lie down beneath the panther and went to tell his friend that she was being eaten by it. The friend rushed to her and struck the panther with his bare fist, knocking it to the side of the road. The girl said that the panther was already dead and that they had wanted to know if he would abandon her in a case of real danger. Which of the three was the bravest? The man, who attacked the panther with only a sword? The woman, who lay under its body in the dead of night, not knowing if another panther would come? Or her lover, who was willing to fight it barehanded? (Equilbecq 1913–1916: I, 247–250).

101:7.   (Mosi)   A man went to bring his friend's wife home from her mother's house. On the way back they were attacked by a lion, and the man killed it. The woman wondered if her husband had not come himself because he feared such an encounter in the bush. She sent the man to tell her husband that she was being eaten by a lion. Naked as he was, the husband ran to his wife, who was lying beneath the dead lion and, with a knife in each hand, threw himself on the lion. After that, the wife knew.... (Guillot 1933: 57; repeated by Bordeaux 1936: 285–286).

Caught by Hair

102:1. (Hausa) Two boys were bringing their girls to their village for a visit. An elder, who disapproved and was hiding in a tree, grabbed the second boy by his hair and held him fast. When the boy ahead noticed his friend's absence, he returned, climbed the tree, and made the elder release him. Now, which of them showed the most determination? (Edgar 1911–1913: II, (44); translated by Skinner 1969: I, 386–387).

Sons or Daughters

103:1. (Nkundo) A man and his wife had no children and they were very old. The man wept constantly for children — before eating, before sleeping, and in conversation — because he had a great desire for them. A ghost promised him twenty children but all of the same sex; it asked the man whether he wanted girls or boys. The man asked his friends for advice. They went into council but still have not returned. Should he choose only boys or only girls? Which is better? Answer: Boys, because a man is a shield, and one can get wives later. If a father has only twenty girls, he is in endless misery, worrying about the return of their bridewealth if they divorce their husbands. Besides, he has no one to help him when he is sick or when he is lonely in his old age, and he has no one to bury him when he dies (Hulstaert and de Rop 1954: 102–105).

Sacrifice Lizard

104:1. (Karekare) A rich man had everything on earth except children, though he had had many wives. Finally he had a son to whom he brought a maiden, hoping he would marry her. But the son died and the father searched for a way to revive him. A diviner said that if the youth's father or mother made a sacrifice, the youth would come to life, but that the one who made the sacrifice would die. The father suggested that a slave make it, but the diviner said that this would not work. Both the father and mother were unwilling to die, but the maiden made the sacrifice. As she fell lifeless to the ground, the youth stood up. Then the diviner sprinkled her with medicine, and she came to life. Who did the best? (Frobenius 1921–1928: IX, 403–404).

104:2.   (Hausa)   A youth took his girl into the bush to talk, and a devil cut off his head. The devil told the boy's mother that if she went through a river of fire, a river of water, and a river of cobras and brought back a land-monitor, her son would be restored to life. His mother refused, but his girl went and returned with the land-monitor, and the boy came to life. The devil then said that if the land-monitor were killed, the boy's mother would die; if not, the girl's mother would die. Well then now — is the boy going to slaughter the land-monitor, so that his own mother dies? Or, on the other hand, will he spare it, so that the girl's mother dies? Which of the two will he choose, do you think? (Edgar 1911–1913: III, (74); translated by Skinner 1969: I, 383–384).

104:3.   (Hausa)   A boy ran off into the forest with a girl and was killed there by the devil. The boy's mother was told that she must go through various dangers to restore her son to life, but she refused. The girl, however, swam through a river of fire and a river of water, entered a hollow tree, thrust out a snake, and returned with a lizard that she gave to the devil. The boy came to life and had to decide whether the devil should put his girl or his mother to death. Choose one. (Harris 1908: 98–100; summarized in Tremearne 1913: 341–342).

104:4.   (Nupe)   A father hid his son in the bush and told him that he would die if he ever slept with a maiden. A maiden came to him and promised to restore him to life if he died; he slept with her. When he died, she went to a hunter who put a lizard on a funeral pyre, saying that if the lizard burned the youth would stay dead, but that he would live if someone rescued the lizard from the flames. The mother and father tried and failed, but the maiden rescued the lizard and the youth came to life. The hunter said that if the youth killed the lizard, his mother would die, but if he spared its life, the maiden would die. What would a true Nupe lad do? Answer: He would kill the lizard at once (Frobenius 1921–1928: IX, 150; translated in Frobenius and Fox 1937: 162–163).

104:5. (Tera) The daughter of a rich man and the son of another rich man were raised together, fell in love, and were betrothed. The girl was bitten by a snake, and a doctor said he could cure her only if her father or mother would burn themselves to death. He built a huge bonfire but neither could do so; however, her lover jumped into it, and the fire died out. The girl revived, but the doctor found a monitor lizard and a knife. The doctor said that if he killed the lizard, either her mother or her father would die, but if he spared it, her lover would die. What should she have done? What would you do? Many people said that the man should kill the lizard and keep the girl for himself. Answer: She killed the lizard because a husband or wife is more important than a father or mother (Newman 1968: II, 384–395).

104:6. (Hausa) To restore his dead son to life, a man was told to throw himself into a large fire. He tried twice and failed, but the boy's mother succeeded. The boy was revived, the fire was turned into a house of gold, and the father was turned into a ground squirrel. The boy was told that if he killed the ground squirrel, he would live with his mother; if not, his mother would die. He killed the ground squirrel and lived with his mother (Tremearne 1913: 340–341).

Part River with Child

105:1. (Limba) A childless wife was told by a medicine man that she would have a son, but that he would die if he were seen. Later the boy was sent to market, and he died. After his father and mother feared to do so, his sweetheart magically restored him to life by walking into fire. They married and set out in search of a chieftainship. They met a woman who declared her love for the youth; she joined them, and when they came to a large river she threw her brother into it, parting the water so that they could cross it. They came to a village where another woman declared her love for him; she saved his life by helping him to point to the chieftainship. Because of this, the former chief was deposed, and the young man became chief. Each of his three wives bore a son. When he died, his sons argued about who was to succeed. Well, of these three people, I want to ask you, who owns the chieftainship? (Finnegan 1967: 148–152).

105:2. (Limba) A chief was told by a medicine man that he would have a son, but that no one should see him. Later a girl saw him standing on the roof and fell in love with him. She came to him and slept with him; the next morning he died. When his father and mother feared to do so, she magically restored him to life by walking into fire. They married and left home and met a woman who gave them food on condition that she also become his wife. They met another woman, who threw her child into a crocodile-infested river, parting the water so that they could cross, also on condition that she become his wife. They came to a village that no stranger could enter unless he could show where the chief's afterbirth was buried. The chief's daughter fell in love with the man and showed him the place, on condition that she also become his wife. The village chief died, the man became chief, and he had children by all four of his wives. When he died, each wife claimed the inheritance for her son. Well, of all these women, whose is the one child who owns the inheritance? (Finnegan 1967: 152–155).

105:3.   (Popo)   A man condemned to die escaped with the help of his wife, and they fled to another kingdom. At the edge of a river he was killed by a snake. A girl and her father came upon the wife, who lay on the corpse, weeping. The girl asked her father to revive the corpse, saying that if it were a woman she would be her friend and if it were a man he would be her husband. The girl ran home to get her father's charm, and the man was restored to life. They were married, and all went to the next kingdom, where the man incurred the wrath of his new king. He was saved by the king's favorite wife, whom he married when the king was killed by his subjects. Each of his three wives had a son. Five years later the man sacrificed a cow, and the three sons fought over its tail, wanting to make a toy of it. The man did not wish to favor any of the sons because he owed his life to each of their mothers. To which child would you give the cow-tail? (Trautmann 1927: 99–100).

105:4.   (Bambara)   The king condemned a man to death, but his girl insisted that she be killed first. When she was beheaded, her head rejoined her body. She told the man to let the king's daughter, who brought him food each day, sleep with him. When he did so, the king's daughter declared her love for him and told him that when the king offered him all kinds of wealth, he should take only a cow-tail. When he did so, the king trembled and went into his house, and the man and his two girls escaped. A ferryman refused to take them across a river, but he was killed by his own daughter, who fell in love with the man. He founded a village, and each of his three wives bore a son. One day the man was killed, and each of the wives claimed the tail for her son.

Which of the three had the most right to it? After each listener has stated his opinion, the narrator continues: The wives were asked if they would abandon their rights, but they refused. The tail was thrown into the air, and when it fell to the ground, it became a ficus tree in the village (Travélé 1923: 169–174).

105:5. (Vai) The king's wife fell in love with a handsome young man and secretly made love to him. When the king became suspicious, the lovers fled during the night, pursued by the king's warriors. They met a woman who gave them food and another who took them across a river in her canoe, each on condition that she also become the youth's wife. They escaped to a kingdom whose ruler demanded that the youth name the secret of his wealth or die, but if the youth could give the right answer, he would become king. The king's beloved daughter fell in love with the youth, told him the secret, and begged him to marry her. The youth announced that the secret was a magical cane, and he became king. Each of his four wives claimed the right to sit in honor beside him. Which one did he take? Decide for yourselves. Converse well together and decide for yourselves (Creel 1960: 27–34).

105:6. (Vai) A king was very fond of the board game but played it badly. When beaten, he would give his magic bracelet to the victor in pawn, but it would return to him the next day. The men who defeated him were executed for having lost the king's bracelet. The king's daughter fell in love with a young man and warned him not to play the game with her father, but he did so and defeated him. The couple fled with the king's soldiers in pursuit. They met a girl who gave them food, a girl who gave them water, and a girl who took them across a river in her canoe, each demanding to become the man's wife. They escaped, and in time each of the four wives had a son. When their father died, each of the sons claimed his property because his mother had saved their father's life. To which of the sons does the property belong? (Ellis 1914: 225–227; retold by Jablow 1961: 103–107).

105:7. (Vai) A king announced that whoever married his daughter must be killed for his funeral. A young man agreed to the condition and married her. When word came that the king had died, he fled with his wife. A second woman gave them water, a third gave them food, and a fourth took them in her canoe, but it could not cross the river until a fifth woman sacrificed her baby. Each woman insisted on marrying the young man. They all escaped to the town of another king, whose daughter also fell in love with the youth. He escaped death by naming the king's possessions; the king fell dead, and he became king. Later each of the six wives had a son. When the man and his wives died, the six sons disputed the inheritance, each claiming it because his mother had saved their father's life. To whom does the money really belong? (Ellis 1914: 255–258).

105:8.   (Mbete)   A man was saved by his wife who told him that someone wanted to kill him. In his flight, he was saved by another woman who took him across a big river in her canoe. Bitten by a snake, a third woman cured him with her medicines. All three wanted to be his only wife. Which should it be? (Adam 1940–1941: 138).

105:9.   (Ewe)   In Dahomey three young men saw three of the king's wives fetching water. They said that they would be willing to die if they could marry them for a few days. They were overheard and taken before the king, who had them locked with the women in a room without windows. At the end of the time they had specified, two of the men were killed and their women were set free. But the wife of the third man helped him to escape, and they fled. A ferryman took them across a river when she promised to reward him, but on the other side the young man was bitten by a snake and died. When a passing man refused to revive him, his daughter also died because she wished to marry the youth. Her father revived them both, and the youth and his two wives went on to another city. There the king's daughter declared her love for him and told him the town's secret. He was called before the council and commanded to tell what was inside a house, on pain of death if he could not answer. He said it was a black bull with a white spot between its horns, and the king was killed, and the bull was killed. He was given the bull's tail and made king. He married the former king's daughter, and in time each of his three wives bore a son. Later, when they grew up, his sons saw the bull's tail, and each of them asked their father for it. He did not know to which one he should give it. And now, my dear friend, to which one would you give the bull's tail? (Prietze 1897: 30–42).

105:10.   (Vai)   To end their poverty, three brothers offered to give their lives if the chief would give the eldest wine, the second food, and the youngest clothes, so that they could enjoy their last five days. The chief granted their requests, and the first two brothers were killed, as agreed. The handsome youngest brother, dressed in fine robes, found the chief's beautiful daughter shut up in an enclosure and made love to her. The two lovers fled at night. They met a maiden who gave them food and a maiden who led them out of a swamp, each on condition that she become the young man's wife. They came to a village whose chief demanded that strangers must identify which of his hundred boxes of gold he had owned in his youth or be beheaded. The chief's daughter fell in love with the stranger, married him that night, and told him which box to choose. When he chose correctly, the chief gave him his daughter in marriage and shared his lands with him. What order would these wives take in his household? (Pinney n.d.: 131–134).

105:11. (Bura) A slave of the chief asked for a sword to behead people so that he would be killed and end his misery. A second asked to go and burn a city so that he also would be killed. A third asked to live seven days with a woman from the chief's house, on condition that he be killed. The chief granted their requests, and the first two were killed, but the third slave and the woman escaped by magic. He was bitten by a snake, but a second woman cured him, on condition that she could also be his wife. A third woman ferried them across a river on the same condition. They escaped to a village whose chief, jealous of the slave's wives, proposed a wager. If the slave could not point out his favorite horse, favorite food gourd, and favorite wife, he would be killed. But if he did so, the chief would be killed. On condition that she could also become his wife, the chief's favorite wife told the slave which ones to choose. The chief was killed, and the slave became chief. Which of the four wives did the most? Not the first, because if the second had not cured the snakebite, he would have been captured. Not the second, because if not for the third, he would have been caught at the river. Not the third, because if not for the fourth, he would have been executed. Not the fourth, because if not for the other three, he would not have met her. Which shall we choose? (Helser 1934: 57–62).

105:12. (Nupe) One man said that if he could be king for a day, they could kill him. Another said that if he could be crown prince for a day, they could kill him. A third man said that if he could have the king's first wife for a day, they could kill him. The first two were granted their wishes and were killed. The third man and the king's wife turned themselves into flies, and the king had them thrown in the Niger river, where they resumed human form. A ferryman refused to take them across the river until persuaded by his daughter, who said that she wanted to marry the man. Continuing their flight, the man was bitten by a snake. A hunter refused to give him medicine until his daughter said that she would not live unless he did, because she wanted to marry the man. They went on to a town where the king said that if the man could identify his first wife, he himself would die and let the man be king. The king assembled his 400 wives dressed in their fineries, but the man said that the first wife was not among them, that she was the woman wearing old clothes. The first wife became his fourth wife, along with the other 400 wives, when he became king. One day the new king was given a coconut. He gave it to his first wife, who had turned him into a fly, but the second wife protested that if she had not begged her father, the ferryman, he would have been killed. He gave it to his second wife, but the third protested that if she had not begged her father to give him medicine, he would have died. He gave her the coconut, but his fourth wife protested that if she had not been present in her old clothes, he would not have become king. The king burned the coconut and soaked the ashes in water. He cooked the water and made salt, which he divided among the four wives. That is how the Nupe learned to make salt (Frobenius 1921–1928: IX, 244–247).

105:13.   (Jukun)   A youth told a man that he could kill him if the man let him sleep with his daughter. A second youth said that he would have nothing to do with women if the man gave him a goat to eat. The man gave him a goat and led the other youth and his daughter to a house where they spent the night. She fell in love with him, asked him to marry her, and helped him to escape. As they fled, the youth was bitten by a snake, but a second maiden took them to her father, who cured him on condition that the youth marry her. They came to a large river where a third maiden had her father take them across on the same condition. The youth built a town by snapping his fingers, but the king who owned the land threatened to kill him if he could not name his first wife; if he could do so, he could kill the king and take his place. The king's first wife declared her love for the youth and told him her name. When he forgot it, people prompted him, and when the king tried to escape, they killed him. The youth became king and married the late king's wife. Then he called his first three wives and asked which one wanted his buffalo tail. All of them asked for it, each claiming to have saved his life. He gave it to his third wife, who had helped them across the river. But the fourth wife said it belonged to her, and he took it back and gave it to her, and she became his chief wife (Frobenius 1921–1928: VII, 265–268).

105:14. (Mano)   A chief allowed three men to stay in his village, warning them that anyone who made a bet or a boast that he could not fulfill would be killed. One man said he could drink a whole calabash of palm wine; he failed and was killed. The next said that he could eat the largest bull in the village; he also failed and was killed. The third said that if the chief would give him a wife, she would have a child by the second time he slept with her. That night he and the wife fled, and the chief sent pursuers to kill them. On the way they met a woman who gave them rice on condition that she also become the man's wife. Another woman threw her child into a river, parting the water so that they could cross over, also on condition that she become his wife. The man built a village and each of his three wives bore a child. He raised a cow, and when it was grown, he killed it and took its tail. The children fought over the cow-tail, and the women went to their husband, each claiming it for her child. Which of the three wives was the chief wife? (Becker-Donner 1965: 115–120).

105:15. (Khasonke)   One man was driven from home by his father because he was never sexually satisfied, a second because his hunger was never satisfied, and a third because he never tired of horse racing. Together they went to the town of the king. The first told the king, "If you satisfy me sexually, you may kill me." The second said, "If you satisfy my hunger, you may kill me." The third one said, "If you let me tire of horse racing, you may kill me." Ten bulls were killed and each was given a share. The greedy one said, "King! I am FULL!" and he was killed. They held a race with all the army's horses. The third one became tired and was killed. To the first man the king gave his favorite wife, but that night she saddled a horse, took the king's gold, bribed the guards, and they fled. They came to a river where they found an old lady and her daughter. When the old lady refused to take them across, her daughter pushed her into the water, and she drowned. The daughter took them across and asked the man to marry her. They came to a village where all strangers were put to death if they could not say where the king's spirit was. The king's daughter told the man that her father would die if he gave the correct answer, but that she would tell it to him if he would marry her. He agreed, gave the correct answer, and became king. When his three wives were about to give birth, a marabout made a paper for the wife he loved best. He could not give the paper to any of them (Monteil 1905: 150–155).

Adulterer

106:1. (Kpelle) Three men, named Intelligence, Fighter, and Adulterer, visited a town. Adulterer immediately demonstrated the appropriateness of his name and was caught. He was about to be beaten when the townspeople heard that to save him Fighter had killed a wicked spirit that had been hurting them. Intelligence brought the news and argued that the net effect of their visit had been helpful. The grateful townspeople gave them a cow and gave each a wife. They went on, raised children, and died. The sons killed the cow for their fathers' funeral feast and then argued over who should have the cow's tail, the symbol of authority in the village (Gay and Cole 1967: 26–27).

Gay and Cole comment:

The discussion was hot. Some defended Adulterer because he began the affair in the village, and because Fighter and Intelligence were merely helping him by killing the spirit and reconciling the villagers. Moreover, one man argued that adultery is the reason for every man's existence, since without sexual relations there would be no children. Others defended Fighter because they said it is only through fighting that we are even able to commit adultery. But the argument was won when one of the town elders presented the case of Intelligence. He said that God gave us reason so we would not seek foolishness. He said we need knowledge both to seek a wife and to win victories. He concluded that the cow's tail belonged to Intelligence, and the rest of the assembled group shouted their agreement.

Shoot Banana Leaves

107:1. (Mano) Four brothers — a hunter, a liar, a trouble-maker, and a diviner — went traveling. A chief said that they could stay in any house in his village except one, which no one must enter. Anyone who broke this taboo would be killed unless he could bring a dead leopard. The troublemaker broke the taboo and was seized. At the diviner's instructions, the hunter cut a bunch of bananas, put magic powder on it, and covered it with a cloth; he shot it with his gun, and it turned into a dead leopard. The liar told the chief that he saw a dead leopard, and they went to bring it to the village. The troublemaker was released, and the brothers left. They met a man, and the troublemaker broke his arm. The liar told their pursuers to go back to their village because three people had died there. The brothers reached another village whose chief said they could stay for a while, but that no one must fight in his village. Anyone who fought would be killed unless he brought a python. The troublemaker started a fight and was seized. At the diviner's instructions, the hunter put powder on a stick, covered it with a banana leaf, and shot it; it turned into a python. The liar told the chief that he saw a python on the road, and they went to bring it to the village. The chief released the troublemaker and gave him a wife. To whom did the wife belong? Answer: After a long dispute in which all four brothers were suggested, a judge decided that she belonged to the diviner, but that he must find goods to compensate the hunter (Becker-Donner 1965: 110–115).

Spear through Chief

108:1.   (Bambara)   A chief, who had a daughter so beautiful that young men could not see her without falling in love with her, did not know how to choose a son-in-law. Together they decided to put charcoal in an underground storage pit and to choose the suitor who could guess what was there. Anyone who failed would be beheaded by a magic sword. Many youths tried, failed, and were killed. Word of her beauty spread to Kayes, and a young man came from there to try. He too fell in love with the girl when he saw her, and she fell in love with him. She told him the answer to the question, reminded him when he forgot it, and they were married. The Fulani attacked the village, and all the men went to defend it except the youth, who stayed with his bride. She accused him of cowardice, but he said he had no weapons. She gave him her father's golden spear, and he joined the battle and drove the spear into a Fulani, who was carried away, with the spear, by his companions. The chief ordered the youth to leave his bride and retrieve the spear immediately. He set out on his horse and found a Fulani girl crying because her brother had been killed in battle; it was the sister of the Fulani whom the youth had killed. She gave him the spear, though she said she would be killed for doing so. She promised to marry him, and he took her on his horse and rode off. They came to a river where a Bozo fisherman refused to take them across in his canoe. The fisherman was killed by his daughter who took them across and begged to be the youth's wife. They came to an old woman who refused to give them water from her well. Her daughter pushed her into the well, gave them water, and begged to become the youth's wife. He returned the golden spear and was joined by his first wife. He returned to Kayes with his five [*sic*] wives and built five houses for them. Each wife became pregnant on the same day, and each bore a son on the same day. He killed a bull and offered its tail to his first wife; but the four other wives claimed it for their sons. To end the quarreling he threw the tail in the air, and a ficus tree appeared at the spot where it landed (Daget 1947: 22–23).

108:2.   (Hausa)   A youth borrowed a spear from a friend and drove it through an enemy chief who fled with the spear through his body. The youth was honored and handsomely rewarded. His friend, who had said he could have the spear as a gift, became jealous and demanded the return of his spear. The young man set out to retrieve it, accompanied by his fiancée, who said that if he were killed she wanted to die with him. They met the enemy chief's eldest daughter; she gave him the spear and declared her love for the youth. The three fled from their pursuers. When the ferryman refused to take them across a river, he was killed by his own daughter who declared her love for the youth and took them across the river. On the other side the youth died, and his three wives mourned him. A fourth girl revived him magically, on condition that she could be his fourth wife. Now, which of these women should be his chief wife? They are still discussing this subject and still have not been able to decide (Landeroin and Tilho 1909: 230–245).

108:3.   (Hausa)   The emir's son and his servant were close friends. During a battle the emir's son told his servant to hold his spear, but the servant spurred his horse and drove the spear into the enemy chief, leaving it in his body. The emir's son sent the servant to retrieve the spear. He found the daughter of the man he had killed, and she fell in love with him. She showed him the spear hut, and he took the spear he had come for. They fled together with her father's men in pursuit. They came to a river where a woman parted the waters for them by tossing a pebble into the river, and the servant returned the spear to the emir's son (Edgar 1911–1913: I, (25); translated by Skinner n.d.: I, (25); summarized by Tremearne 1913: 324–325).

108:4.   (Hausa)   A woman gave a horse and a bride to the son of her co-wife, who was poor. The king asked him to bring the spear of the king with whom they were at war. He set out with his wife and met the enemy king's daughter. She showed him a house full of spears, and he chose that of her father and asked her to return with them. They came to a river where a girl called, causing canoes to appear. They reached home and delivered the spear to the king. The king divided his city in two and gave half to the boy, who ruled it with two wives (Tremearne 1913: 323–324).

Spear through Animal

109:1. (Nkundo) A wealthy younger brother lent his best spear to his poor elder brother to kill wild pigs that were raiding his manioc garden, but on the condition that he must die if he did not return it. The poor elder brother speared a boar, but it escaped with the spear in it. The younger brother ordered him to follow and not to return without it. He came to an old woman and washed her, plaited her hair, and cut her nails. She gave him food, the spear, seventeen other spears, a dog, and a pipe. When he invited the rich younger brother to come and smoke, he swallowed the pipe, and the elder brother demanded his pipe. He cut his younger brother open, took the pipe from his belly, and sewed him up again. The younger brother lived but became poor and unimportant, and the elder brother became wealthy. Did the younger brother behave well? Answer: No. He deserved what he got because he wanted to kill his elder brother for a spear and because he drove his own brother away like an animal (Hulstaert and de Rop 1954: 50–57).

109:2. (Mongo) A poor man borrowed the harpoon of his rich younger brother to kill elephants that had overrun his field. He speared an elephant, but it escaped with the harpoon. The younger brother demanded his harpoon, and their relatives could not settle the case. The elder brother set out in pursuit of the elephant and met the spirit of his dead mother, who told him that the wounded elephant was her husband. She gave him the harpoon and a calabash of hemp. Following her instructions, he assembled the people and publicly returned the harpoon to his younger brother, who afterwards demanded the calabash. Later he broke the calabash and when the elder brother asked that it be returned, the elders in council awarded him the wives of his rich younger brother (Hulstaert 1965: 194–197).

109:3. (Mongo) A prosperous man scorned his poor elder brother but lent him a harpoon to kill elephants that had ravaged his fields. A wounded elephant escaped with the harpoon, and the younger brother said he must return it or die in the forest. Eventually the elder brother came to the house of an old woman who told him to bathe her, clear her eyes, plait her hair, cut her nails, and make up her face. Doing as he was told, he also cut bananas, cooked food, and ate. The next day he met his dead mother who had a dog that cleaned house and cooked for her and that brought him hemp to smoke. His mother told him that the elephant he had wounded was his father. Having retrieved the spear, his mother sent him home with hemp and other provisions and her dog. Stopping to see the old lady, the dog magically built a new house for her and, on their return, a house for him. The man gave away hemp for men to smoke, and the news of his return spread throughout the country. He returned the harpoon to his younger brother in front of all the people. The younger brother sent for hemp and a calabash, but he swallowed the calabash while smoking. His wives gave him enemas, but the calabash did not come out. The elder brother slit open his belly and took out the calabash, and the younger brother died. This abbreviated tale continues with another tale type (Hulstaert 1965: 428–443).

109:4.   (Mongo)   A man borrowed a lance from a friend to kill an elephant, but it escaped with the lance in its body. The friend demanded that the lance be returned, and the man set out in search of the elephant. He met his dead sister, whose husband returned the lance, saying that they were not really elephants but humans dressed like elephants. He returned the lance to his friend and the affair was ended (Hulstaert 1965: 52–55).

Pinch Brother's Neck

110:1.   (Nkundo)   A youth was jealous of his wealthy elder brother. When they went to the forest together to hunt caterpillars, he took his charm, hoping to use it to kill his elder brother. When the elder brother found a tree with many caterpillars, he told his younger brother to climb it. The younger brother took the charm from around his neck in order to climb and asked his elder brother to wear it. When he was high in the tree, he sang to the charm, "Pinch the neck. Pinch the neck." It pinched the neck of the elder brother, who also had magic, and he slapped the tree and sang to it to climb. The tree shot up into the air, and when the younger brother could no longer see the earth, he sang to his charm to release the neck. Then the elder brother called to the tree to come down, and the younger brother climbed out of it. Each asked the other why he had attempted murder. They went home and put the case to the judges. Who of these acted badly against his companion? Answer: The younger brother, who took his charm to kill his elder brother. If a child of your mother has wealth, even though you have nothing, you should rejoice over it (Hulstaert and de Rop 1954: 120–123).

Senior Son Succeeds

111:1. (Nkundo) A man had two wives. The junior wife had a son, and later the first wife had a son. The sons grew up, and the father died. People came to make the child of the second wife the father's successor, but the other son claimed this right because his mother was the first wife. The elders stopped their quarreling and said they would settle the matter. Who will receive their father's authority? Answer: The child of the second wife, because the first-born of a lineage is he who is first-born of his father (Hulstaert, and de Rop 1954: 116–119).

Loyal Son Succeeds

112:1. (Nkundo) A man had two sons. The elder son did not treat his father well, but the younger one did, and when the father died, he gave the younger brother the authority to wear the leopard skin. The elder brother was angry and fought his younger brother, who took the case to the judges and told them what had happened. The elder brother admitted that his father had not given him the symbols of authority but claimed that they were his by virtue of seniority. How will this palaver be settled? Answer: Despite his seniority, the elder brother loses because the father refused him the authority and gave it to the younger brother (Hulstaert and de Rop 1954: 114–117).

Dispensing Justice

113:1. (Anyi) A man told God that he wanted to be king, and God told him that he first must travel around the world. During his travels he saw animals and men dispensing justice, and he learned that against a lion a monkey is always wrong, against an elephant an insect is always wrong, and against a man a monkey is always wrong. He learned a lot about life and justice, but he still wanted to be king, though not as much as before. Finally he saw some troubles between the monkeys of the town (men) and the monkeys of the country (chimpanzees) and ran to tell God. God asked him what decision had been reached, but he did not know because he had left the discussion too soon. God said, "Bring me the answer and you will be king." The man never returned because there was no verdict. But what would you have decided? The man who knows the answer will be the king (Dadié 1955: 149–156).

Fall into Latrine

114:1–2. (Hausa)   A man fell into a latrine up to his chin. His enemy found him and threw a stone at his head. Should he duck down into the faeces or stay upright? Which would be better? They are still arguing, and we still haven't found who's right (Edgar 1911–1913: III, (188); translated by Skinner 1969: I, 402). A second Hausa version ends with the questions, "Will he choose to duck? Or to get his head cracked?" (Edgar 1911–1913: III, (13); translated by Skinner 1969: I, 403).

Slave in Latrine

115:1.   (Nkundo)   A man had three wives. The first dug a latrine pit; the second built a little house over it; the third fed their husband rotten fish. That night he had diarrhea and went to the latrine, where he found an escaped slave hiding. The next morning his three fathers-in-law came to ask for a slave: one for the restitution of his sister's bridewealth, another for bridewealth for his own wife, and the third for a funeral sacrifice. The man gave the slave to the father of the woman who had dug the pit, but the other two wives claimed it for their fathers. The three wives began to fight and called the judges to settle their dispute. Which wife wins the palaver? Answer: The slave belongs to the woman who dug the pit because she began the work (Hulstaert and de Rop 1954: 12–15).

Slave on Farm

116:1.   (Nkundo)   A man went to the forest to clear his wife's field, but she did not bring him food. So he went to the field of his other wife for sugar cane, and on his way he met an escaped slave and took him as his own. To which wife should he give the slave? Answer: To the first wife, because it was for her that he went to the forest and because it would have been her fault if the husband had died there (Hulstaert and de Rop 1954: 28–33).

116:2. (Nkundo) A man went to the forest to clear his wife's field, but she did not bring him food. So he went to the field of his other wife for sugar cane and found an escaped slave stealing it. He took the man as a slave, and each wife claimed him, the first one arguing that she would have been blamed if their husband had died. The case was taken to the headman. Who do you think will be the owner of the slave? Answer: The second wife, because the man was caught stealing her sugar cane and owed indemnity to her (Hulstaert and de Rop 1954: 32–39).

Slave on Farm to Widow

117:1. (Nkundo) A woman saw a very strong young man armed with weapons in her maize field. She told her husband who took his weapons and told the villagers to arm themselves and look for the youth. The youth killed one of the villagers with his arrow but was captured and taken home. The widow asked for the prisoner as a slave because her husband had been killed, but the couple who owned the maize field claimed him because the woman had discovered him. A large gathering was called together to settle the dispute. Who will ever win it? Answer: The widow is given the slave in place of her husband, and the couple loses because, without reason, the man called the people to fight the strong man (Hulstaert and de Rop 1954: 118–121).

Child Born on Farm

118:1. (Vili) A man cleared separate gardens for his two wives. When the second wife took some beans from the other's garden, they quarreled, but eventually they agreed that anything born on the farm of either should belong exclusively to her. Later the first wife came to the second wife's garden and asked for tobacco; while she was smoking she gave birth to a child. The second wife claimed it as her own because it was born on her farm, and the elders decided that she was right (Dennett 1898: 58–59; retold as a Loma tale by Jablow 1961: 108–110).

Abandoned Farm

119:1. (Nkundo), A man cleared the undergrowth for a garden but abandoned it. A second man saw the unfinished garden, felled the large trees, did part of the burning, and then abandoned it. A third man finished the burning, raked, took away the tree stumps, and planted fruit. When they were ripe, he guarded them and sold them. The first and second man claimed that the fruit was theirs, and the elders intervened. How will the palaver be settled? Answer: The one who began the garden owns the fruit because without him the others would not have thought of continuing (Hulstaert and de Rop 1954: 90–93).

Tobacco in Mouth

120:1. (Kono) A hunter asked his friend for tobacco. His friend said it was in his mouth but ate as if nothing were there. The hunter shot him, and a genie appeared and poisoned the hunter. Who was the most guilty, the man with the tobacco, the hunter, or the genie? (Holas 1952: 81–82).

The First Smoke

121:1. (Vai) One man had a pipe, one man had tobacco, and one had matches. They fought over who should have the first smoke and took the case to the judge. He could not decide and turned it over to the people. Which of the three men was really entitled to the first smoke? (Ellis 1914: 196).

Girl from Ashes

122:1. (Limba) "Three men. One had a pipe, but he had no tobacco. Another said, 'I have tobacco, but I have no match.' Another said, 'I have a match.' The one who owned the pipe said, 'Give here the tobacco.' The one who owned the tobacco gave it. The other said, 'I have a match.' He gave the match. He put the tobacco in the pipe. He lit it. They smoked, all of them, the three. They finished smoking. The one who owned the pipe took it, he knocked out the ashes from the pipe. A girl came out from there (the ashes), a beautiful girl. Of those three, which is the one who owns the girl?" Finnegan notes that this short dilemma tale, told here in full, which she heard several times, can give rise to fairly lengthy (but light-hearted) discussion (Finnegan 1967: 230).

122:2. (Baule) One man asked another for his pipe, filled it, and began to smoke. The smoke changed into a beautiful woman, and the two men began to argue over her. They took their quarrel to the Sky God, who said that the woman belonged to the owner of the pipe. Therefore, if someone asks you for something, you should give it to him because you can never know how good deeds will be rewarded (Himmelheber 1951: 27–28).

Girl from Pool

123:1. (Limba) A girl told a boy he could marry her if he could catch her, but she disappeared into a pool of water. The next day the same thing happened to the boy's twin brother, and he followed her into the pool. A fly and a dog helped him identify the girl, and he brought her back with him. Both twins claimed the girl. Which one owned her? Answer: The one who brought her back (Finnegan 1967: 212–214).

123:2. (Limba) One twin did all the farm work while his brother only made love. A girl appeared first to the farmer, then to the lover who followed her into a pond. An old woman, a dog, and a tsetse fly helped him identify the girl, and he was handsomely rewarded. The twins agreed that the farmer should have the girl and that the lover should keep his reward (Finnegan 1967: 263–267).

123:3. (Kpelle) Another of Mengrelis' incomplete tales begins in the same manner: An elder brother farmed while his younger brother did nothing but smoke his pipe in the village. A very beautiful girl appeared to the elder brother and promised to marry him if he could catch her, but she jumped into a river (Mengrelis 1950: 191–192).

Carving a Wife

124:1. (Kabyle) A fisherman pulled up an ape instead of a fish. The ape made him wealthy, and they went to a town whose chief had killed all the suitors of his beautiful daughter. Putting the ape inside his clothing, the fisherman asked for her hand in marriage. The chief agreed on condition that he move her to talk to him; if not he would be killed. (The foregoing is much abbreviated.) When the fisherman and the girl were seated, the ape told a story: "A woodcarver once made a very realistic carving of a woman. Traders dressed her in beautiful clothing; others made up her face with cosmetics; and a prophet breathed life into the wooden figure. I have asked myself to whom she belonged. I think that her greatest thanks are due to the woodcarver." The girl cried, "No! The prophet earned her since he gave her a soul." The fisherman said, "You have spoken," and she replied, "Yes. Now I will become your wife." The fisherman went home, took the ape out of his clothing, and thanked it for helping him to obtain a wife. The ape replied, "Who really earned the woman, you or I?" (Frobenius 1921–1928: III, 98–101; AT 945).

124:2. (Swahili) A carpenter carved a wooden figure, a blacksmith riveted its limbs to its body, a weaver made its clothing, a silversmith made jewelry for it, and a learned man prayed and God granted his request. The figure came to life as a beautiful woman. Which of these five men should have her? Answer: The learned man, because a soul is priceless and because all of the other men are craftsmen who are paid for their work (W. E. Taylor 1932–1933: 6–8; cf. Farnham 1920: 263, 266, 268–269).

Cloth for Woman

125:1. (Kpelle) Two brothers — a trapper and a weaver — went to live in the forest when their parents died. The trapper said that they must make a clearing and build a house. The weaver said, "Leave me in peace so I can weave my cloth." The trapper cleared the land, brought lumber, and asked his brother to help build the house. The weaver kept on weaving. The trapper built the house and invited the weaver to live in it with him. The trapper brought game, but the weaver would not help him butcher it. He called the weaver to eat, but he kept on weaving. The trapper dried and stored meat and planted rice. The weaver wove and stored his cloth. The trapper had four granaries full of rice, two houses full of dried meat, and a house full of oil. One day the trapper found a group of women near his trap, but he could not capture them. Finally he told the weaver, and they went to the trap together, the weaver taking his cloth. When he showed it to the women, they came running and followed the men home. The two men argued over the women. To whom did the women really belong? (Westermann 1921: 422–423).

125:2. (Kpelle) A trap maker saw a chip of wood floating down a river and realized that there was someone upstream. He found a palm wine tapper and later a weaver joined them, and they founded a village in the forest. The trapper spotted the footprints of a woman, but they could not take her by force. The trapper offered her meat which she refused. When the weaver offered her cloth, she accepted it and went to live with the men. To which man did she belong? (Gay and Cole 1967: 26).

Gay and Cole comment on the ensuing discussion and the resolution of the dilemma:

The answer might seem clear to an American — she belonged to the man whose gift she had accepted. But the discussion waxed furious, with the debate shifting back and forth between advocates of the trap maker and the weaver. They chose sides, apparently for the sheer joy of the debate. Basically, the argument in favor of the trap maker was that he had been first in the forest, had brought the other two men to the site of the village, and thus had primary rights over the produce of the area, including the woman. As evidence in his favor it was claimed that the first hunter to see an animal owns it, even though another may actually kill it. It was pointed out by the trap maker's advocates that he had first found the woman's footprint, and had tracked her down.

Those who supported the weaver gave the argument Americans might prefer, yet couched it as an alternative expression of traditional values. Someone suggested the analogy of a rice farm. The supporters of the trap maker said that the man who cleared the farm should claim the rice. Supporters of the weaver said that the man who harvests the rice owns it. At this point the argument began to center on one of the possible traditional values, and several persons were of the opinion that even if the palm-wine producer alone had captured the woman, he should give her to the weaver, who had customary rights. It was at approximately this point that the discussion ended, with the decisions of the group given by a village elder in favor of the trap maker, on the basis of traditional privilege.

125:3. (Vai) An elder brother made a trap, and his younger brother wove a cloth. Each day a woman came and set rice by the trap, and the elder brother ate it. One day they asked the woman to come home with them, but she refused, saying that she had no cloth. The younger brother gave her his cloth, and she went home with them. Both brothers claimed her, and they took their quarrel to the king. The king said that the younger brother should let the elder have the woman, that the elder brother should make another trap and that the next woman they found should belong to the younger brother. When they returned home, they found another woman sitting there, and the younger brother took her (Ellis 1914: 235–236).

Deaf and Blind

126:1.   (Nkundo)   A blind man heard the sounds of war and fled, guided by his friend who was deaf. They hid in the forest, where the deaf man captured a woman who was also fleeing. When the battle ended, they returned home, and both men claimed the woman as his wife. Who owns her? Answer: The blind man, who heard the sounds of battle and who heard the woman in the forest (Hulstaert and de Rop 1954: 10–13).

Woman in Trap

127:1.   (Mano)   A farmer ate only his crops and a hunter ate only meat. Each refused the other's food, thinking that it would kill him. Later they ate soup with rice together. The hunter set his trap and left the farmer to watch over it. It caught a beautiful maiden, but the farmer forgot to look at the trap, and the hunter found her. The farmer claimed the maiden because the hunter was his guest, but the hunter refused to give her up. Who won this argument? (Becker-Donner 1965: 106–109).

Food for Hunter

128:1.   (Kono)   Two women lived at opposite ends of a stream. One ate dry rice, the other only sauce. One day they met and ate rice with sauce together, and both liked it. A hunter passing by greeted them, and the women invited him to share their food. One put a handful of rice on the sauce in the pot, and the other handed it to the hunter. Which of the two women was worthier? (Holas 1952: 86).

House or Food

129:1.   (Kpelle)   Two rich women fell in love with a poor man who lived in the forest. The first woman built him a fine house, made him a garden, put cattle and goats in the nearby fields, and sent a messenger to bring him to town. The second went to the forest to find him, gave him rich food and wine, and brought him back to town. Which of the two women deserved him? (Pinney n.d.: 84–85).

Four Bad Cooks

130:1. (Nkundo) A man had four wives. The first did not prepare all her food at the same time, only a little each day. The second knew how to find good food, but she cooked it all together; she gave it all to her husband and found new food the next day. The third kept no food; when she had a little, she prepared it all at once and gave it to her husband, but the next day she had nothing and complained of hunger. The fourth wife was stingy; what little food she had she kept for a long time, giving her husband food only three times a week. Their husband became angry because of the weaknesses of his wives and complained to the notables. They deliberated over which wife had the greatest weakness. Which of these four women will be sent away? Answer: The fourth wife, because even if a woman is stingy, she should not be stingy toward her husband; a woman who is so, is a witch (Hulstaert and de Rop 1954: 130–135).

Naked Prince

131:1. (Bandi) The son of a chief, whose chiefdom had been completely destroyed, had nothing. He was naked and lived in a hollow tree, living by his sword. Two beautiful daughters of a chief to the north and chief to the south heard of his pride and bravery and set out to marry him. Each was accompanied by 1,000 warriors and slaves who carried riches. The maiden from the south arrived first. When she found that he was not in his tree, she sent 500 warriors to town to hunt naked men. They captured 100 naked men — men bathing, men undressing, men lying in bed with their wives, and the naked prince. When the maiden from the north arrived, she asked for him by name. She had her slaves set food before her rival's warriors, and they released him. When he was bathed, she rubbed him with fragrant ointments and gave him food and wine in golden bowls. Then the maiden from the south came and dressed him in robes of gold and silver thread, precious jewels, and perfumes. Both maidens claimed him as her husband, but he ordered them to stop quarreling and married them both. But which of them had the right to be his first wife? (Pinney n.d.: 26–27).

Choosing a Wife

132:1.   (Pygmy)   A young man wanted to get married and went to
visit three girls suggested by his father. The first was an expert at fishing,
the second was an excellent cook, and the third knew well how to make
love. Which one did he choose? (Trilles 1932: 273–276).

Choosing a Husband

133:1.   (Pygmy)   Turtle Dove was a very pretty young girl who was
good at fishing, cooking, and dancing. When the time came for her to
marry, she had three suitors. The first youth, called Chimpanzee, was
big and strong; he had already killed two elephants, and all the women
ran after him. The second youth, called Arrow of the Forest, was small
and slender; he was always gay and singing, the best dancer you could
find. He ran after all the girls, knew well how to talk with them, and
had children in several villages. The third was called Toadstool. The day
he was born, his mother had cooked a large dish of mushrooms in which
a poisonous one was found, and his father died. He did not hunt or
fish, but he brought much game and fish because he was a great medicine man and knew how to cure sickness. He had blood in the corner
of his eye, one tooth stuck out of his mouth, one shoulder was higher
than the other, and he never looked others in the face. Each of the
youths claimed Turtle Dove as his wife. To whom should she be
married? Men and women, old and young, each gave a different advice.
I prefer to leave the choice to others (Trilles 1932: 276–278).

Showing her Love

134:1.   (Vai)   Three young men went to woo the king's daughter. For
one she prepared his bath and gave him fresh clothes and a cover for
his bed. She prepared a big feast for the second and his attendants. She
gave nothing to the third, but at sunset she walked with him among the
trees and flowers. They argued about whom she liked best and submitted
the case to the judge. The judge could not decide, and the girl is still
unmarried (Ellis 1914: 211–213).

134:2.   (Nkundo)   Three youths came to woo a woman who did not
like men at all and had refused all her suitors. She gave one a chair to

sit on, gave food to the second, and in the evening she gave a bed to the third. To which of the three has she shown love? Answer: The second, for whom she prepared food (Hulstaert and de Rop 1954: 130–131).

Raising Grain

135:1. (Luba) A man's three wives made their gardens. They brought grain from the home of the first wife and hoes from the home of the second wife; the third wife's family called down rain. At harvest time each wife claimed all the crops, and they took their quarrel to the chief. He ruled that each was entitled to one third of the harvest but because they all had the same husband, he should own all of the gardens and all of the crops. The chief claimed one tenth of the harvest for hearing the case (Burton 1961: 151).

135:2. (Songye) Rain, Blacksmith, and Farmer were friends, and each had a daughter. The three girls were friends and farmed together, but one day they fought over the division of their maize. One said that her father had provided their seed. Another said her father had made their hoes. The other said that her father had made the rain. The three men heard the argument and took back the maize, the hoes, and the rain, each claiming that his daughter was right. The fields were not cultivated, and there was no harvest. Farmer ate up his maize and died. Rain died, and Blacksmith died. Rain, farm tools, and seed belong together (Frobenius 1921–1928: XII, 279–280).

Arrowhead

136:1. (Nkundo) A man had four wives. The first bought an arrowhead, the second an arrow shaft, the third a bow, and the fourth a bow string. The man killed an animal, and each wife claimed it. Which wife deserved it? Answer: The animal must be shared, but the largest portion should go to the first wife because the arrowhead is most valuable, because it is made by specialists, and because without it no one would have looked for a shaft, a bow, or a bow string (Hulstaert and de Rop 1954: 4–5).

Blowgun and Arrows

137:1.   (Betsimisaraka)   A hunter borrowed one man's blowgun and
another man's arrows and killed 100 birds. Each of the three received
thirty-three birds, and each claimed the one remaining. Which of the
three should have it? (Renel 1910: II, 117).

Dividing a Hare

138:1.   (Unidentified, Sierra Leone)   A hunter wounded a hare. A
farmer's dog caught the hare and took it to its master, and the hunter
and the farmer argued over it. The villagers joined in the argument,
taking sides, and it reached the ears of the chief. A young boy asked the
hunter and the farmer why they wanted the hare. The hunter said he
wanted its skin to make a drum; the farmer said he wanted its meat.
The boy told the chief to have the hare divided between them. Later,
when the chief died, the boy was made chief (Baharav 1963–1966: I,
26–27).

Who Owns the Pig?

139:1.   (Nkundo)   A hunter killed a pig, another man made a fire,
and a third man cooked it. They argued over the meat. Who do you
think owned it? Answer: The hunter, who may share it with his helpers
(Hulstaert and de Rop 1954: 16–19).

139:2.   (Nkundo)   Long-Leg helped his friends across a river. Long-
Bow killed a pig, and Long-Nail butchered it. They fought over the pig.
Who do you thing owned it? Answer: Long-Bow, who should share it
with his helpers (Hulstaert and de Rop 1954: 6–9).

Who Owns the Leopard?

140:1.   (Mano)   Not knowing of each other's presence, two hunters
saw a leopard in the bush. The first man shot and dropped his gun.
The second, who also shot, found the gun and took it; he butchered the
leopard and put it in a basket. The townspeople argued about who had
shot the leopard and who owned its meat (Becker-Donner 1965: 96–
98).

Trapping a Leopard

141:1. (Nkundo) A man offered to guard the animals of his friend who had no place to keep them, and he guarded them well. When a leopard came to catch his friend's animals, he made a trap and caught and killed it. He ate a portion of the leopard and sold a portion. His friend heard of this and demanded his share because both men had animals inside the enclosure, and he took the case to the judges. Who will ever win it? Answer: The first man wins because he constructed the fence, made the trap, and caught the leopard (Hulstaert and de Rop 1954: 128–129).

Sharing the Game

142:1. (Nkundo) Jilo was a stingy hunter who did not share his game with those who helped him hunt. Because of this Yoto refused to hunt with him, but after Jilo promised to treat him well, he agreed, warning Jilo that if he did not treat him well, something would happen to him. They killed four wild pigs, and Jilo gave Yoto only one. When he refused to give more, Yoto fell down dead. Jilo called to him and begged him to stand up, but Yoto remained dead. Jilo returned to the village and found Yoto singing at a beer party. He went back to the forest and found Yoto there dead. He ran back to the village and found Yoto sitting and talking. He returned to the forest and found Yoto's body at the point of decomposing. He was surely dead. Fear seized Jilo, and he wanted to return home, but Yoto stood up and said Jilo had seen his punishment for being so stingy. Jilo offered to be more generous, but he gave Yoto only a pig and a flank. Yoto threatened to die again and stay dead. Jilo said that it was his dog and his nets that they had used, so the pigs were his. But he gave Yoto two pigs, and they returned to the village to tell the people about their argument. Who will win the palaver? Answer: Yoto wins because if people help you hunt, you should share the game with them equally and because if you die or are injured in the forest, they will help you (Hulstaert and de Rop 1954: 106–111).

Dog Finds Ivory

143:1. (Unidentified, Cameroun) Three men went on a journey, one to sell his dog, another his meat, and the third his vegetables. At the suggestion of the third, they stopped to eat; they shared their food, the dog receiving a bone. Starting on their way, they noticed that the dog had stayed behind with its bone, and they returned, calling out and beating the bush. Suddenly each of them saw two elephant tusks, only two, when there were three men. The first man said that the tusks had been found because of his dog. The second said that the dog had stayed behind because of the bone that he had given it. The third said that he was the one who had suggested they stop to eat. The argument continued (N'Djok 1958: 84–86; repeated by Fouda, de Julliot, and Lagrave 1961: 14).

N'Djok comments:

People are at ease, and as the rights of each are considered at length and the arguments are exchanged, the tone of voice . . . rises. One plays the game. The truly Bantu game of railing at the adversary, of introducing the most irrelevant details, of responding to a question with another question, of attributing to him what he had not said, of invoking God as a witness, . . . of all speaking together, of watching for your partner to run out of breath so as to deafen him, in his turn, with a verbal deluge, punctuated with extravagant but very eloquent mimicry. That is the art! Finally they are all agreed: The one who carried vegetables will have nothing; only the dog and the meat (bone) caused the discovery. Their two owners will each take a tusk. But what excellent exercise to prepare for the arguments of the village and those of the court! Woe to the inexperienced official! And what preparation again for the political game of the future!

143:2. (Bulu) Three men went courting and met at a crossroads. One had a dog, another some cassava, and the third peanut butter wrapped in a leaf. The second asked what they could eat with his cassava, and the third man offered his peanut butter. They ate together and threw the leaf into the bushes. The dog went to lick the leaf and found a dead elephant. When the men had gone on a way, the first man returned to look for his dog. He found the elephant and claimed it because his dog found it. The third man claimed it because the dog had gone after his peanut butter, and the second claimed it because they would not have stopped to eat if he had not brought his cassava. After they had quarreled a long time, they asked people in the next town to settle their dispute. We ask you, gentle reader, how would you settle this delicate question? (Krug and Herskovits 1949: 354–355).

143:3. (Bulu) Three men went on a journey together. One had cooked food wrapped in a leaf; one had cassava; one had only a dog. They ate together. When the first man threw away the leaf, the dog went to lick it, and when the third man went to look for his dog, he found it eating an elephant. He took a tusk and returned to the others. The three men quarreled over the elephant and went to town to have their dispute settled. The owner of the dog was given one half of the elephant, and the other two shared the other half (Krug 1912: 118; retold by Jablow 1961: 59–61).

143:4. (Nkundo) Three men went on a journey. One had meat, another had manioc, and the third had only his dog. When they stopped to eat, the first two shared their food but gave nothing to the third man or his dog. They threw away the leaf from which they had eaten and went on. The dog found the leaf, placed it on an elephant tusk, and began to lick it. When the third man returned to look for his dog, he found the tusk. The first man claimed it because the dog had run after the leaf with the meat on it. The second man claimed it because he had suggested eating. The third man claimed it because they had refused food to him and his dog and because his dog had found the tusk. They went to town and presented the case to the judges. Who, now, is the owner of the elephant tusk? Answer: The owner of the dog, for the reasons he stated, and because the others had thrown the leaf away (Hulstaert and de Rop 1954: 68–73).

Wealth from Termite Hill

144:1. (Kpelle) One man went upstream and slept, and the other went down to the settlement and slept there. They slept very long. One slept on a mountain peak, the other at the mouth of the river. Termites built a town over one, but he slept there for six years. Two boys went hunting in the forest and saw a hole in the termite hill. Inside they found a man and asked what he was doing there. He said that he was sleeping, but that he should wake up and go to town. Out of his hand came five bundles of cloth, seven horses, and five cows. He said they were his property, but the boys claimed them. To which of these three people do these things belong? (Westermann 1921: 431–432).

Horses from Gourd

145:1. (Soninke) A man's mare died, and he buried it in a field next to his house. The owner of the field planted gourds where the mare was buried. One of the vines grew toward the house of the first man, coiled around the stake to which the mare had been tethered, and bore a gourd. The second man said, "Take care of my gourd and I will pick it when it is ripe," and, as a good neighbor, the first one did so. When the second man came to pick it, it was so big that he cut it in two. Out came two healthy young horses. The two men argued over them and took their case to the judge. What do you think the judge decided? Answer: Each received one horse (Monteil 1905: 23–25).

Village from Gourd

146:1. (Mano) A younger brother did nothing but watch a calabash that he had planted while his elder brother brought water, rice, sheep, and chickens. When the calabash was grown, the younger brother cut it in two, and a village appeared. The village elders argued about who owned the village. Some said it belonged to the younger brother, but others said that if he had not been fed by his elder brother, he could not have raised the calabash (Becker-Donner 1965: 103–106).

146:2. (Vai) Three brothers, grieved at the death of their parents, went to live in the bush. The eldest made a rice farm that attracted wild animals. The second set a trap that caught a pot that said they would die if they touched it. The third, wanting to die, broke the pot, and a large town appeared. Each brother claimed the town. They called the judge to settle the matter, and the judge said he could not decide and turned it over to the people, who have not settled it yet (Ellis 1914: 187–188).

Village from Egg

147:1. (Bulu) A foolish man who did nothing but smoke ordered bales of tobacco and went to live in the forest. He was joined by a foolish hunter who killed much game every day. The smoker refused the hunter's meat, but a giant came and took it all. The hunter threatened to shoot the smoker if this happened again. When the giant returned for more meat, the smoker explained his predicament. The giant gave him a brass egg shell and told him to throw it on the ground if the hunter threatened him. When he did so, a large village appeared. Who is the owner of this village? You, my friends, who read this, may settle this difficult palaver (Krug and Herskovits 1949: 353–354).

147:2. (Mano) A hunter and a weaver lived together, and all the houses in the village were filled with the hunter's dried meat. A forest spirit asked the weaver for some meat and paid for it with "medicine" to make the village become large. The weaver divided the medicine with the hunter, but the hunter demanded it all, and they began to fight over it (Becker-Donner 1965: 109–110).

147:3. (Kpelle) A hunter and his companion went into the forest to hunt. But the companion stayed in camp to smoke his pipe while the hunter killed wild game, and he refused to help the hunter butcher it. One day while the hunter was hunting, a forest spirit came to the pipe smoker and bought some of the hunter's meat. When the hunter returned, he demanded that the smoker bring him payment for the meat. The smoker went to the spirit and was given a hen's egg as payment. Then the two men began to fight over the egg. They broke it, and a city appeared. They quarreled over the city and took the case to the king. The king ruled that the city belonged to the hunter (Westermann 1921: 392).

Village from Snake

148:1. (Kpelle) A hunter saw a raffia rib in a river and knew that there was someone upstream. He found a man and asked for food. The man cooked fish and rice for him, but the hunter refused to eat it, saying there were too many bones in it. The hunter killed an ape and gave it to the other man. Then he asked for it back so that he could eat its tail. But when the man brought it, the tail was gone. The man said that "a big thing" had taken the tail. They went to the big thing which denied taking the tail. They went to a leopard which did the same. They went to a long snake, killed it, split open its belly, and cut a city out of it. To which of the two did the city belong? (Westermann 1921: 391).

Perverse Brother

149:1. (Mano) In a lengthy tale, two orphans climbed a tree after killing a leopard cub that had fed them. When the perverse younger brother urinated in the leopards' food, people began to chop down the tree. He killed the lizard that mended the tree and broke the wings of the eagle that carried them away. They fell and were killed. The younger brother killed the tortoise that revived them, and the brothers separated. An old woman gave the younger brother a frog. He roasted it and gave it to her child, then roasted the child and gave it to a frog. The child's father put him in a basket to be thrown on the fire, but he induced the man's other child to take his place. He returned to his brother and killed a bush-devil. Out of its mouth came a village that grew ever larger. To whom did the village belong? (Becker-Donner 1965: 121–130).

149:2.   (Temne)   After a series of adventures, a perverse younger brother saved a snake from fire, and it told him how to revive a man's favorite wife whom it had bitten (as in number 50). After further adventures, a king lodged the two brothers and gave them two virgins, whom the younger brother killed. They climbed a tree, and the younger brother urinated and defecated on the king. When people began to chop down the tree, he killed the lizard that mended it, the hawk that carried them away, and the tortoise that revived them when they fell to earth. An old woman gave him a cricket to roast for her child, and he roasted the child for a cricket. After several other adventures, including the common one of selling some Fulani a lion as a dog, the brothers returned to town and opened a shop. The tale ends unexpectedly with the question: "Who is the rightful owner of the shop – the older one or the younger?" (N. Thomas 1916: III, 18–42). Again no attempt has been made to retrieve African non-dilemma versions of this tale.

Chicken Finds Gold

150:1.   (Unidentified, Cameroun)   A poor man went to tell his woes to a forest spirit, which gave him four charms: a chicken, a dog, a cow, and a seed. As directed, the man planted the seed, and in seven years it bore 1,000 boys and 1,000 girls. With each peck the chicken brought up silver and gold from the ground. Many sacks of rice were found wherever the dog slept. Each evening, when the cow returned from pasture, it brought a calf, a bundle of millet, and a large calabash of milk and food. One day the chief sent his woodworker to fell the tree. A lion killed the cow; a panther killed the dog; an eagle carried off the chicken. I ask, of these four charms, which would you have tried to save? (Fouda, de Julliot, and Langrave 1961: 15).

150:2.   (Fulani)   A very poor man was given a chicken, a dog, a cow, and a seed. He planted the seed, as instructed, and in seven years it produced a tree that bore 1,000 boys and, the next year, 1,000 girls. The chicken, scratching for food, found silver and gold with each peck of its beak. Wherever the dog lay down, a granary full of rice was found. And every day the cow brought a calf, a bundle of millet, and a large calabash of milk. But a chief sent his messenger to cut down the tree. A lion came to kill the cow, a panther to kill the dog, and a *sirou* to carry the chicken away. Which would you save? (Equilbecq 1913–1916: II, 148–150).

150:3. (Unidentified, Senegambia) A man had a mother who could make porridge out of sand, a son who could shoot an arrow into the air and have it return with a piece of meat, a cock that brought him ten pieces of gold each day, a cow that had a calf every morning, a goat that gave palm wine instead of milk, and a cotton plant that had ten beautiful cloths on its branches every day. He was very happy. But one day his mother was captured and carried away, his child fell in a well, a lion ate his cow, a jackal ate his cock, and his goat was strangled in its rope. What should the poor man do? (Bérenger-Féraud 1879: 245–246; repeated in Bérenger-Féraud 1885: 240–241).

150:4. (Ewe) In time of hunger a boy refused to sell his hen to buy food. The hen began to excrete gold, and the boy built a large house. The house caught fire, and both his mother and his hen cried, "Save me!" Which of them will he save first? (Schönhärl 1909: 105–106).

Reward for Clothing

151:1. (Temne) A fisherman asked the Alulu bird to divine for him and find why his traps were always empty. The bird told him to take a whip and hide by the river; there he would see who was stealing his fish. He saw a spirit take off its clothes, go into the water, and lift a fish trap. The fisherman broke wind, and the spirit heard him. It ran away, leaving its clothes, which the man took home. The man and his two brothers then returned the clothes, asking payment for the stolen fish. The eldest, who owned the traps, took a chisel that always gave him palm wine; the next took a rope tied to which he found a cow each morning; the youngest took a purse that was always filled with money and gold. Of these three, who was the wisest? (N. Thomas 1916: III, 55–58).

151:2. (Temne) A fisherman confronted a spirit that had been stealing from his traps, but it escaped, leaving behind its clothes, bag, and knife. With his two brothers, he returned the spirit's possessions but demanded payment for the stolen fish. The eldest brother chose a knife that always gave him plenty of palm wine. The youngest chose a rope at the end of which he found a new cow each morning. The fisherman chose a purse in which there was always plenty of money. Now, which one made the best choice? (Musson 1957: 16–19).

Wife Doesn't Scold

152:1. (Tsimihety) A man and wife had only a cock, a bull, and a ram, which they decided to sell to buy other animals to breed. The husband traded them for rice, maize, and manioc, which he ate. He met the king, who wagered 100 cows that his wife would scold him. When the man told his wife, she showed no annoyance and even smiled a little, saying that they would work together again. The king heard and gave her 100 cows. Now, which was the happiest, the wife with her cattle, her husband, or the king who had among his subjects a woman who did not sulk? It must be the king (Rabearison 1967: 67–68; AT 1415).

Food Under Bowl

153:1. (Vai) A woman cooked rice for one man and a bird for another, putting them in separate bowls under a cover. She told the first man where his rice was, and he ate both the rice and the bird. He claimed she had given him the bird, which she denied. The two men took the case to a judge, who decided that the owner of the rice was guilty, but popular opinion held that he was innocent. What is a proper decision in the case? (Ellis 1914: 202–203).

Buying a Sun

154:1. (Nkundo) A man gave his two sons money to buy a sun in another land. The younger brother spent all his money on women, but when they reached their destination he took as his concubine the daughter of the man who sold suns. She freely gave him a sun, locked in a trunk, and gave him the key. The elder brother took the trunk home and told his father that he had bought a sun while his younger brother had squandered his money on concubines. The father called the people, but the elder brother could not open the trunk. He said that the trunk had no key, but at that moment the younger brother arrived with it. He admitted he had spent his money on women, but said that he had been given a sun and his brother had taken it. Thereupon, he took the key and opened the trunk, and all saw the sun. Which of these two sons acted well? Answer: The younger brother; the elder brother had stolen and lied (Hulstaert and de Rop 1954: 156–161).

Snorer and Singer

155:1.   (Mende)   A chief allowed two strangers to sleep in the guest house, warning them that if they snored they would be killed in their sleep. One man awoke to hear his companion snoring and the villagers sharpening their knives. He composed a song and sang loudly so that the villagers could not hear the snoring, and they took up the song and began to drum and dance. The next morning the chief rewarded them for the fine song, and when they were out of town they argued over the larger share. The snorer claimed it because, if he had not snored, his companion would not have composed the song. The singer claimed it because, if he had not sung, his companion would have been killed. They could not decide. Can you? (Jablow 1961: 43–45; repeated by Feldmann 1963: 200–201).

155.2.   (Unidentified, Africa)   "Two travelers, welcomed at an African village, learn of the village taboo against snoring. Despite their anxiety about the taboo, one of them sleeps and snores. The other sings to cover the sound. The singing sets the villagers, who are assembling to punish the snorer, to dancing instead. While the villagers dance, thieves make away with the chief's yams. The snoring traveler awakens, sees them, and pursues them. He recovers the yams and traps the thieves. When the chief learns what has happened, he presents both travelers with a single sack of coins. As the travelers depart, the quarreling begins. Who deserves the largest share?" (From the film *The Travelers and the Thieves: An African Folktale* produced by Eothen Films).

Don't Steal or Waken

156:1.   (Vai)   The king proclaimed a fine of fifty dollars if anyone stole or if anyone awakened a person who slept in the daytime. An old woman stole a plantain, fell asleep, and was awakened by a boy sent by the owner of the plantain. Both were taken to the judge who asked, "Who should pay the fine?" (Ellis 1914: 205–206).

Charm for Wealth

157:1. (Betsimisaraka) A poor man had absolutely nothing, though his father and brother were rich. He promised a slave to a sorcerer in return for a charm that would bring him wealth. As soon as he received the charm, his father died, and he inherited all his father's slaves. When the sorcerer came for his payment, the man refused, saying that he had been given an evil charm, not a charm for riches. The sorcerer objected, saying that without the charm he could not have become wealthy. Which of the two was right? (Renel 1910: II, 113–114).

Cure for Blindness

158:1–2. (Limba) A man was blinded when he saved his friend from a dangerous spirit. A vulture told the friend that he could cure the man's blindness by killing his own child and smearing its blood on his eyes. When his wife gave birth, he did so. The two friends argued amicably, each maintaining that the other was the greater friend (Finnegan 1967: 127–129). Finnegan (1967: 30) says that she thinks she heard a dilemma added in one version of this tale.

158:3. (Vai) A man was blinded when he saved his friend from an enormous snake. A diviner told the friend that he could cure the man's blindness by killing his own son and washing his face in his son's blood, and he did so. Which one was the greater friend? (Ellis 1914: 214–216; retold by Jablow 1961: 115–117).

158:4. (Fulani) A man went to get married, accompanied by his friend. On the way they met a vulture that said that a while after the marriage, the man would be killed by a crocodile. It was the man's custom to spend the night in the forest, but his friend took his place and killed the crocodile when it came. On their way home they met the vulture again; it said that the man's bride was pregnant and would give birth to a son, but that his friend would become blind and could only be cured with the brains of the son. When the child was born, the friend became blind. The man told his wife that the brains of their child would cure his friend. She said, "Kill it, your friend is worth more to us than this child." The husband killed it, put the brains on his friend's eyes and cured them. Which of these loved the other most? Answer: The one who killed his son for the sake of his friend (Gaden 1913–1914: I, 182–185).

Cure for Impotence

159:1. (Hausa) A friend gave a man a magical armlet that cured his impotence. Later he saw his mother, who had been lost in a slave raid, in a gang of prisoners. He begged his friend to use his magic to release her. The friend agreed on one condition — that the armlet be returned. What shall his choice be? (Fletcher 1912: 90–92).

Knocked with Baobab

160:1. (Hausa) A youth carried his girl through the rain to the home of her former suitor and left her to spend the night there. In the morning she cracked open a baobab fruit on the head of her former suitor and gave it to the first youth to suck. Which of the two young men had the worst of it? (Edgar 1911–1913: II, (53); translated by Skinner n.d.: II, (53).

Husband's Rough Buttocks

161:1. (Hausa) A man and his wife came upon the wife's lover bathing in a river. The husband, who was carrying a load of salt, girt up his loincloth to wade across. The wife's lover said, "Well, just fancy, my dear! I never knew what rough buttocks your husband had!" and he rubbed mud on them. And so, what people ask is this: Should the husband throw his load of salt into the water and fight his wife's lover — or should he ignore him? (Edgar 1911–1913: III, (69); translated by Skinner 1969: I, 394).

Father Takes Son's Brides

162:1. (Nkundo) A wealthy man provided bridewealth for two of his three sons but refused to do so for the eldest. The youth went to look for a wife himself and came to a village of women. He asked an old woman if she had a daughter he could marry. She said that her daughters were bathing and that if he liked one of them, he should bring back her clothing. When the daughter came for her clothes, her mother said that the youth was her husband. After two months they returned to his village. When his father saw how beautiful his son's wife was, he took her as his concubine. The youth killed his father and was brought to trial by his family. How will the judges settle this palaver? Answer: The son wins because it is a father's duty to provide a wife for his son and because the father did wrong in taking his son's wife from him (Hulstaert and de Rop 1954: 88–91).

Deer Escapes

163:1. (Mano)   A woman asked a man to set a trap for a deer that had been eating rice on her farm. When the deer was caught in the trap, she ran and told the man. Then she ran back to the deer, undressed, and lay down beside it. The man had intercourse with her, and the deer escaped. Was it the man or the woman who let the deer escape? (Schwab 1947: 447–448; retold by Jablow 1961: 56–58).

Fouls His Trousers

164:1. (Hausa)   The chief's son committed adultery with a hunter's wife whenever the hunter was away hunting. One day the hunter returned while they were together. The wife hid the chief's son under a mat and told her husband to shoot an arrow through it. The hunter was reluctant, and while his wife urged him to do so, the chief's son fouled his own trousers. Well, which of them played the worst trick on one of the others? (Edgar 1911–1913: III, (112); translated by Skinner 1969: I, 395–397).

Sleep with Corpse

165:1. (Bambara)   When it was dark, a young man went to bed with his mistress, who was dead. Her husband came, sat down, sang his wife's praises, and called for her divine benediction. The lover said to himself, "Oh! Then I am sleeping with a corpse." He got up and fled, but he bumped into the husband before reaching the door. The lover thought that the husband had caught him, and the husband thought that his wife's corpse had arisen against him. At the place where they met, a large piece of excrement was found. To which of the two did it belong? (Travélé 1923: 84).

165:2. (Kpelle) A woman had a love affair with another man and was to take an ordeal. She told her mother, who said, "My child, you are silly. When a woman dupes her husband, she must treat him with care. Whatever he says to you, you must not contradict. Your father and I have lived together a long time. I had my lover, but I handled your father so that he did not know." The father overheard this, struck his wife, denounced her wickedness, and drove her away. Bitter at heart, he went to an old man and told him what had happened. The elder said, "I sympathize with you, but it is an old story in the world. Since the time God sent us here, women have not stopped treating men badly. If God has sent you a bad wife, if you beat her, even if you kill her, the matter rests on you, and not on her character." And the old man told a story:

"A beautiful woman in our town had a lover, and her husband did not know it. When the husband went on a trip, the lover would come to her at night. One day she died, and her husband laid her in bed and went to inform her relatives. That night her lover came, caressed her, and spoke to her, but she did not answer. He asked what he had done that she would not speak to him. Just then the husband returned. As he entered the door, he asked, "Oh God, what shall I do?" At this the frightened lover jumped up, bumped into the husband in the doorway, and said, "I come from the city of God." The townspeople came to see what was happening. When they looked for the lover, who had escaped, they found a piece of excrement at the spot where the two men had collided. They asked, "Whose is it?" This is a matter of dispute until to-day (Westermann 1921: 406–408; cf. AT 1418*).

165:3. (Vai) A man's daughter died, and he left her in bed. That night her lover came and thought that she was asleep. He called to her, but she did not answer. He asked her what he had done that she treated him so, but she remained still. Her father heard the lover and thought he was a ghost, and the lover heard the father, talking to himself, say that she had died. They ran into each other trying to make their escape and fled to the next town, where they told what had happened. The affair was reported to the king, who told the old man that he had not heard a ghost and that he should go and bury his daughter (Ellis 1914: 204–205).

Blind Man's Proposition

166:1. (Hausa) A blind man came begging to a house, but its owner ignored him, saying nothing. When his wife answered, the blind man asked if her husband was away and, when she said yes, offered her 400 cowries if she would lie with him. She refused, saying that her husband might catch them. The blind man offered 500, then 600 cowries. At this point the husband spoke up, demanding the blind man's gown, trousers, turban, and the 600 cowries he had offered the wife. The blind man went home wearing only his loincloth. Well, which of the two — husband or wife — incurred guilt in his treatment of the blind man? (Edgar 1911–1913: III, (95); translated by Skinner 1969: I, 359–360).

Four Lovers

167:1. (Limba) A woman had four lovers. She served one maize, one rice, one guinea corn, and one millet which she had mixed together and cooked together in the same pot. That night she slept with each of her lovers in turn. In the morning the men left and came to a big river. One of the men smoked, and they crossed the river on the smoke. Now, of them and the girl, which is the greatest? (Finnegan 1967: 166–167). Finnegan says, "The men, apparently, are to be thought remarkable because they accepted a situation with so many known rivals.... The general verdict after the narration was that they were all equally amazing, and the telling generally caused much amusement."

Revenge on Chief

168:1. (Hausa) A man praised his horse more than his wife, and she said he could not approach her unless he killed the horse. Another man heard of this and impersonated the husband. When told to kill the horse, he did so, and then he slept with the woman. When her husband returned, she promised to seek revenge. She found the other man, slept with him again, cut off his penis, and started home. A pursuer caught her but, instead of killing her, asked her to sleep with him. She agreed, on condition that he cut some palm leaves. When he climbed the tree, she rode home on his horse, which was just like the one that had been killed. She showed the penis to her husband and gave him the horse. Well, now, which of them would you say got done — the girl, her husband, the other man, or the pursuer? (Edgar 1911–1913: II, (63); translated by Skinner 1969: I, 391–393).

168:2. (Limba) A man begged his chief for spinach leaves. When the chief refused, he stole them, and the chief killed him with his sword. The man's pregnant wife went elsewhere to live and gave birth to a beautiful girl who grew up and promised to avenge her father's death. She sought out the chief, married him, killed him with his sword the first night, and fled with her wedding gifts. She was overtaken by the chief's son on horseback, but when he was about to kill her, she offered to marry him if he would first pick a leaf from a tree. When he climbed the tree, she rode home on her horse and showed her mother the chief's sword. Thus, even if you are a chief, don't kill someone who disobeys your word (Finnegan 1967: 131–137).

REFERENCES

AARNE, ANTTI, STITH THOMPSON
  1964   *The types of the folktale: a classification and bibliography* (second printing). Folklore Fellows Communications 184.
ADAM, JÉRÔME
  1940–   Nouvel extrait du folklore du Haut-Ogooué. *Anthropos* 35-36:
  1941   131–152.
ANONYMOUS
  1956   Fables juridiques Nkundo. *Annales N.D. Sacré Coeur* 67:154–155.
APPIAH, PEGGY
  1967   *Tales of an Ashanti father.* London: André Deutsch.
  1969   *The pineapple child and other tales from Ashanti.* London: André Deutsch.
AREWA, E. OJO
  1966   "A classification of the folktales of the northern East African cattle area by types." Unpublished doctoral dissertation, University of California at Berkeley.
  1971   Two subtypes of dilemma tales from the East African cattle area: the rationale for the distinction. *Anthropos* 66(1/2):229–231.
ARNOTT, KATHLEEN
  1962   *African myths and legends.* London: Oxford University Press.
  1967   *African fairy tales.* London: Frederick Muller.
BAHARAV, GENE
  1963–   *African folktales told in Israel,* three volumes. Haifa: International
  1966   Training Centre for Community Services.

BARKER, W. H., CECILIA SINCLAIR
1917   *West African folk-tales.* London: George G. Harrap.

BASCOM, WILLIAM
1965   "Folklore and literature," in *The African world: a survey of social research.* Edited by Robert A. Lystad, 469–490. New York: Fredrick A. Praeger.
1969   *Ifa divination: communication between gods and men in West Africa.* Bloomington, Indiana: Indiana University Press.
1972   "African dilemma tales: an introduction," in *African folklore.* Edited by Richard M. Dorson, 143–155. Garden City, New York: Doubleday.

BATEMAN, GEORGE W.
1901   *Zanzibar tales, told by natives of the east coast of Africa.* Chicago: A. C. McClurg.

BECKER-DONNER, ETTA
1965   *Die Sprache der Mano.* Österreichische Akademie der Wissenschaften, Philosophisch-Historischen Klasse, Sitzungberichte 245(5).

BENDER, C. J.
1922   *Die Volksdichtung der Wakweli: Sprichwörter, Fabeln und Märchen, Parabeln, Rätsel und Lieder.* Beiheft zur Zeitschrift für Eingeborenen-Sprachen 4.

BÉRENGER-FÉRAUD, L.-J.-B.
1879   *Peuplades de la Sénégambie.* Paris: Ernest Leroux.
1885   *Recueil de contes populaires de la Sénégambie.* Collection de Contes et Chansons Populaires 9. Paris: Ernest Leroux.

BERGER, P., O. GEMUSEUS
1932–   Konde Texte. *Zeitschrift für Eingeborenen-Sprachen* 23:110–154.
1933

BERRY, J.
1961   *Spoken art in West Africa.* London: School of Oriental and African Languages.

BORDEAUX, HENRY
1936   *Nos Indes noires.* Paris: Librairie Plon.

BOUCHE, PIERRE
1884–   Contes Nagos. *Melusine* 2: columns 49–60, 121–128, 313–320.
1885

BOUVEIGNES, OLIVIER, DE
1938   *Entendu dans la brousse: contes Congolais.* Les Joyaux de l'Orient 10. Paris: Librairie Orientaliste Paul Geuthner.

BROWN, GODFREY N.
1966   *Stories from the south of Nigeria.* London: George Allen and Unwin.

BURTON, W. F. P.
1961   *The magic drum: tales from Central Africa.* London: Methuen.

CARDINALL, A. W.
1931   *Tales told in Togoland.* London: Oxford University Press.

CAREY, MARGRET
1970   *Myths and legends of Africa.* London: Hamlyn.

CHARLTON, LIONEL EVELYN OSWALD
1908 *A Hausa reading book.* London, New York, and Toronto: Henry Frowde, Oxford University Press.

CHATELAIN, HELI
1894 *Folk-tales of Angola.* Memoirs of The American Folklore Society 1.

CHRISTALLER, J. G.
1894 Negermärchen von der Goldküste. *Zeitschrift des Vereins für Volkskunde* 4:61–71.

COLE-BEUCHAT, P.-D.
1957 Riddles in Bantu. *African Studies* 16(3):133–149.

COURLANDER, HAROLD
1963 *The king's drum and other African stories.* London: Rupert Hart-Davis.

COURLANDER, HAROLD, GEORGE HERZOG
1947 *The cow-tail switch.* New York: Henry Holt.

COURLANDER, HAROLD, ALBERT K. PREMPEH
1957 *The hat-shaking dance.* New York: Harcourt, Brace.

CREEL, J. LUKE
1960 *Folk tales of Liberia.* Minneapolis: T. S. Denison.

CRONISE, FLORENCE M., HENRY W. WARD
1903 *Cunnie Rabbit, Mr. Spider, and the other beef.* London: Swan Sonnenschein; New York: E. P. Dutton.

DADIÉ, BERNARD B.
1955 *Le pagne noire.* Paris: Présence Africaine.

DAGET, JACQUES
1947 La légende du Dubale. *Notes Africaines* 36:22–23.

DENNETT, R. E.
1898 *Notes on the folklore of the Fjort.* Publications of the Folk-Lore Society 41 (1897).

DOKE, CLEMENT M.
1947 Bantu wisdom-lore. *African Studies* 6:101–120.

EDGAR, FRANK
1911– *Litafi na tatsuniyoyi na Hausa. Litafi na farako,* three volumes.
1913 Belfast: W. Erskine Mayne.

ELLIS, GEORGE W.
1914 *Negro culture in West Africa.* New York: Neale.

ENNIS, MERLIN
1962 *Umbundu: folk tales from Angola.* Boston: Beacon Press.

EQUILBECQ, F. V.
1913– *Essai sur la littérature merveilleuse des noirs, suivi de contes in-*
1916 *digènes de l'Ouest Africain Français.* Collection de Contes et Chansons Populaires 41–43. Paris: Ernest Leroux.

FAESSLER, GERARD
1962 Wieder auf dem Afrikanischen Alverna. *Acta Tropica* 19(3):217–247.

FARNHAM, WILLARD EDWARD
1920 The contending lovers. *Publications of the Modern Language Association* 35(3):246–323.

FELDMANN, SUSAN
1963   *African myths and tales.* New York: Dell.
FIKRY-ATALLAH, MONA
1972   "Oral traditions of the Wala of Wa," in *African Folklore.* Edited by Richard M. Dorson, 397–440. Garden City, New York: Doubleday.
FINNEGAN, RUTH
1967   *Limba stories and story-telling.* Oxford Library of African Literature. Oxford: Clarendon Press.
FLETCHER, ROLAND S.
1912   *Hausa sayings and folk-lore with a vocabulary of new words.* London: Oxford University Press.
FOUDA, BASILE-JULÉAT, HENRY DE JULLIOT, ROGER LAGRAVE
1961   *Littérature Camerounaise.* Club du Livre Camerounais (Cannes) 7.
FROBENIUS, LEO
1921–   *Atlantis.* Veröffentlichung d. Forschungs-Institut für Kulturmor-
1928   phologie 1–12. Jena: Eugen Diederichs.
FROBENIUS, LEO, D. C. FOX
1937   *African genesis.* New York: Stackpole Sons.
FROGER, FERNAND
1910   *Étude sur la langue des Mossi (boucle du Niger), suivi d'un vocabulaire et de textes.* Paris: Ernest Leroux.
FUNKE, E.
1911–   Die Familie im Spiegel der Afrikanischen Volksmärchen. *Zeit-*
1912   *schrift für Kolonialsprachen* 2:37–63.
GADEN, HENRI
1913–   *Le Poular: Dialecte Peul du Fouta Sénégalais,* two volumes. Col-
1914   lection de la Revue du Monde Musulman. Paris: Ernest Leroux.
GAY, JOHN, MICHAEL COLE
1967   *The new mathematics and an old culture: a study of learning among the Kpelle of Liberia.* Case Studies in Education and Culture. New York: Holt, Rinehart and Winston.
GBADAMOSI, BAKARE, ULLI BEIER
1970   *Not even God is ripe enough.* African Writers Series 48. New York: Humanities Press. (First published 1968.)
GIRARD, J.
1967   *Dynamique de la société Ouobé: loi des masques et coutume.* Mémoires de l'Institut Fondemental d'Afrique Noire 78.
GREEN, LILA
1967   *Folktales and fairytales of Africa.* Morristown, New Jersey: Silver Burdett.
GUILHEM, MARCEL
n.d.   *Cinquante contes et fableaux de la savane,* two volumes. Paris: Ligel.
GUILLOT, RENÉ
1933   *Contes d'Afrique.* Numéro spécial du Bulletin de l'Enseignement de l'A.O.F.
1946   *Contes et légendes d'Afrique noire.* Paris: Société d'Éditions Géographiques Maritimes et Coloniales.

HARRIS, HERMANN G.
1908   *Hausa stories and riddles*. Weston-super-Mare: Mendip Press.

HAUENSTEIN, ALFRED
1967   *Les Hanya: description d'un groupe ethnique bantou de l'Angola*. Veröffentlichungen des Frobenius-Instituts an der Johann Wolfgang Goethe-Universität zu Frankfurt/Main, Studien zur Kulturkunde 19.

HELD, TONI VON
1904   *Märchen und Sagen der Afrikanischen Neger*. Jena: H. W. Schmidt's Verlagsbuchhandlung.

HELSER, ALBERT D.
1930   *African stories*. New York: Fleming H. Revell.
1934   *Education of primitive people*. New York: Fleming H. Revell.

HERSKOVITS, MELVILLE J., FRANCES S. HERSKOVITS
1958   *Dahomean narrative*. Northwestern University African Studies 1. Evanston, Illinois: Northwestern University Press.

HIMMELHEBER, HANS
1951   *Aura Poku* (second edition). Eisenach: Erich Röth-Verlag.

HOLAS, B.
1952   Échantillons du folklore Kono (Haut-Guinée Française). *Études Guinéennes* 9:3–90.

HULSTAERT, G.
1965   *Contes Mongo*. Académie Royal des Sciences d'Outre Mer, Classe des Sciences Morales et Politiques, n.s. 30 (2).
1970   *Fables Mongo*. Académie Royal des Sciences d'Outre Mer, Classe des Sciences Morales et Politiques, n.s. 37 (1).

HULSTAERT, G., A. DE ROP
1954   *Rechtspraakfabels van de Nkundó*. Annales du Musée Royal du Congo Belge, Sciences de l'Homme, Linguistique 8.

JABLOW, ALTA
1961   *Yes and no. The intimate folklore of Africa*. New York: Horizon Press.

JEFFREYS, M. D. W.
1967   Some Ibibio folk-tales. *Folklore* 78:126–136.

JOHNSON, JANGABA, BAI T. MOORE
1972   "Vai tales," in *African folklore*. Edited by Richard M. Dorson, 389–394. Garden City, New York: Doubleday.

JOHNSTON, H. A. S.
1966   *A selection of Hausa stories*. Oxford Library of African Literature. Oxford: Clarendon Press.

JUNOD, HENRI A.
1897   *Les chants et les contes des Ba-Ronga*. Lausanne: Georges Bridel.

KILSON, MARION DE B.
1960– Mende folk tales. *West African Review* 31(397):87–91 and 32
1961   (398):45–48.

KLIPPLE, MAY AUGUSTA
1938   "African folk tales with foreign analogues." Unpublished doctoral dissertation, Indiana University.

KRUG, ADOLPH N.
1912   Bulu tales from Kamerun, West Africa. *Journal of American Folklore* 25:106–124.

KRUG, A. N., M. J. HERSKOVITS
1949   Bulu tales. *Journal of American Folklore* 62(246):348–374.

LADEMANN, GEBHARD, LUDWIG KAUSCH, ALFRED REUSS
1910   *Tierfabeln und andere Erzählungen in Suaheli*. Archiv für das Studium Deutscher Kolonialsprachen 12.

LANDEROIN, M., J. TILHO
1909   *Grammaire et contes Haoussas*. Paris: Imprimerie Nationale.

MABENDY, GUISSÉ
1966   Contes et fables recueillis au Mali. *Notes Africaines* 111:103–109.

MACDONALD, DUFF
1882   *Africana; or, the heart of heathen Africa*, two volumes. London: Simpkin Marshall; Edinburgh: John Menzies; Aberdeen: A. Brown.

MATOLA, LESLIE
1907   A Swahili riddle story. *Central Africa*, 296:214–216.

M'BOW, AMADOU MAHTAR
1971   Le nouveau dossier Afrique. *Marabout Université* 210:311.

MENGRELIS, THANOS
1947   La queue du boeuf, conte Guerze. *Notes Africaines* 35:29.
1950   "Contes de la forêt" in Le Monde Noir, *Présence Africaine* 8-9:185–192.

MISCHLICH, A.
1929   *Neue Märchen aus Afrika*. Veröffentlichung des Staatlich-Sächsischen Forschungsinstitutes für Völkerkunde in Leipzig, Erste Reihe, Ethnographie und Ethnologie 9. Leipzig: R. Voigtländers Verlag.

MOCKLER-FERRYMAN, A. F.
1902   *British Nigeria*. London: Cassell.

MONTEIL, C.
1905   *Contes Soudanais*. Collection de Contes et Chansons Populaires 28. Paris: Ernest Leroux.

MÜLLER, FR.
1902   Ein Beitrag zur Kenntniss der Atakpame. *Zeitschrift für Afrikanische, Ozeanische, und Ostasiatische Sprachen* 6:138–166.

MUSSON, MARGARET
1957   *Mr. Spider and his friends*. The Oxford Story Readers for Africa. London: Oxford University Press. (First published 1953.)

NASSAU, ROBERT HAMILL
1914   *Where animals talk: West African folk lore tales*. London: Duckworth.
1915   Batanga tales. *Journal of American Folklore* 28:24–51.

N'DJOK, KINDENGVE
1958   *Kil'lam, fils d'Afrique*. Paris: Éditions Alsatia.

NEWMAN, PAUL
1968   *Tera folktale texts*, two volumes. New Haven, Connecticut: Human Relations Area Files.

NICOLAS, FRANÇOIS J.
1954 Énigmes des L'éla de la Haute-Volta (A.O.F.). *Anthropos* 49: 1013–1040.

PARSONS, ELSIE CLEWS
1923 *Folk-lore from the Cape Verde Islands.* Memoirs of The American Folklore Society 15(1–2).

PAULME, DENISE
1961 Littérature orale et comportements sociaux en Afrique. *L'Homme* 1:37–49.

PECHUËL-LOESCHE, EDUARD
1907 *Volkskunde von Loango.* Stuttgart: Verlag von Strecker und Schröder.

PINNEY, PETER
n.d. "Legends of Africa." Mimeographed manuscript.

PRIETZE, RUDOLF
1897 Beiträge zur Erforschung von Sprache und Volksgeist in Togo-Kolonie. *Zeitschrift für Afrikanische und Ozeanische Sprachen* 3:17–64.

RABEARISON
1967 *Contes et legendes de Madagascar.* Tananarive: Imprimerie Luthérienne.

RAMÓN ALVAREZ, HERIBERTO
1951 *Leyendas y mitos de Guinea.* Madrid: Instituto de Estudios Africanos.

RATTRAY, R. SUTHERLAND
1913 *Hausa folk-lore,* two volumes. Oxford: Clarendon Press.
1930 *Akan-Ashanti folk-tales.* Oxford: Clarendon Press.

REHSE, HERMANN
1910 *Kiziba: Land und Leute.* Stuttgart: Verlag von Strecker und Schröder.

REINISCH, LEO
1889– *Die Saho-Sprache,* two volumes. Wien: Alfred Hölder.
1890

RENEL, CHARLES
1910 *Contes de Madagascar.* Collection de Contes et Chansons Populaires 37–38. Paris: Ernest Leroux.

REUSS, ALFRED
1931 Märchen der Wazeguha, nach den Kisuaheli-Aufzeichnungen des Ali bin Kikunguru as Mgambo (Bezirk Pangani). *Mitteilungen des Seminars für Orientalische Sprachen* 34(3):116–138.

ROP, A., DE
1956 *De gesproken woordkunst van de Nkundo.* Annales du Musée Royal du Congo Belge, Sciences de l'Homme, Linguistique 13.

RUSKIN, E. A.
1921 *Mongo proverbs and fables.* Bongandanga: Congo Balolo Mission Press.

SCHÖN, J. F.
1885– *Magána Hausa: native literature, or proverbs, tales, fables, and*
1886 *historical fragments in the Hausa language* (with English translation). London: Society for Promoting Christian Knowledge.

SCHÖN, J. F., CHARLES H. ROBINSON
1906   *Magána Hausa.* London: Society for Promoting Christian Knowledge.

SCHÖNHÄRL, JOSEF
1909   *Volkskundliches aus Togo.* Dresden and Leipzig: C. A. Kochs Verlagsbuchhandlung.

SCHWAB, GEORGE
1914   Bulu folk-tales. *Journal of American Folklore* 27:266–288.
1919   Bulu folk-tales. *Journal of American Folklore* 32:428–437.
1922   Bulu folk-tales. *Journal of American Folklore* 35:209–215.
1947   *Tribes of the Liberian Hinterland.* Papers of the Peabody Museum of American Archaeology and Ethnology 31.

SEIDEL, AUGUST
1896   *Geschichten und Lieder der Afrikaner.* Berlin: Schall and Grund.

SKINNER, NEIL
n.d.   "Hausa folk tales and miscellanea," (a translation of *Litafi na tatsuniyoyi na Hausa,* by Frank Edgar), three volumes. Unpublished manuscript.
1969   *Hausa tales and traditions: an English translation of Litafi na tatsuniyoyi na Hausa, originally compiled by Frank Edgar,* volume one of three. London: Frank Cass.

SMITH, EDWIN W., ANDREW MURRAY DALE
1920   *The Ila-speaking peoples of Northern Rhodesia,* two volumes. London: Macmillan.

SOCÉ, OUSMANE
1948   *Karim: Roman sénégalais, suivi de contes et légendes d'Afrique noire* (third edition). Bibliothèque de l'Union Française. Paris: Nouvelles Éditions Latines.

SPIETH, JAKOB
1906   *Die Ewe-Stämme: material zur Kunde des Ewe Volkes in Deutsch Togo.* Berlin: Dietrich Reimer.

STEERE, EDWARD
1899   *Swahili tales, as told by natives of Zanzibar* (second edition). London: Society for Promoting Christian Knowledge. (First published 1869.)

TAUXIER, L.
1924   *Nègres Gouro et Gagou.* Études Soudanaises. Paris: Librairie Orientaliste Paul Geuthner.

TAYLOR, ARCHER
1951   *English riddles from oral tradition.* Berkeley and Los Angeles, California: University of California Press.

TAYLOR, W. E.
1932–   A Swahili tale in the dialect of Mombasa. *Zeitschrift für Einge-*
1933   *borenen-Sprachen* 23:1–24.

THOMAS, JACQUELINE M. C.
1970   *Contes, proverbes, devinettes ou énigmes, chants et prières Ngbaka-Ma'Bo (République Centrafricaine).* Langues et Littératures de l'Afrique Noire 6. Paris: Éditions Klincksieck.

THOMAS, LOUIS-VINCENT
1958– *Les Diola: Essai d'analyse fonctionnelle sur une population des*
1959 *Basse-Casamance.* Institut Française d'Afrique Noire Memoire 55(1–2).
1968 Divertissement chez les Bandial. *Notes Africaines* 119:65–77.
1970 Nouvel exemple d'oralité négro-africaine: Récits Narang-Djiragon, Diola-Karaban, et Dyiwat (Basse-Casamance). *Bulletin de l'Institut Fondemental d'Afrique Noire*, série B, 32:230-309.

THOMAS, NORTHCOTE W.
1916 *Anthropological report on Sierra Leone*, three volumes. London: Harrison and Sons.

THOMPSON, STITH
1951 *The folktale.* New York: Dryden.

TIENDREBEOGO, YAMBA
1963 *Contes du Larhallé, suivis d'un recueil de proverbes et devises du pays Mossi.* Ouagadougou: privately published.

TRAORÉ, DOMINIQUE
1944– Cinq contes africains. *L'Éducation Africaine* 33–34:25–28.
1945

TRAUTMANN, RENÉ
1927 *La littérature populaire à la Côte des Esclaves.* Travaux et Mémoires de l'Institut d'Ethnologie 4.

TRAVÉLÉ, MOUSSA
1923 *Proverbes et contes Bambara.* Paris: Librairie Orientaliste Paul Geuthner.

TREMEARNE, A. J. N.
1909– Fifty Hausa folk-tales. *Folk-Lore* 21:199–215, 351–365, 487–503
1910 and 22:60–73, 218–228, 341–348, 457–473.
1913 *Hausa superstitions and customs.* London: John Bale, Sons and Danielsson.

TRILLES, H.
1932 *Les Pygmées de la forét équatoriale.* Anthropos Ethnologische Bibliothek 3(4).

TUTUOLA, AMOS
1953 *The palm-wine drinkard.* New York: Grove Press. (First published 1952.)

WALKER, BARBARA K., WARREN S. WALKER
1961 *Nigerian Folk Tales.* New Brunswick, New Jersey: Rutgers University Press.

WATERMAN, RICHARD, WILLIAM BASCOM
1949 "African and New World Negro folklore," in *Funk and Wagnalls standard dictionary of folklore, mythology, and legend.* Edited by Maria Leach, 1:18–24. New York: Funk and Wagnalls.

WEEKS, JOHN H.
n.d. *Congo life and jungle stories* (second edition). London: The Religious Tract Society.

WERNER, A.
1906 *The natives of British Central Africa.* London: Archibald Constable.

WESTERMANN, DIEDRICH

1907   *Grammatik der Ewe-Sprache.* Berlin: Dietrich Reimer.

1921   *Die Kpelle: ein Negerstamm in Liberia.* Göttingen: Vandenhoeck and Ruprecht; Leipzig: J. C. Hinrichs'sche Buchhandlung.

1922   *Die Sprache der Guang in Togo und auf der Goldküste, und fünf andere Togo-sprachen.* Berlin: Dietrich Reimer.

WITTE, AL, DE

1913–   Evenaarsfolklore. *Onze Kongo* 4:177–187.
1914

WOODSON, CARTER GODWIN

1964   *African myths together with proverbs.* Washington, D.C.: The Associated Publishers. (First published 1928.)

YOUNG, W. P.

1933   *The rabbit and the baboons and other tales from northern Nyasaland.* Little Books for Africa 43. London: The Sheldon Press.

Biographical Note

WILLIAM BASCOM was born in Princeton, Illinois on May 23, 1912. He received his B.A. degree in Physics in 1933 and his M.A. degree in Anthropology in 1936 from the University of Wisconsin. Following field research among the Yoruba of Nigeria, he received his Ph.D. from Northwestern University in 1939. From 1939 to 1957 he taught in the Department of Anthropology at Northwestern, except for a leave of absence from 1942 to 1946 when he was in West Africa as a civilian employee of the United States government. Meanwhile he did ethnological field work among the Kiowa Indians of Oklahoma, the Gullah Negroes of South Carolina and Georgia, on Ponape in the Caroline Islands, and in Cuba. In 1950–1951 he returned to Nigeria with his wife, Berta, for a second year of research among the Yoruba, and in 1952–1954 he served as President of the American Folklore Society. In 1957 he moved to the University of California, Berkeley, as Professor of Anthropology and Director of the Robert H. Lowie Museum of Anthropology.

Ethnic Index